FOOL *Me* ONCE

Center Point
Large Print

Also by Catherine Bybee and available from Center Point Large Print:

Wife by Wednesday

CATHERINE BYBEE

FOOL *Me* ONCE

BOOK ONE IN THE
FIRST WIVES SERIES

CENTER POINT LARGE PRINT
THORNDIKE, MAINE

This Center Point Large Print edition
is published in the year 2019 by arrangement with
Amazon Publishing, www.apub.com.

Originally published in the United States
by Amazon Publishing, 2017.

The text of this Large Print edition is unabridged.
In other aspects, this book may vary
from the original edition.
Printed in the United States of America
on permanent paper.
Set in 16-point Times New Roman type.

ISBN: 978-1-64358-246-7

Library of Congress Cataloging-in-Publication Data

Names: Bybee, Catherine, author.
Title: Fool me once / Catherine Bybee.
Description: Center Point Large Print edition. | Thorndike, Maine : Center Point Large Print, 2019.
Identifiers: LCCN 2019016383 | ISBN 9781643582467 (hardcover : alk. paper)
Subjects: LCSH: Large type books.
Classification: LCC PS3602.Y344 F66 2019 | DDC 813/.6—dc23
LC record available at https://lccn.loc.gov/2019016383

This one is for Tracy Brogan
For obvious reasons

Chapter One

Divorce cake was so much sweeter than wedding cake, and when that cake was served to a room full of women celebrating the freedom of a newly single, incredibly wealthy thirty-year-old, it tasted even better.

Lori lifted her tumbler in the air and caught the gaze of Samantha Harrison from across the room.

Another successful Alliance contract executed.

Another payday for the both of them.

Avery Grant, the divorcée of the hour, laughed over the volume of the music pumping through the expansive speaker system in the high-rise condominium. The unit sat several floors above Lori's in the same Los Angeles complex.

The lofty space had been stripped of most of its walls before Avery moved in. She wanted it open, with massive views of the city twinkling below after sunset. Her husband of sixteen months liked his living space to resemble a Civil War–era colonial home, complete with cubicle-style rooms and drafty halls. It wasn't surprising to see Avery make a completely opposite choice for her home.

"You're Avery's attorney, aren't you?"

The voice on Lori's right belonged to Avery's mom, Adeline.

Lori extended her hand. "I am. It's Mrs. Grant, right?"

"Did Avery speak of me?"

No, but Lori had sat on the sidelines of Avery and Bernie's wedding nearly a year and a half before. She hadn't stayed for the reception. A divorce attorney at a wedding sometimes created gossip, something Lori and Sam's team avoided like socks on newly polished toes.

"Avery showed me pictures from the wedding," Lori lied.

Mrs. Grant lifted her nose a little higher. "Disgraceful. Who shows a divorce lawyer pictures of what failed?"

They both glanced at Avery, who was working her way into a wicked hangover.

"Their split was amicable." A direct quote from the tabloid that blasted the finality of the divorce earlier that week.

"Amicable or not, it shouldn't have happened. Avery always was impulsive, making the wrong choices. Bernie was perfect for her, grounded, good family."

Rich!

"He was a bit older than your daughter." Eighteen years, to be exact. Not to mention the male-pattern baldness and five foot ten height. When Avery appeared at his side in anything but flats, she towered over him. Not that Bernie had minded. He had wanted a trophy wife, and with Avery, he'd gotten what he ordered.

Laughter caught their attention again.

"This is disgraceful. Who has a divorce party?"

In Lori's line of work, lots of women.

"If you'll excuse me, Mrs. Grant, I see someone I need to speak with."

The older woman pinched her lips a little tighter and pivoted toward the kitchen.

Lori worked her way to Sam's side and lifted her cocktail. "Cheers."

"Looked like Mom wasn't happy."

"Not at all." Lori lowered her voice. "If I remember right, Avery wanted a reprieve from her parents nagging her to settle down." Her brief marriage and subsequent divorce had given her that.

"I wonder how long Mom will wait before going at her again?"

"Anyone's guess."

"Well." Sam placed her half-empty glass on a nearby table. "At least Avery has the financial freedom to avoid her overcontrolling parents."

"I've never seen domineering parents loosen their grip on their children."

"Perhaps Avery will pry their fingers off."

A fast-paced song had the woman of the hour bouncing to the beat. "She is certainly breaking loose tonight."

"What is she drinking?"

"It's called a ball and chain, otherwise known as Fireball and tequila shots."

"That's gonna hurt in the morning."

A chattering of women increased in volume and brought both their attention to the front door. A tall, muscle-bound twentysomething walked in wearing the fakest cop's uniform Lori had ever seen.

Sam shook her head. "When the stripper arrives, that's my cue to leave."

Lori waved her off. "Go home to your hot man. I'll stick around and make sure our client doesn't do anything tabloid perfect."

Sam kissed the side of Lori's cheek before skirting around the crowd.

Someone handed Lori a plate full of cream cheese frosting smothered cake.

Strippers and sugar.

It could be worse.

The sound of glass crashing to the floor brought Lori's eyes wide open.

In front of her, the world shimmered into focus.

Bright light glared.

Avery's condo . . . commando stripper . . . it all came back in a breath.

Fuzzy pain sat in the back of her neck and threatened serious pain if she didn't change position.

She shifted and closed her eyes.

The guttural sound of someone attempting to empty their stomach shot her into action.

Lori zeroed in on the noise.

Avery, God love her, had made it halfway to the stone and lacquer bathroom before losing the previous evening's indulgence.

Choking back the involuntary desire to follow Avery's stomach, Lori swallowed hard, moved past the mess, and grasped the girl's hair as she found the toilet.

"Oh, God."

Lori wasn't sure who was praying to the porcelain throne, Avery or her . . . but one of them was exclaiming something.

"I got ya," Lori said as she closed her eyes and thought of rainbows and unicorns.

Avery emptied her stomach, the hard way, into the pristine white Kohler toilet.

Just when Lori thought the worst was over, it wasn't.

"Oh, damn."

Lori sucked air in through her mouth.

Only when the sound of the toilet flushing hit her ears did Lori open her eyes. "You good?"

Avery heaved.

Nope.

Two minutes later . . .

For every day she sat at her desk charging five hundred dollars an hour for her efforts, this wasn't one of them.

Nurses, Lori decided then and there, deserved a half-off deal when they showed up looking for representation.

"One too many tequila shots."

Avery's comment had Lori grinning. "Or five."

Avery leaned against the tub, head in her hands. "You said my divorce wasn't going to be painful."

Laughing, Lori said, "Your divorce was final before Patrón and Detective Dan."

Avery opened one eye. "Was that his name?"

"I never got his name."

"He was firm."

Lori grinned, thinking of the fake stripper cop. "Everywhere."

They both laughed.

"Stop, it hurts."

"C'mon." Lori helped Avery to her feet and down the hall.

"I need to clean that." Avery turned her head away from her own mess.

"I got ya." Or she'd call someone from an emergency maid service with combat pay who would get it.

After placing Avery on her sofa, Lori turned to the open kitchen. "Coffee."

Avery moaned.

"For me. You get crackers and ice chips until noon."

A fancy single serving coffee dispenser was

a divorce gift from one of Avery's friends. Lori had cracked it open after midnight in an effort to sober up a few guests before they left.

Most of them went by way of overtipped Uber drivers.

"That party was epic."

Lori felt five years past the epic days of her life. "It was memorable."

A coffee cup made it under the stream of hot cappuccino. Just the smell helped her headache.

"I'm really divorced?" Avery asked on a sigh.

"Yep."

"And my bank account has five million dollars in it?"

"Yep."

Avery's laugh started low and built. Lori smiled as she lifted the coffee cup for her first taste.

"Bernie's a nice man, he just needs . . ."

"Someone closer to his age?"

"Yeah."

Lori avoided conversations with her clients during their marriages unless something legal came up. And since most of the time she represented both parties in these "arranged marriages," from prenup to divorce, it was best to stand clear.

Alliance, a successful marriage-for-hire service for the rich and famous who needed a spouse quickly and quietly, was Sam's brainchild. The marriages were designed to be temporary, twelve to twenty-four months, including a six-month uncontested divorce grace period. Sam often fostered the relationship with the payees, mainly women, where Lori dealt with the payers, often men. Lori wasn't an employee of Alliance per se, but she did financially benefit from every prenuptial agreement she wrote up, and again when the couple split.

Once the divorces were final, Lori often took on the role of transitioning the divorcées from "married to a rich man" to "cast-off wife." And yes, Sam paid her for that service as well.

Even though her role with Alliance went beyond the professional scope of a divorce attorney, she didn't mind. Her involvement kept her clients out of the papers and on the path to the happiness they sought when they entered into their counterfeit marriages.

The irony lay in how many times Alliance marriages actually worked out. Between Sam's vetting of the couples involved, the extensive background checks, and the overall matching process, it wasn't uncommon for the couples to have a physical attraction that sometimes grew deep roots filled with *I love you* and *forever.* Considering the divorce rate was 50 percent in the normal world of happily ever after, the fact that the fabricated marriages that Samantha Harrison's company arranged had a 28 percent success rate was astounding.

And those success stories alone kept Lori in the mix.

As jaded as a divorce lawyer with one failed marriage under her personal belt was, she liked to believe happily ever after existed.

"Was it really that easy? Taking the job as Bernie's wife paid me over nine grand a day."

It was too early for math.

"Uhm . . ."

"Five million and the condo."

Yeah . . . the condo had cost Bernie close to two million after renovations. Every client was different.

Every client had a price for a year or two of their personal freedom.

Not to mention the gifts Bernie had bestowed upon his wife during their marriage. All a facade.

Even now, Bernie was happily hooking up with a woman slightly older than Avery with the real possibility of that happily ever after in his future. It seemed having a trophy wife broke down some of his personal demons that prevented him from seeking out relationships.

There were pitfalls for Avery, however . . . things she'd discarded when she'd signed contracts that she would now face. Dating after being labeled a gold digger would be challenging. Not to mention the opportunistic men out there who would try to hook up with her to get a piece of her bank account. Avoiding the lottery curse and blowing the five million she gave up a portion of her life for was also something Lori and Sam both tried to help their clients avoid. Hence the reason Lori was standing in Avery's condo and not hers at nine in the morning with puke dripping off the walls. Avery already trusted and respected her, but now that the marriage and divorce were over, Lori hoped their relationship could develop into a friendship so Avery would seek her advice during what could be a challenging transitional year.

"Water?" Lori offered.

Avery shook her head.

Lori leaned against the kitchen counter.

"You need to ease your life out of purgatory just a little bit longer," Lori warned. "Give the papers someone new to follow."

Avery laughed with half-open eyes.

"Avery?" The younger woman caught Lori's gaze. "This isn't going to be easy."

"Yeah, yeah . . . you told me people would call me a gold digger, a user. I know."

Avery Grant had been ostracized by her parents' crowd for not conforming to the plaid skirt wearing teen or the perfectly polished Stepford wife type as an adult. Her wealthy, Ivy League–educated family didn't know what to do with her wild, unorthodox personality. Her parents sent her to one boarding school after another, never letting Avery develop any lasting friendships. Avery continued the pattern by floating in and out of three colleges before graduating with a liberal arts degree after five years. Avery said she was bulletproof after her unsettled childhood.

"It's more than being called a name," Lori said.

"You've told me this before, Lori. I'm good."

Lori's phone rang like an exclamation point.

She followed the ringtone until she found her cell plugged in by the kitchen sink.

It was Sam.

"Good morning."

"You left before all the fun." Detective Dan had earned his three hundred bucks.

"Are you sitting down?"

Sam's abrupt tone shook the remaining cobwebs from Lori's head. "No."

"Sit."

Lori took the seat opposite Avery. "I'm sitting." And her heart was beating too fast.

"They have art."

They and *art* were never a good combination. "Last night?"

"Yeah. A picture of Avery letting Detective Dan take a Jell-O shot off her belly is making the rounds." Sam rambled off the tabloid that had managed to obtain pictures from the previous night's party.

"That's not good."

Sam sighed.

Avery opened both eyes as she took in half the conversation.

Lori faked a smile. The reaction was pre-programed in her head in an effort to keep control of her emotions when she felt her blood pressure rising.

"That's not all."

"I'm listening."

"Fedor Petrov squeezed the trigger of his .45 millimeter point-blank to his head last night."

Lori's stomach protested. She swallowed. Hard. "God, no."

"I wish I was joking."

"Where is Trina?" Petrov was their payer, and Trina was the temporary wife halfway through her two-year contract.

"Secluded in Petrov's estate in the Hamptons."

"This is bad." Lori closed her eyes and envisioned Trina the last time she saw her. She was packing up her apartment after her brief fake honeymoon and moving back east. "How did you find out?"

"Trina called, hysterical."

"My God, is she okay?"

"No. I'm not sure it's possible for her to be okay right now. My plane leaves in two hours."

"I'll be ready."

Chapter Two

By the time Lori and Sam landed in the Hamptons, every newscaster, rag, and wannabe paparazzo had beat them there. Cameras blinded them as the car passed through the gate of the Petrov estate.

Thankfully, the media had no idea who Lori was, so she rushed in first. But when Sam stepped out of the car, cameras renewed their frenzy. Sam had already established herself as Trina's friend, so her presence wouldn't be questioned.

Lori found Trina sitting on a chaise in her bedroom with an empty bottle of wine at her side.

The dark skinned, ebony haired woman looked up when Lori entered the room.

She'd been crying. A broken shell of the woman Lori had last seen just six months before.

One look in Lori's direction and Trina's tears flowed again.

Lori folded Trina into her arms and listened as she sobbed.

Through hiccups, Trina spoke.

"I didn't sign"—Lori patted Trina's back—"up for this."

"It's okay . . . you're going to be okay."

Trina buried her face in Lori's shoulder.

Lori looked up at the sound of Sam's footsteps. She and Sam kept eye contact for several seconds of silence.

"I should have seen this coming," Trina managed once Sam sat on the other side of her.

"Did Fedor say anything to you?"

"Nothing."

"Then how could you have known this would happen?" Lori asked.

"I'm his wife."

Lori glanced to the closed bedroom door. "In name only."

"People are going to blame me for not seeing this coming."

Lori couldn't argue with that. "It's not your fault."

"Doesn't matter. He'd been quiet this last month. Almost never away from the hospital. I thought the changes in him were about his mom. I asked him how he was doing, but he didn't offer more than that he was holding up. He obviously wasn't holding up," she cried.

Fedor was a devoted son, his mother was his world. Suffering from cancer, Alice Petrov had been on her deathbed for the last few months, and Fedor knew it would bring her peace to see him married.

Cancer was stealing her lungs, and a stroke had left her in a wheelchair. In the past week, she'd had a second stroke and no longer recognized anyone. The doctors didn't give her long to live.

Sam's theory behind Fedor's suicide was that he couldn't cope with his mother's impending death. And since she no longer recognized him, he wasn't hurting her by exiting this life.

"Did you find a note, a suicide letter?" Lori asked.

"No, nothing."

"We're going to get you through this," Sam told her.

Trina's tears were drying up. "Two years and I'd have the means to be able to start my own company. That's all I wanted." Her eyes welled again. "I didn't think anyone was going to die."

While there were clauses in the prenuptial contracts for the unlikely event of one of the spouses dying during their marriage, in the history of Alliance, they'd never had to revisit the clause.

A knock on the door caught their attention. "Mrs. Petrov?"

Lori recognized one of the housekeepers. "Yes?"

"Your parents are here."

Trina blinked a few times before she spoke. "Give me a minute."

The housekeeper nodded and closed the door behind her.

"Do they know the truth about your marriage?" Sam asked.

Trina shook her head. "No. I've told no one."

Lori attempted to put Trina at ease with a smile. "It needs to stay that way."

"I know."

"Do you want us to stay while you talk with your parents?"

Trina closed her eyes. "No. I need to talk to them on my own."

"We'll go, then."

Trina's eyes opened wide in protest.

"To one of the spare rooms," Sam assured her.

"Okay. Don't leave."

Lori stood. "We won't. We're here for you, Trina. We'll get you through this."

Sam and Lori kept quiet until they were shown the rooms they were going to occupy. Once alone, they started to plan. "She looks awful," Lori said straight out.

"She's a sensitive soul."

"Does she have any friends here?"

"Not close ones," Sam told her.

Lori looked around the dark walls of the old estate. The black clouds outside didn't help the somber mood inside. "We'll have to get her away from here as soon as possible."

"I think that's a sound plan. Someplace warm and sunny . . . and far enough away that people won't recognize her."

"And where is that?" Lori wasn't sure such a place existed.

"Europe, on the sea . . . I don't know. Let's help her get through the funeral, give her the support she needs to dig out of this mess, and remove her from this sadness."

Lori leaned against the dresser. "I've never transitioned a client after a spouse's suicide."

Sam blew out a slow breath. "This is going to take more than one-on-one. She's going to need more than you and I talking her through this."

Lori thought of the client she'd left in LA. "Let's include Avery . . . it's hard not to smile around that woman."

"I like that idea. Take them both—" Sam's phone buzzed. She reached for it.

"You know who else would be helpful?"

Sam glanced at the screen on her phone, promptly dropped it onto the bed. "Who?"

"Shannon." One of the highest profile divorces Lori had to date. If anyone could be a sympathetic shoulder, it was the former first lady of California. The one client that Lori had failed to help readjust after her marriage was over. Not that she'd stopped trying. "Maybe this would be helpful for all of them. An intimate group in the know about their marriages."

"I like this idea, Lori."

They both heard Trina sobbing from across the hall when someone opened a door.

Lori's heart sank in her chest.

• • •

An angry male voice pulled Lori from the few hours of broken sleep she'd managed.

Trina was yelling, her voice wavering.

Lori jumped from the bed, grabbed the robe, and shoved her arms into it as she fled into the hall and down the stairs.

Before she reached the bottom step, she caught sight of Ruslan Petrov, Fedor's father, shaking his fist in Trina's face. Lori remembered the man from his pictures, big, unmoving . . . a man you didn't want to find yourself alone with in a dark place.

"Your fault. My son was fine before you."

Trina stepped away.

From behind Lori, someone barreled down the stairs, nearly knocking her over. Trina's father, a man half the size of Ruslan, shoved his frame between the two of them.

"Get away from my daughter."

Ruslan shoved his chest forward and said something in Russian that Lori didn't understand. From the way he spat the words, she assumed the insult would have resulted in a thrown fist.

Trina winced.

Lori found herself inching forward.

"My son is dead." Ruslan squared his shoulders, looked past Trina's dad, and glared.

"My daughter did not pull the trigger."

Ruslan looked at the crowd that had gathered behind Lori on the stairs, and then directly at Trina. "I will find his reason. And that *person* will pay." He shook his meaty fist toward Trina.

As threats went, that was one for the courts.

"You need to leave." Trina's father pointed toward the door, which was flanked by two of Petrov's suit-wearing bodyguards, who were easily the size of small buildings.

"This is my son's house."

Trina lifted her chin. "A house you've never stepped foot in."

Ruslan glared.

"My husband was quiet about many things, but his distaste for you was something we spoke of often."

"My son was destroyed by the women in his life."

Lori sensed the tension rising again and took the remaining steps to Trina's side.

"You've been asked to leave, Mr. Petrov. I suggest you do before we need to call the authorities to remove you."

His round face grew red with anger.

He spewed more angry Russian words before he turned and stormed out the door.

A sigh of relief went through the house-guests.

Sam flanked Trina as the widow's face turned

white. “I’m going to call Neil. We need security.” Neil was the head of Sam’s personal security team, and if anyone could trump Ruslan in terms of size, it was him.

Lori nodded and looked around the room as Sam walked away. Studying Trina’s file on the airplane was coming in handy. “Mrs. Mendez?”

The sixtysomething woman focused on Lori. “Do I know you?”

Lori shook her head. “No. Why don’t you help your daughter get ready for the day?” Lori glanced at the wide-eyed housekeeper. “Cindy, right?”

The woman nodded.

“We need coffee. I need to know how many rooms are available for guests.” There was a funeral to plan, and someone needed to take control of the details.

“Yes, ma’am.”

Lori turned to Trina, placed a palm to her face, and offered a calm smile. “Go shower. I’ll take care of everything.”

The adrenaline of Ruslan’s outrage passed through everyone like an angry ocean hitting the shore, and now Trina stood in silence, like a zombie, unsure of what direction to go. “Okay . . . okay.”

Flanked by her parents, Trina mounted the stairs.

Less than a week later, Fedor Petrov was

laid to rest with over four hundred attending guests.

Two days after that, Alice Petrov took her last breath.

Chapter Three

There were reasons why Lori's caseload was lighter than that of the average divorce attorney to the rich and famous. She spent very little time in front of judges hashing anything out. Her practice was built on prenuptial agreements and premeditated divorces. These took up over half of her calendar and added to her retirement plan faster than any divorce lawyer could have dreamed.

When cases like Trina Mendez-Petrov's took a significant turn for the worse, she had ample time to deal with them and enough professional clout to obtain the required court delays with her current inbox of clients.

Lori stood poised, with massive sunglasses covering her eyes, a wide-brimmed hat covering her head, and her chin held high in the lobby of the Mandarin Oriental Hotel in Barcelona. The hotel dripped opulence and sophistication. It screamed money, and lots of it. Attendants stood everywhere, their uniforms crisp, their smiles painted on. Fresh flower arrangements featured exotic plants Lori couldn't name. Looking past the sleek lines and gold trim of the decor, she watched the glass doors leading outside as one of many limousines stopped in the valet turn-around.

Wearing a white jumpsuit few women could pull off, Shannon Redding, the ex-wife of Paul Wentworth, the current governor of the state of California, climbed out of the back of the limo and donned sunglasses similar to Lori's. She said something to one of the bellmen, who placed a soft black bag onto a cart, and preceded her luggage into the lobby.

They hugged. "Hello, Shannon."

"It's good to see you."

Lori tilted her sunglasses. "I'm glad you could make it."

"Two years is long enough to sulk." Shannon said the right thing, but Lori could see a shadow still lurking in the woman's smile.

Someone behind Shannon called out, "Lori?"

Lori placed a hand on Shannon's arm and moved past her. "You're early."

Avery wore her hair in a ponytail and smiled like she'd enjoyed her in-flight drinks. "My mother was driving me crazy, so I caught an earlier flight."

Lori turned toward Shannon and made the introductions.

"Shannon, this is Avery."

Shannon's poised and practiced smile met Avery's grin. The two couldn't be more different and still have so much in common.

The women knew they were both Alliance brides, but the details would only be spoken of in private.

"Is our fourth party here?" Shannon asked as they walked toward the elevators.

"She is."

They kept the small talk to conversation about their flights and lack of sleep until they entered the double doors of the penthouse suite.

Lori tipped the bellmen and closed the door behind them.

She removed her sunglasses and hat, tossing them on the foyer table.

Avery pointed a finger in Shannon's direction. "You're the governor's wife."

Shannon placed her purse on the table and sat. "Ex-wife, but yes. Paul Wentworth was my husband."

Avery's jaw dropped. "An Alliance husband?"

"Guilty. And who was your husband?"

"Bernie Fields."

Shannon looked up as if searching her memory for some recollection. "Hedge funds?"

Avery smiled. "Not to mention his trust fund. But yes, that's Bernie."

Shannon smiled. "I can't picture you with him."

"He wanted tall and blonde."

"And beautiful, I assume."

Avery's grin grew wider. "Thank you."

"I thought I heard voices."

Lori turned as Trina walked from one of the bedrooms.

Shannon sucked in air and Avery blew out a breath. "Katrina Petrov?"

"Call me Trina," she corrected Avery.

Shannon moved her stare to Lori. "When you said you had a client that could use some friends in the know, you weren't kidding."

Trina's disaster of a life had been front-page news in as many as a dozen countries.

Avery stood and crossed the living room space to the open kitchen. "I think we're going to need liquor."

Shannon extended her hand to Trina. "Shannon Redding."

"Trina Petrov."

"You're keeping his name?"

"For now."

Trina looked the grieving widow. Sullen eyes, the spark all but gone. At first the media had painted her as a young bride in the thick of tragedy. Then, somewhere right after Fedor's funeral and before Alice's, fingers started pointing, and Trina was the center of gossip. She'd come from nowhere to marry a rich man, into an oil-rich family, and suddenly all the people holding the money were dead. Never mind Alice's condition wasn't new or that Fedor took his own life . . . Trina found blame placed on her shoulders, just as she'd predicted.

“I’m so sorry,” Shannon said.

Avery popped the cork from a bottle of red. “I’m Avery Grant. I didn’t take Bernie’s name from the get-go.”

Lori helped Avery with the glasses and took a seat beside Shannon. “I need to play lawyer for just a few minutes, then I promise to play something else for the rest of the week.”

Avery nudged her, grinning.

“I brought you all here for different reasons, you’ve all signed confidentiality agreements and understand that everything we speak of is in the strictest confidence.”

“We know, Counselor.” Avery was the snarky one in the group.

“With so much secrecy around your actual married life, Sam and I thought it would be helpful if you have a friend or two you can confide in when times get hard.”

Trina tried to grin but failed.

“I’ve brought Shannon because she’s two years postdivorce and has probably the highest profile of all of you. I know it seems as if everyone is talking about you, Trina, but Shannon can attest that it could be worse and it will get better.”

Shannon lifted her glass before taking a sip.

“I brought Avery to remind you both about the excitement you once had entering into your arranged marriages.”

"Whoop-whoop," Avery exclaimed before drinking.

"And Avery might think it's all fun and games, but there are some pitfalls to look out for."

Lori's comment was met by Avery rolling her eyes. "You worry too much," Avery said.

"How long have you been divorced?" Shannon asked.

"Little over a month."

"How long has it been since you've had sex?"

Avery's smile fell. "Too long!"

"Who did you date before you married Bernie?" Lori asked.

"A long string of assholes, sadly."

"So you're a bad judge of character?" Shannon's question sounded almost like a statement.

"I wouldn't say that. I just don't think there are that many good guys out there."

Shannon shrugged. "You have a point there."

That wasn't something Lori could argue and win. It had been so long since she'd met a man worthy of a second cup of coffee, let alone anything more. "Finding a guy who isn't using you for your money, or who doesn't think you're after his, isn't easy," Lori reminded her.

Avery lifted her glass. "I don't want to find *the* guy, just *a* guy. Why should men be the only ones out there playing?"

Trina sat there during their conversation with a

small smile and took it in without saying a word.

"*That* guy isn't easy to find," Shannon informed Avery.

"Don't tell me you have a hard time getting laid." If Avery's colorful language offended the others, it didn't show on their faces.

"Oh, I can find a man for that. But one that won't go to the tabloids when it falls apart . . . not so much."

"You were married to a Republican governor. So does that cross off every Democrat?" Trina asked with a hint of a grin.

"Almost."

Lori sat back and sipped her wine.

"So is that why we're going on the cruise? The Mediterranean doesn't have Republicans or Democrats?" Avery asked.

"That, and there aren't many who will know who Bernie Fields is, or care that you're his ex-wife," Lori said.

"What about Fedor? I don't think I'll escape the media's scrutiny about his suicide, even here."

"We aren't here to escape your life, or his suicide," Lori told her. "We're here to pull ourselves together without the distractions of our daily lives. Which is why we're going on a cruise. New ports every day. If the media is about, chances are they aren't going to row after a cruise ship to follow us. You speak three languages, Trina, and can blend. You need a break and you're far too young for those frown lines on your face," Lori said.

"Three languages, really?" Avery was obviously impressed.

"English, Russian, and Spanish. Which makes Italian a little easier to grasp."

"Good thing we're going to Rome," Avery said.

"This week is about finding a way to move forward after your marriage, figuring out where you need to go from here, and what path you will need to take. Maybe even discover what kind of man should come along for the ride."

Avery opened her mouth to speak, then closed it with a laugh.

Lori lifted her glass. "A week to get this First Wives Club off the ground."

"First Wives? Wasn't there a movie with that title?" Avery asked.

Trina grinned. "Yeah, but those women were all older, with husbands that left them for younger women."

"But we're the young ones," said Avery.

"And rich," Shannon added.

Avery narrowed her gaze in Lori's direction and questioned, "Rich?"

"What are you looking at me like that for? I arrived in a private plane, you guys schlepped in first class."

Trina laughed for the first time since Lori had walked into the Petrov estate. Lori wasn't sure if it was the liquor or the company . . . or the combination of both. But already her plan to wipe the frown from Trina's face was working.

"No one schleps in first class," Trina said.

"So you're young and rich . . . but you've never been married," Avery proclaimed.

Lori lifted her chin higher. "How I wish that were true."

All three of them lowered their glasses in shock.

"Wait, you're divorced? Alliance?" Shannon asked.

"Yes, divorced, but not through Alliance. I made the fatal mistake of marrying for love."

Avery picked up the bottle and topped off her glass. "Looks like we all have some secrets to spill this week."

"I would never have guessed you'd taken the plunge."

Lori met Avery's eyes. "It isn't something I plan on repeating." The image of her long-ago ex scratched at her memory. She'd fallen hard and early, and the experience gave her a hardened, jaded edge to make her a kick-ass divorce attorney who happily helped Alliance arrange fake marriages for a price. Unfortunately, after years of witnessing the cycle of love, marriage . . . failure, it was difficult to start anything in her own life without seeing the end before the second orgasm.

Lori shook her personal thoughts from her head and lifted her glass. “To the *First Wives* . . . divorced or widowed.”

“Cheers!”

Lori’s bags were in her room before she opened the door. “Wow,” she sighed. The pictures didn’t do the space justice.

Anytime one scored over eight hundred square feet of cruise ship cabin space, you knew they were paying dearly for it. Lori’s room as well as the First Wives’ rooms were centered around a private pool, private dining room, and exclusive lounge that could only be accessed by the ultimate of first-class passengers. Some considered cruising a vacation for the budget minded, but among the patrons in this section of the ship, *budget* wasn’t in their vocabulary. While the butler service was way over-the-top, Lori wasn’t about to complain. She’d researched the cruise ship and their accommodations extensively to assure their privacy and high-end lodgings. Alliance spared no expense. No matter what level of socialization the women wanted, they could get it on board the outsize floating city.

She went to the balcony door and pushed it open. From behind the small dividing wall, she heard Trina. “What a view.”

Lori peeked around the partition. “Beautiful,

isn't it?" Barcelona buzzed from beyond the ship while passengers funneled on board.

"This balcony is bigger than my college dorm room," Trina said.

"I'm glad you like it."

A soft knock on the open door behind her captured Lori's attention. A short Filipino man dressed in a formal black-and-white uniform stood smiling. "Ms. Cumberland?"

She nodded. "That's me."

"I'm Datu, I'll be your butler while onboard." He stepped inside the room, placed his hand on her luggage. "I understand you're here with a few of your friends?"

"That's right." She gave Datu the names of the others.

"Most wonderful. I'll see to unpacking your things. Might I suggest you enjoy our cocktail of the day with your companions before we set sail? Perhaps you can plan your evening. I'm happy to make any reservations on your behalf, or bring you anything you might need."

"Thank you, Datu. That would be wonderful." She pointed to her laptop case. "Please leave that case out so I can get some work done."

Datu narrowed his eyes. "Work, Miss?"

"Sadly. No worries, I plan on playing quite a bit."

"Wonderful." Datu opened her suitcase as she moved past him.

"Oh, Datu?"

He turned. "What is your cocktail of the day?"

"It's called rebellious fish. One of my favorites."

"What's in it?" The question no sooner left her lips than she waved off any answer he might have. "Never mind, I don't want to know."

With her room key tucked into a small clutch, Lori made her way to the exclusive bar.

She found Avery already flirting with two young male passengers, her glass half-full.

"There you are." Avery had managed to don a pair of tight shorts and a tank top destined to give the tops of her breasts a tan before they left port.

"It's been less than thirty minutes since we checked in," Lori told her.

Avery offered a flirty smile at the bartender, as if the two guys talking to her weren't enough. "She'll have one of these. It's a rebel something."

"Let me go out on a limb and say you know a thing or two about being a rebel," said the man to Avery's right, who had a thick Italian accent and equally thick hair.

"Why would you guess that?"

"I'm Lori," she chuckled and introduced herself.

"Oh, I'm sorry. Lori, this is Mr. Married, and this is Mr. Engaged."

Lori lifted an amused eyebrow.

Mr. Married lifted both palms in the air as if apologizing. And Mr. Engaged, the one who nailed Avery as a rebel, flirted with his eyes. "We will have to find you Mr. Single, Miss Rebel."

"It's a big ship, and I'm going to need more than one." Avery sipped her drink.

The bartender put Lori's colorful drink on the bar and moved away.

"So that's how it is?" Mr. Engaged said.

Avery played with the straw using the tip on her tongue. "Yep. At least two for me and one for each of my friends."

"That didn't take you two long," Shannon said as she joined them. Trina walked beside her with large sunglasses hiding her eyes. Those sunglasses had become a shield in the past month, whether to keep the media from recognizing her or to hide the pain in her eyes, Lori wasn't sure. She made it a goal to see those glasses gone by the end of the week. Or at the very least, put away when the sun wasn't shining on Trina's face.

"The rooms are phenomenal," Shannon told Lori.

"I can't imagine we'll spend much time in them," Avery said.

Lori finally sipped her cocktail. Rum, she thought . . . and a bunch of other stuff. It went down way too smooth.

Avery did another round of introductions,

keeping with the theme of Mr. Married and Mr. Engaged. Something told Lori that she'd never remember the men as anything other than that. More drinks were ordered, and before she knew it, her shoulders started to relax.

This might be a working vacation, but Lori was determined to enjoy herself.

When Mrs. Married and Miss Engaged found their men, the eye flirting ended and resulted in Avery looking around the deck in search of a fresh catch. The space slowly filled up as passengers made it from their rooms to the bar. Two kids, both boys, ran past them en route to the pool in the center of the deck.

"You look familiar," Mrs. Married told Trina.

Both Lori and Shannon tensed.

"My first time in Barcelona, so I doubt we've met."

"You're American, right?"

The married and engaged party of four was from Sicily. All of them spoke English.

"Oh my God, Shannon, I almost forgot. We were supposed to meet those French guys on the main pool deck when we pulled out of port."

Shannon caught on quickly. "Oh, that's right." She put her arm through Trina's and turned her away from the Italians. "Lovely meeting you. I'm sure we'll see you again."

Lori held back to sign for the bar tab.

One of the Italians muttered something about

the French before they took their drinks to another part of the lounge.

By now, the barkeep was elbow deep with orders. With tractor-beam eyes, she watched the man in hopes of gaining his attention.

"The death stare usually works faster." Lori felt her lips peeling back in a smile before pivoting her head toward the amused male voice.

She took him in from the ground up. Slacks, not jeans or shorts like many of the men milling about on deck. Trim waist that bloomed into thick shoulders covered by a pullover, three-button shirt. Arms that spent some time holding something other than a pen flexed under the short sleeves and made her wish he was sunbathing by the pool instead of standing at the bar. Strong jaw, freshly shaven, could only be described as chiseled, or maybe that was the faded scar that slid along his left cheek, a little more than an inch long. His eyes were dark with thick lashes most women would pay to have. His chestnut hair was a little long, and not as well cut as the rest of him. She thought, briefly, that his hair didn't fit. Then she shook off her odd thoughts and realized she was staring.

Lori forced herself to look away only to find the bartender on the other side helping out a gaggle of early twentysomethings wearing as little as possible.

"The key to the death stare is never letting

your eyes wander away," Lori said, and when it appeared the bartender was turning around, she lifted her hand in the air.

He didn't see her.

"I messed you up, my apologies." He pushed in closer, their shoulders brushed against the other's.

"I can have him put your drink on my room." The realization that he was hitting on her created a swirl of chaos inside her. Lori's job was to acclimate the First Wives into their new single life, not trying to get lucky on her weeklong cruise.

Lori turned to find him watching from a good five inches above her head. She liked them tall. "That would be rude of me, seeing as I don't even know your name."

He extended his hand, his palm warmed hers with a spark. "Mr. Single."

Lori hesitated and then laughed. "You were listening."

"Three beautiful women show up at the bar, and men watch."

Lori cocked her head. "There were four of us."

"Three beautiful and one captivating." He squeezed her palm before letting go.

Her cheeks warmed. "Are you a salesman, Mr. Single?"

"I can be."

She looked him up and down, made sure he knew she was sizing him up this time. “Personal trainer?”

“Every day but Sunday.” He met her eyes with a full kilowatt of charm.

He was joking, but she liked the flirty banter. “What’s wrong with working out on Sunday?”

“Nothing. I prefer to take my workouts outside of the gym on Sunday.” He had a decent tan, so she assumed that meant the beach, or maybe a hiking trip. “What about you? Professional model?”

Lori rolled her eyes. “Really? Your lines were better a minute ago.”

“You’re right. You seem much too put together for such a flighty profession. Doctor?”

Lori played along, mainly to avoid him asking the next question and suggesting *lawyer.* Because for some strange reason, announcing she was a divorce attorney while on the cruise with three of her female clients didn’t feel right. Besides, the less this stranger knew about her, the better. “You guessed it. Doctor.”

“Of?” He didn’t believe her.

“Anthropology.”

He snickered.

“What, I could be. Especially in a bar on a cruise ship sailing the Mediterranean. Lots of great people to study here.”

“That would make me an anthropologist in

training, since watching people is my greatest strength."

The bartender walked by and Lori shouted out the need for her check.

"Body language is important when selling used cars."

His smile slid, but his eyes did that twinkle thing. He sized her up slowly. "I bet you're into yoga?"

"Only on Sunday," she said with a laugh.

"Why only Sunday?"

"Because the rest of the week I'm shimmying up a pole and collecting one-dollar bills all night."

If she had to guess, the way he shifted his hips meant her comment made his mind go there.

"Now that I'd like to see."

The bartender handed her the bill and walked away. She wrote her room number and scribbled a signature.

"Next time you're in Vegas, let me know. I'll hook you up."

Mr. Single leaned back as their flirting came to a close. "A pole dancing stripper needs to work a lot of hours to afford a cruise like this."

"Nawh, she just needs a sugar daddy, now if you'll excuse me, my friends are waiting."

He turned as she walked away. "Until next time, Miss Single."

She lifted her hands. “I’m here all week.”

“Lucky me.”

Lori laughed as she walked away, ignoring the heat of his stare on her ass.

Chapter Four

Sugar daddy. Reed couldn't help but wonder if Miss Single had one of those, past or present. He enjoyed the view as she sashayed away. Honey blonde hair, a sparkle in her blue eyes that wasn't flighty like her overly animated friend's. There had been a smirk behind her serious expression, and when she had started on the pole dancing line. She had curves, and that ass . . . yeah, a week on the open sea pursuing that one was a challenge he happily accepted. His eyes landed on the bill, which had her room number on it. One of the penthouse suites. He wasn't surprised. This woman, and those she surrounded herself with, dripped with sophistication and money.

He took a pull on his longneck beer and opened the daily itinerary the ship provided. He reached for the pen left behind by Miss Single and circled a singles mixer dance party for later that night. None of the women Miss Single was with wore wedding rings, so it was safe to say he'd find them among the unattached on the ship.

His phone buzzed. A number from the States displayed without a name.

"Reed," he answered, 99 percent sure who the caller was.

"How is Spain?" the female voice asked.

"Balmy."

"I trust your accommodations are satisfactory."

He glanced around the deck. "They'll work," he said without humor.

"Anything to report?"

"I've located my target."

"Well, I hope so. That suite didn't come cheap."

Reed looked around the Haven's private accommodations and was glad he wasn't paying the bill.

"She's traveling with friends."

"Who?"

"I don't know yet, I've been on board less than an hour."

She muttered something crass. "I will call you in Rome."

"Until Rome." He hung up and signaled the bartender for his bill.

"Don't look."

Funny how when someone tells you not to look, that's exactly what you want to do. Lori found her eyes drifting from the spinning ball on the roulette table.

Shannon elbowed her gently.

Lori snapped her attention away from the table.

"He cannot take his eyes off you."

"Who?"

The croupier called out the number, placed his

marker on the board, and paid out the winners. Sadly, Lori wasn't one of them.

She took the moment to pick up her drink and briefly scan the room.

Sure enough, Mr. Single stood on the opposing side of the craps table, watching her.

Instead of pretending she didn't notice him, she lifted her glass in salute and smiled. It felt good to flirt, even though it was against her better judgment.

His answering grin was mixed with mischief.

"That's the guy you were telling us about, isn't it?" Shannon asked.

"Sure is."

"Wow, he is something to look at."

Lori hummed.

"Needs a haircut, though."

Lori broke eye contact with him and turned to Shannon. "I know, right?" She set her chips on the table and stood back.

"Place your bets," the croupier told them. Shannon leaned across Lori to reach the higher numbers.

When Lori looked back up, Mr. Single was gone. A hair of disappointment wiggled up her spine.

"Thirty-one black."

Shannon high-fived Lori. "Whoop, whoop!"

Her five-dollar chip sat on the line between thirty-one and twenty-eight.

"Next round is on you," Lori teased.

Shannon collected her money and generously placed her bets. She glanced up. "Where did he go?"

"Who knows?" Lori looked at her hand of dwindling chips, promising to walk away if she didn't win on the next turn of the wheel. Just then her skin prickled and her palms started to itch.

"Red." His voice came from behind her, his lips close to her ear.

She forced herself not to smile. "You're sure?" she asked.

The croupier spun the wheel and released the ball.

"Forty-eight percent sure."

She looked up and down the table, remembered the green zero and double zeros. She put twenty on red and scattered another twenty bucks on various red numbers.

"No more bets."

The ball started to bounce.

Lori held her breath.

"Fourteen, red."

"Okay, then. I guess I owe you a drink," Lori said as she peeked over her shoulder to find Mr. Single staring.

"Hello." Shannon peered from Lori's other side.

"Hello," he replied, then narrowed his eyes. "Aren't you—"

Lori panicked and lifted a finger to his lips as if she had a right.

His amused eyes widened as he reached to touch her hand.

"My *friend* is on vacation." Lori hoped her words kept him from bringing unwanted attention to Shannon. "*Far* away from home."

His eyes told her he understood. With a tiny squeeze of her hand, he let her go.

Shannon tilted her head. "Thank you. Do you have a name other than Mr. Single?"

"You've been talking about me."

Lori felt like she was sixteen years old, caught talking about the new kid in school. She tried to hide her embarrassment.

He reached across Lori. "I'm Reed."

"Nice to meet you, Reed. This is my friend Lori."

"Lori." It sounded as if he was testing her name with the weight of the sigh he used when saying it.

The heat on her neck felt unnatural.

"Now that we have the names straight, what should I bet on now?"

The ball was already rolling.

"Let it ride on red."

"I never let it ride."

He stopped her hand from pulling her chips away. His lips moved close to her ear again. "What are you worried about, losing Sugar Daddy's money?"

Before she could pull the chips away, the croupier waved a hand over the table, indicating she'd lost her opportunity to back out.

"Twenty-seven, red."

She sighed, and once she'd been paid out, she removed her chips. Not that she worried about losing forty dollars. Hell, she was down two hundred and she'd only been in the casino for forty minutes. Gambling in general was outside her control spectrum. A little bit was fine, exciting even . . . but if any real money was involved, she'd probably break out in hives before the ball settled on a number.

"No guts to do it again?" Reed asked.

She pointed to the table. "Where's your bet?"

"Touché." He removed his wallet, placed a hundred-dollar bill on red.

The croupier made quick work of removing the cash and replacing it with several green chips.

Less than a minute later, *twenty-one, red* was called.

Lori stood back to watch, her hands tightening in on themselves with each rotation of the ball.

All she noticed was the color when the ball dropped.

Red.

Reed let it ride.

"You're nuts," she whispered.

Lori wasn't sure if his reckless gambling was because of his cocky self-assuredness or if he was just a man using his money to flirt with her. Either one was slightly flattering.

Four spins later, Reed was up sixteen hundred dollars. Only then did he pull off the hundred dollars he started with.

"You're going to leave it there?"

He shrugged with a grin.

The other players at the table were watching. Others were putting their money on black, muttering his luck was about to run out.

Lori held her breath, the ball bounced. "Twelve, red."

Even Shannon was speechless.

Lori was sweating, and it wasn't her money.

"You're not a gambler," he observed.

She looked up to find his eyes laughing at her. "Apparently not."

"Sir?" the croupier caught Reed's attention.

He smirked like it was a natural thing for him to leave three grand on the table riding on a color. "Leave it," Reed told him.

By now a small crowd had gathered to watch.

Lori leaned in. "You're crazy."

He leaned closer. "Life begins at the end of your comfort zone, Lori. You should try it."

None of the other players placed bets on the table as the ball rolled.

"Three, red."

"Dude is lucky."

"Holy crap," a man behind them said.

The noise grew around them as spectators took in Reed's pile of chips, chips equaling six thousand dollars that looked like a pot of gold to Lori.

"Sir?"

"Well, Lori, should I walk away?"

Walk, hell, she'd be running.

Her heart sped and she found herself shaking her head. "Let it ride." She couldn't believe the words came from her lips. She wanted to retract them but heard an opposing counsel in her head shouting "objection."

He winked. "You're learning."

Shannon leaned close. "Crazy."

The croupier signaled his manager.

The delay in spinning the wheel had Lori looking around. She glanced at the plaque on the table indicating a five-thousand-dollar limit.

The manager spoke with the croupier and glanced at the previous winning red numbers on the digital board above the table. A single nod and the ball spun.

Lori gripped the edge of the table, her eyes following the ball, with suspended breath.

Just when the ball bounced onto twenty-one, red, it flipped out and settled on four.

"Four, black." The deep tone of the croupier sounded as disappointed as Lori felt.

A collective sigh from those watching hummed in the air, and the six thousand dollars in chips were taken away.

Lori hung her head, her hands still buzzed with excitement.

Reed reached across the table, leaving the hundred dollars he started with at the croupier's side as a tip.

"Well, that was fun," Shannon said with a lift in her voice.

"How about that drink?" Reed asked Lori.

The music from the singles mixer was blaring through the doors of the ship's nightclub.

Lori was keenly aware of the proximity of the man moving beside her. She hadn't felt this high on a man's attention in so long that she had forgotten how warm and fuzzies felt.

"There's Avery and Trina," Shannon said over the noise of the music and people.

The three of them weaved through the crowd until they reached the high-top table their friends were standing around.

Avery sized Reed up before saying hello. "Are you Mr. Single?"

Lori felt her cheeks burn with embarrassment.

He reached out a hand. "I'm Reed."

Avery made a little growling noise and winked at Lori before introducing herself and Trina.

"You need one of these." Avery took a pen and self-sticking nametags from the table and started to write down their names.

"What's this for?" Shannon asked.

"It's a mixer. We need to mix," Avery said as if that explained everything.

It wasn't long before a cocktail waiter took their order, delivered their drinks. There weren't any real rules except one. Every time the bell rang, you moved to another person.

Lori started in front of Reed.

"You have a wild look in your eyes."

She looked over to find Trina fidgeting while she spoke with a man twice her age who slid up beside her at the first bell.

"I do?" Lori didn't meet his gaze.

Reed paused. "You're worried about your friend."

Lori watched for signs of distress on Trina's face. "She's, uhm . . ." Lori didn't finish her sentence when the bell rang. Without another word, she rushed to cut off another guy walking Trina's way.

"You okay?"

"This isn't blending," Trina pointed out.

Lori looked around, saw Shannon being hit on by a redhead. A single nod and Shannon got the hint. "It's a twenty-minute meet and greet, and we're done." Lori made light of it and extended her hand. "Hi, I'm Lori."

Trina smiled. "I'm being silly."

The bell rang, and Shannon took Lori's place.

Lori found Reed in front of her again. "Do you always take care of your friends?"

"Don't you?" she asked.

"You're assuming I have friends."

She wasn't sure if he was joking or not. The man had quite the poker face. "A man without friends . . ."

The bell rang.

Avery took Lori's place, and Lori moved back to Trina.

"The men are going to think I'm a lesbian," Trina said.

Lori glanced around them . . . "Are you ready to talk to a stranger?"

Trina placed both hands on her head. "This used to be easy."

"Let them speak first, then switch languages if you don't want to interact."

"That's a great idea," Trina said with a strangled smile.

The bell rang and Lori turned to find a hard-bodied Spaniard grinning down at her. He said something in Spanish that she didn't understand, but his grin and wink were enough. "Oh, you're too much for me." Lori looked at Avery, who was still talking to Reed. She pulled the other girl over in front of Mr. Spanish Charm. "Switch," Lori said.

Reed was grinning. "So Avery you feed to the wolves, and Trina you protect."

The bell rang again, and instead of moving, Lori reached for her drink. "This is exhausting."

• • •

Lori rose the next morning to find a note attached to the daily itinerary slid under her door. The yoga class was circled in red with a note: *Since you missed your Sunday ritual.*

The man put a smile on her face. Maybe because she hadn't taken the time to flirt or get to know a member of the opposite sex in several months. Not because she was opposed to the thought, but she'd burned out on the dance. At thirty-five, she'd dated plenty of men. Only half of whom were emotionally available. And of those, half of them only wanted sex. The rest couldn't handle her success or she couldn't handle their egos.

When she'd turned thirty, she'd decided that she never wanted to marry again. On some level, she knew that made her less emotionally available than the men who asked her out. Once the men found out what she did for a living, they assumed she was single by choice, which either turned them on or completely off.

Where did Reed fall?

Temporary.

If for no other reason than they were on a cruise ship.

Lori glanced at the clock and wondered if Reed would show up at her yoga class.

Only one way to find out.

"Good morning, Miss Lori." She dressed,

bolted out the door, and ran right into the resident butler.

"Morning, Datu. Can you tell my friends when you see them that I'll meet them poolside at eleven?"

"Of course. Any other requests?"

"How about fruit and yogurt in my room around ten?"

"Coffee?" he asked.

"Yes, please." Lori was all smiles as she walked away. A butler was something she could get used to.

The fitness center was lined with bikes, ellipticals, and treadmills, all facing a massive window looking out over the Mediterranean Sea. Since this was the only full day at sea, the place was packed with hard bodies and even a few soft ones trying to combat the opulent food on board.

She spied Trina lying on a mat in the far corner of the classroom. Lori removed a mat from a stack in the corner and took the spot next to her.

"Good morning," she whispered over the calming music.

Trina opened her eyes and smiled. "Morning."

The room was library quiet, with only a few mumbling students settling in.

"I didn't know you liked yoga," Lori told her.

"Been a while. But I thought it would help . . . you know."

A wave of guilt crashed over Lori when she

realized she'd been preoccupied with herself. Her job was these women. Especially Trina, since her world was falling apart.

Reed had stolen her attention the moment she'd laid eyes on the man.

Lori mentally kicked herself.

Refocus.

Thoughts of a temporary anything with Reed should not be dominating her head before reaching the twenty-fourth hour on the ship. Trina, Shannon . . . Avery, that's what she was there for, not Reed and his sexy smile and cocky gambling techniques.

The instructor started to speak, and Lori took her place on the mat and pushed Reed out of her head.

Chapter Five

If Reed stood in the window to the yoga room much longer, someone was going to tell his voyeur ass to move along. He wasn't surprised to see Lori bending and stretching in ways the body didn't normally move, but the sight of her butt held tight by a pair of black yoga pants . . . that's what snagged his attention and wouldn't let go. He was half-willing to join a yoga class just so he wouldn't be so obvious.

His eyes kept level with her ass as he walked by the glass doors. He snapped out of his trance and quickly looked around the gym. He decided to burn through a few miles of frustration with the free weights until the yoga class was over.

Reed worked through his daily routine in half his normal time, his eyes tracking on the yoga door.

A tall blonde wearing a purple sports bra and shorts that should be illegal anywhere other than by a swimming pool stopped in front of him. "*Ar det tungt*?"

"Excuse me?" He didn't recognize the language, and with over forty different nationalities on board, he didn't want to guess.

"American?" she asked, her smile full of flirt.

He nodded.

She pointed to her chest, which spilled from the sports bra. “Swedish.”

“I don’t speak Swedish.”

“I know English. Not perfect, but some.”

Any other time, she’d be fun. But just then the volume of voices in the room increased, and Reed noticed the yoga door opening and people spilling out.

“Maybe later,” he said with a wink before he stood and started toward the exit.

He lingered at the door, half an eye on the people leaving, the other half on his cell phone in an effort to not be obvious about his intentions.

“I think someone is following you,” he heard a woman say.

He looked up to see Lori and Trina walking toward him.

Moisture gathered on their skin. *Does yoga make you sweat?*

“No, he’s a gym rat.”

“A big one,” Trina said.

“Morning, ladies.”

Trina moved out of the way of the people moving through the door. “I’ll see you by the pool, Lori.” She glanced at him. “Bye, Reed.”

“I see you found my note,” he told Lori once Trina left.

“I did. Great suggestion.”

Something in her voice told him something had changed since the night before.

"And here I thought your line about yoga was a fabrication."

"It was."

Short answers with an edge to her voice. Her eyes kept moving past him. Yep, something had changed.

"By the way, how did you know what room I was in?" He couldn't tell if the question was curious or accusatory.

He considered lying but didn't. "When you signed for the bar bill."

"Ahh." She started to frown. "I'm not sure if I should be flattered or creeped out."

He thought of his sister and wondered how he would feel if someone had obtained her room number the way he had. "I'm harmless," he lied, "but you might want to be more careful."

She paused. "I will."

Miss Swedish took that moment to walk past. She eyed Reed, then turned her attention to Lori. With a lift of her eyebrow, she parted with a swaying of her hips.

He caught Lori laughing under her breath. "Enjoy your day, Reed."

Yep, something was definitely off. "You too, Lori."

The conversation from the night before played in his head. Did he say something to put her off?

No. He'd flirted, she flirted back.

Time to switch things up. Avery was the party girl. Reed needed one of Lori's crew on his side and he'd be where he wanted to be. He paused, wondering exactly what his goal was again.

There were many things to enjoy on a cruise ship. Sitting poolside with a fruity drink that's sporting an umbrella before noon was only one of them.

Buried in a sea of bodies on the main pool deck with the sea breeze was better than being huddled in the exclusive pool on the Haven's deck. Seemed as if more eyes were watching the four of them in their private "haven" than on the most populated area of the ship. It was probably all in her mind. Her concern for the women she'd taken under her wing on this trip was becoming a moving force in her brain. One she couldn't ignore.

The ladies pulled up four lounge chairs, grabbed a few towels, and settled in.

"What did you think of Rogelio last night?" Avery asked after they'd lathered up with suntan lotion.

"The sexy Spaniard who didn't speak a lick of English?" Shannon asked.

Avery smirked. "Yeah, that one."

"He doesn't speak English," Shannon said as if that answered Avery's question.

"That man drips with charisma," Trina said from the sidelines.

Lori turned toward the woman she assumed was sexually dormant, surprised that she'd noticed Rogelio's sex appeal.

"And he was into you last night," said Trina.

"He doesn't speak English!" Shannon didn't want to let the language barrier go.

"It's a cruise," Trina reminded Shannon. "What happens in the bedroom doesn't need words."

"I'm starting to really like you," Avery told Trina.

The two women clicked their umbrella-sporting drinks together.

"And what's with you and Reed?" Avery asked Lori.

"The gambler?" Lori asked as if that defined him. Sexy man of chance . . . she dreamt of him the night before and woke frustrated.

"The hot guy from the casino, the nightclub, and the gym this morning," Trina said.

She rested her sunglasses over her eyes and lay back. "Nothing."

"Didn't look like *nothing* last night."

"You see something in everything, Avery," Lori reminded her.

"She has a point, Avery," Trina agreed.

"That man is into you," Avery said.

Lori tilted her sunglasses. "He snagged my room number from the bar bill."

All three sets of eyes zeroed in on her.

After explaining what she meant, Lori turned her attention to the people bobbing in the pool. "Besides, I'm here for you three this week."

After several quiet seconds, she turned to find all three of them staring.

"Last time I looked," Shannon started, "we're all adults. And while you may have brought us together, that doesn't mean we're your charges. You're not *Aunt* Lori."

"You're not even our *lawyer* on this trip," Trina said.

"I'm always your *lawyer.*" Lori whispered the last word and looked around as if she'd said a dirty word.

Avery pointed to her chest. "I'm not paying you five hundred dollars an hour this week . . . what about you, Trina?"

"Nope . . . you, Shannon?"

"My bill has been paid."

Lori rolled her eyes.

"Guess that means you're just one of the First Wives. No more or less than any of us." To Avery, everything was that simple. Lori wasn't sure if that was a good thing or bad. Was she right?

"We are here on behalf of Alliance. And I'm the ambassador. You're my priority, not a hard-bodied, charming gambler."

"Oh, please. When was the last time you got laid?" Avery asked.

A woman in a chair in front of them responded by taking her child by the hand and leading her away with a dirty look.

"I manage," Lori said quietly.

"Nice diversion, Counselor," Shannon said.

"I'm fine."

Lori's terse response halted the conversation for a few moments.

"I tell you what," Avery broke the quiet.

Lori was almost afraid to ask. "What?"

"If two out of the three of us hook up, then you let your hair down."

Lori lifted a hand to her ponytail, her eyes landing on Trina. Yeah, Trina wasn't looking at her. Then there was Shannon. The chances of her letting loose were slim . . . and Avery? Yeah, Avery was a sure thing for hooking up. The woman was beyond ready. If two out of the three of them did manage to find some male companionship, then Lori's idea for this weeklong trip would have been worth the effort.

Life begins at the end of your comfort zone.

"I'm not a gambler, but I'll take that bet."

"I haven't been pressured into going on a date by a woman since high school," Shannon said.

Trina raised her hand. "College, and he was French."

Avery giggled. "The one language you don't speak."

"There are a lot of languages I don't speak."

The women spoke of college and friendships as they soaked up the sun while Lori closed her eyes.

"*Hola*, ladies."

Miguel and Rogelio from the dance club stood shirtless and smiling.

"Hello, boys." Avery flirted without effort. She scooted her legs off her lounge chair. "Sit." She patted the space next to her.

Rogelio took her offered spot, his eyes sweeping her skimpy bikini.

"We hoped to see you again," Miguel said, sitting on the edge of Trina's lounger.

Trina was smiling. Reserved, but smiling.

Miguel said something to Avery in his thick Spanish accent as he lifted her hand, kissing the back of it.

Shannon leaned over and whispered. "I hope you weren't counting on winning your bet."

Rogelio spouted off in Spanish, and Miguel spoke beside him as if finishing his sentences. "Do you think we can win the competition?"

"Really, both of you?" Trina asked Miguel.

"What?" Lori asked, missing some key words in the conversation.

"They're entering the Mr. Epic contest," Trina translated.

"What's that?" Shannon asked.

"A male body pageant. They want us to join them," Trina said.

"Join? As in parade onstage?" Lori saw that as

a great way to be noticed when they were trying hard to blend.

Trina shook her head.

"I'll be the oil girl," Avery offered.

Miguel started laughing, and translated for Rogelio.

Rogelio leaned over Avery, rested a hand on her leg. There was heat between their eyes.

Oh, yeah . . . someone was getting lucky before dinner.

"Sounds like fun," Lori said.

Trina sat forward, grabbed her wrap. "What the hell. It's like Vegas, right? What happens here stays here."

"That's right," Shannon encouraged her.

"Let's go, Miguel. Lead me to the oil."

Miguel flashed a smile. "Would you like to join us?"

Lori didn't get a chance to respond.

"Go, six is a crowd," Shannon told him.

Trina and Avery wasted little time following Spanish Playboy Number One, and Spanish Playboy Number Two to the stage.

"Oh, boy," Lori sighed.

"That's what we're here for, right? Reconnect with life?"

"It is," Lori said.

"So what are you worried about?"

Lori lifted her sunglasses from her eyes. "I'm paid to worry."

"Good thing you can afford Botox, then. You're gonna need it."

She rolled her eyes.

One of the rotating cocktail waiters covered them in shade. "Can I get you something?"

Shannon answered for both of them, "How about two of your specials."

"Good choice."

Lori watched him as he walked away. "My liver is going to need a good detox."

"It's five o'clock somewhere."

Ten minutes later, sipping something that tasted of coconut and rum, Lori changed the conversation. "What's your story?"

Shannon peeked from behind her glasses.

"You of all people know my story."

"No, not the marriage . . . your life after the marriage? Has there been anyone? Anything?" It had been close to two years since Shannon and Paul had separated. A year and a half since their divorce. Her high profile world was littered with the paparazzi for months after their split.

"It's easy."

"Oh?"

Shannon sipped her drink and shrugged. "I fell in love with him."

Lori's smile fell with the last hope that she was wrong. She'd guessed that Shannon had fallen hard. So had Sam, but they never asked.

"I'm sorry."

Shannon set her drink down, looked beyond those in the pool. "Not your fault. You cautioned me, Sam and Eliza pointed out Paul's past. I should have been more guarded."

There was a time when Lori and Sam hoped to hear that the first couple of California was going to stick the marriage out. Only like clockwork, the week their contract was up, Paul showed up in Lori's office and asked to sign the papers to end his in-name-only marriage.

Their polite divorce shook the state. Media had a field day and made crap up when there was nothing gossip worthy to report. First it was that Paul had found another woman, then that Shannon had an affair . . . none of it validated with facts. A few pictures leaked of Paul dating, but never with the same woman twice. His handlers kept the media out of his personal life as much as they could. Alliance helped Shannon with the media for the first year. Since then, there was little to report.

Shannon moved out of Sacramento and into the house she and Paul had shared before he was elected. Everything was as they'd contracted. Paul even added a security detail for her and kept in contact with Alliance to make sure she was cared for. It was as if he knew he'd left a foot-print on her heart and still wanted some control over her life.

"He's a great man. Just not the kind to settle for one woman."

Lori placed her hand over Shannon's. "I'm sorry."

"I'm fine. Please, let's not talk about ancient history. It's time for me to move on."

Lori lifted her drink with a reluctant toast. "To moving on."

Chapter Six

"Antonio!" Reed greeted the man he'd met the night before.

They shook hands.

Around them swam a sea of bikini-wearing women sporting suntan lotion and consuming copious amounts of liquor. The DJ pumped music loud enough to bust eardrums, and a walkway was set up in the middle of the deck.

"What's going on?" Reed asked the Italian.

"Male exploitation."

"Male what?"

"Male fashion show without clothes."

Naked? That didn't sound right.

Antonio pointed to the lineup of men wearing Speedos and shorts. Reed noticed Trina and Avery spreading oil all over two of the men that were part of the previous evening's party.

"Looks like someone is having fun."

"That Avery is a party."

"Looks like it's rubbing off on her friend." Reed looked around to see if Lori was nearby.

Sensing what he was searching for, Antonio pointed toward the massive swimming pool. "The others are over there."

"Should we drag them over here?" Reed asked.

“I’m not walking on that stage.”

Yeah, neither was Reed. “I’ve never met a single woman who didn’t appreciate this kind of thing.”

“Let’s go.”

Antonio led the way, weaving through the deck chairs and kids running around.

He spotted the two lone women stretched out on chairs, large sunglasses covering their faces.

He’d pegged the conservative woman for a one piece. He was wrong. Lori wore a black bikini, revealing more skin than he was prepared for.

“Bella!” Antonio announced their presence before they stood over them.

Reed couldn’t see Lori’s eyes, but he felt them.

“Hey.” Shannon lifted her sunglasses.

“We’ve come to drag you away from this boredom,” Reed told them.

“I’m not bored,” Lori countered.

Shannon pushed up from her reclined position. “What did you have in mind?”

Lori slapped at Shannon’s arm.

“We’re good.”

“Come, Bella, sitting in the sun you can do at home.”

Shannon stood, reached for Lori’s hand. “C’mon. I need my wingman.”

Reed liked Shannon more and more.

He reached for Lori’s wrap and handed it over once she was standing. Not that he wanted her to cover up. That yoga butt looked even better in a bikini than it did in pants.

The four of them found a spot on the north side of the stage right as the cruise director took the mic. "Ladies and ladies, and a brave few gentlemen. What is a day at sea without a lot of suntan oil and skin?"

Reed kept an eye on Lori as the translators made sure everyone on board caught the information.

The cruise director and her staff were wearing bright shirts and equally bright shorts with comfortable shoes. They worked the crowd, encouraging them to drink the cocktail of the day and to get the most out of their cruise by entering as many competitions, events, and gatherings as humanly possible. *If you're bored on the ship, it isn't from a lack of activities to take part in!*

"I'm starting to have college flashbacks," Lori said loud enough for all of them to hear.

The DJ turned up the music, making conversation difficult.

The judging at this competition was based completely on applause and audience participation. One at a time, the men took the stage. Most of them owned it, chins in the air, smiles on their faces. More than one of the men sported bodies by beer, complete with several extra inches around their stomachs. Lori looked away when one guy tested his own beer gut with both hands and gave it a good shake.

It wasn't until Rogelio and Miguel took their turns, one after the other, that Lori and Shannon started to clap.

From the side of the stage, Reed saw Avery blowing a loud whistle between her fingers and Trina waving some kind of pom-pom that one of the staff had been using to rev up the crowd.

"Now it's time to show us your best Schwarzenegger pose." The announcer lifted her arms in the air, flexed what little muscles she had in example.

Several men impersonated the Hulk, complete with grunts and growls. The first beer gut guy showed up on stage with a can of brew and flexed a bicep as he drank the whole thing in one swallow. The crowd went a little crazy.

Rogelio and Miguel took the stage together, turned around, and showed off their backs with a pose. Lori leaned over to Shannon and said something Reed couldn't hear. From the way the women smiled, they appreciated the view.

He pointed to the stage and said, "You like?"

She rolled her eyes but didn't answer.

The last hops and barley dude had changed his board shorts for Speedos. The crowd laughed, and Shannon watched through a slit in her fingers. As if the European male bathing suit wasn't enough, he turned his back to the audience and flexed his hips to the music. Every dimple in his butt was one too many bags of chips.

The last part of the competition weeded out the weak quickly.

Pushups.

The women went crazy, especially when one of the harder bodies did his impression of a stripper giving a lap dance.

Lori reached over and grasped Shannon's arm before pointing to Trina and Avery. Both of them were being dragged onstage.

Avery jumped onstage, while Trina had to be coaxed.

The men started to clap when both women were lying on the stage, faceup. The cruise director encouraged the crazy, and as the music took on a more sultry beat, Miguel and Rogelio gave the crowd a show worthy of any Magic Mike performance.

Reed wondered if he needed to up his pushup performance in order to make Lori blush like she was doing while watching her friends.

Shannon took pictures with her cell phone, something he considered himself. But he decided to hold this in his memory instead of his data plan.

Once the "contest" was over and the majority of the men took away T-shirts, Miguel and Rogelio each managed a T-shirt, free drinks, and a crown. The beer gut guys received a bucket of beer.

The music kept playing as the people on deck started to spread out for other activities. It wasn't long before Avery, Trina, Miguel, and Rogelio joined them.

"That was fabulous," Shannon told them.

"Crazy." Trina looked at Lori, slight worry marring her brow.

Lori placed a hand on her friend's arm. "I'm sure it's fine."

The statement sounded out of place.

"You ladies stole the show," Reed told them.

Rogelio slid a hand around Avery's waist, the familiarity of his touch raising a few eyebrows among the women. Miguel didn't take the same approach, instead he said to Trina, "You make doing pushups onstage worthwhile."

Color rose in her cheeks.

"How about some drinks," Lori suggested.

Miguel pulled out a drink card. "Free for us today. What can we get you?"

Less than half an hour later, Rogelio and Avery peeled away from their party to "swim." Only instead of heading for the pool, they headed toward the stairs.

"That's one," Shannon said to Lori. Her eyes skirted over to Reed.

"One what?" he asked.

"Nothing!" Lori said too quickly.

"Hey, Antonio, do you ever have the feeling that there is a whole conversation going on between women that you have no idea about?"

"Every day, my friend."

"Everyone has secrets," Shannon told them.

Lori's gaze moved between Reed and Shannon. Out of nowhere, she stood and reached for his hand. "Do you swim?"

For one brief moment, he thought maybe she was suggesting they head in the direction that Avery had with Rogelio. But when Lori pulled his hand and led him to the pool, he realized his signals were being crossed again.

Lori's heart flipped a little when she saw Trina take the stage. Avery's marriage and divorce wouldn't be considered high profile on the Mediterranean Sea. A rich American man who divorced his trophy wife simply wasn't newsworthy enough in this part of the world. Trina Petrov, however . . . might easily get picked up. Infamous in both Russia and Germany, Ruslan was a well-known businessman with as many allies as he had enemies. Those who knew him knew of Fedor's death. And then there were the oil interests of Fedor's mother, Alice—the reaches of their story captured worldwide attention. So far, the only person who looked twice at the four of them with any recognition was Reed.

She grasped his hand and pulled him to the pool. The warm salt water was easy to slide into. And since the pool was more for lounging than for swimming, they stood waist deep along the side of the pool before she started to talk.

"I didn't want to swim."

His eyes lingered on her wet skin. "That's too bad."

"You're incorrigible."

"Guilty."

She dodged the splash of a man playing with his kids.

"You recognize Shannon." She was certain he had.

"Hard not to. I do live in California."

Lori knew she stared. "You do?"

"I thought I told you that."

She scrolled through their conversations and didn't even know where he would have suggested they spoke of where they lived. Lori knew for a fact she hadn't told him anything about where she lived. "No."

His fingers found her elbow and led her deeper into the pool. "Don't look so stressed," he said.

She tried to relax. "They're my friends. We planned a vacation far away to avoid recognition."

"I would think Shannon would be used to the spotlight by now."

"Doesn't make it comfortable. Lots of people judge out there."

Reed splashed water on his arms. "I'm not judging, and I don't think anyone else was snapping pictures of Shannon to sell to the media."

"If you see anyone taking pictures, tell me." She hesitated. "Please. Or any of my friends."

His eyes narrowed. "Should I know who they are, too?"

"No," she said, straight-faced.

"You're a beautiful liar."

She shivered. "Please. I could use another set of eyes."

He blinked his a few times. "That's a simple request."

"Good." She turned to leave the pool.

"On one condition."

A slow pivot and she was inches from his body. "What's that?"

"Dinner tonight. You and me."

Dripping wet, with a sly smile on his lips, he was hard to resist. When was the last time she had a romantic dinner with a man?

"I need to watch over my friends." Her excuse was lame, even to her ears.

"You're not old enough to be their mother."

"I'm their—" She caught the word *lawyer* before it fell from her lips.

"You don't look like sisters either." Reed traced his fingers along her arm. "What are you scared of, Lori? I asked you to dinner, not skydiving."

"Something tells me skydiving is next."

He smirked. "Let's start with dinner. We'll meet up with your friends after . . . that is, if Avery and Rogelio come out for air before tomorrow."

"They were kinda obvious."

"They have the same goals."

What were Reed's goals? Would he tell her? Should she ask?

Did she want to hear them?

"Okay, dinner. I can do dinner."

"All right then." Reed left a hand on the small of her back as they exited the pool.

His touch lingered long after they were among friends and separated by conversation.

Chapter Seven

Lori slipped into a midcalf-length sundress and jeweled sandals. The sun had given her face more color than she normally had, so makeup consisted of mascara and lip gloss. Strange how living in Southern California didn't add a glow to her face, yet less than three days on the Mediterranean had.

She glanced at the time when someone knocked on her door.

"You're early," she called out.

"It's Trina."

Lori hustled to the door to let her in.

"You look nice," Trina said, closing the door behind her.

"It's just dinner." And she was more nervous than she cared to admit.

"If my opinion is wanted, I think Reed is a decent guy."

"We've known him less than forty-eight hours."

"And I'm sure there is a lot to know, but if this is a weeklong affair, what does it matter?"

Lori had been asking herself that question since she met the man. "You're right." She shook her head. "I'm overthinking this."

"I'm glad you said that. It isn't like you just

buried your husband, or just divorced your husband . . . or had it bad for your ex-husband. You should be the first one from the First Wives Club that should be having a fling."

Hearing Trina paint the truth in black and white cleared up her resolve. She'd go to dinner, see if any warning bells rang. Lori sat on the edge of her bed. "How are you holding up?"

A slow smile inched across Trina's lips. "I forgot about Fedor for over an hour today."

"Let me guess: somewhere between the lap dance and oiling Miguel?"

"Or the other way around." Her smile fell. "I feel guilty."

Lori reached out and grasped both of Trina's hands, encouraged her to sit next to her on the bed. "Stop it. You have no reason to feel guilty. Fedor did this to himself. We may never know why he did what he did, but it *was* his choice."

"He was my husband."

"No. He was a contract. He may have been given the title of husband, but he wasn't."

"The world won't think that."

Lori leaned down until Trina met her eyes. "Which is why we're miles away from his life and the details of his death. Find the strength it took for you to take the plunge into his world, and use it to catapult out of it."

"I'm trying."

"Good. Now do me a favor. Every time you

think about Fedor as your husband, take that word out of your thoughts and put in *business partner.* You don't owe your *business partner* who killed himself anything."

Trina slapped her palms on her thighs and stood. "You're right. He shouldn't have done this to me. We had become friends, and friends don't exit without an explanation."

"He shouldn't have!" Lori agreed.

Now that Trina was moving out of the denial stage of her grief, it was time for her to get mad. With any luck, this trip would help her move through the five stages quickly. The sooner she accepted Fedor's death and the murky waters he left behind, the better.

A knock on the door brought Lori back to reality.

Trina kissed Lori's cheek. "Go have fun. Shannon and I are going to check out the ice bar."

"Brrr, that sounds cold."

"If you need a cold shower later, join us," Trina said.

Lori laughed as she opened her stateroom door.

Reed wore slacks and a button-up short sleeve shirt. His hair was wet, as if he'd just jumped from the shower. He'd shaved.

"Hi."

His eyes swept her. "You look nice."

"Thank you."

"Okay, three is a crowd." Trina pushed past Reed. "You kids have fun. Don't keep her out too late, we have an early morning," she teased.

"Yes, ma'am."

Trina giggled and scooted past him and into the hall.

Lori studied her feet, feeling a little bit like she had when she'd dated in high school and her dates had to meet her parents before taking her anywhere.

"Ready?" he asked.

"Let me grab my purse."

"Do you know anything about French food?" Reed asked as they left the room.

"I know enough to avoid escargot."

When his hand found the small of her back, her cheeks warmed. Crazy how a simple touch declared that she was with him . . . if only for a meal.

They worked their way through the halls and decks of the ship, which were a mix of everything from people still in bathing suits to others dressed to the nines.

The low lighting and music of the French themed restaurant certainly paved the way for romance. Couples filled most of the tables, whereas families spent most of their time in louder locations on the ship.

"Do you cruise often?" Lori asked him once they were seated.

"This is my second," he told her. "What about you?"

"I've done my fair share."

"With your friends?"

She shook her head, thinking of Trina and the others. "Not with . . ." she stopped herself. "With other friends." She'd taken a one-on-one cruise with a previous Alliance bride in the past. This was the first time she had a group of four.

"Other friends who might have strangers taking pictures of them?"

The waiter saved her from having to answer his question. They ordered a bottle of wine and listened to the chef's recommendations.

"Tell me about yourself," Lori changed the subject.

He lifted one questioning eyebrow but didn't bring up her travel companions again.

"What do you want to know?"

Everything . . . but then, if she started asking about what he did for a living, he'd ask her. "Tell me more about this philosophy of yours."

"Which one?"

"Living life beyond your comfort zone."

He leaned back. "That's easy. As kids, we learned to take risks every day. Jumping into a lake without a life preserver and learning to swim because of it. Do you remember your first roller coaster?"

"Not really."

"Do you remember being afraid to go on one?"

"Yeah. I still get that way."

He lifted his hands in the air. "But you still go on them."

"They're fun."

"The thrill comes from fear."

"Like watching six grand ride on the color red."

"Exactly."

The waiter returned with the wine and took their order.

"Sometime between the age of eighteen and thirty we forget to take risks, and the fun in life is lost on us," Reed told her.

"You've been skydiving, haven't you?" Lori asked.

"More than once. You should try it sometime."

"I'll stick to the inside of airplanes, thank you."

"Chicken."

She couldn't help but laugh. "What is this, junior high?"

"Maybe. What are you afraid of?"

Lori lifted her wineglass. "Oh, I don't know . . . hitting the ground at two hundred miles per hour."

"It's only about a hundred and twenty."

"That sounds *so* much better."

Reed had an addictive smile. "What's the most adventurous thing you've ever done?"

Lori blinked . . . twice. "I traveled to China by myself."

Reed stared at her. "China? That's it?"

"Hey, I don't speak Chinese. It was scary." What she failed to mention was that she was meeting a potential client of Alliance. A businessman looking for an American bride. The scary part took place when, on behalf of Alliance, she passed on the man as a client. He had a violent side she picked up on shortly after meeting him in person. "What about you?"

"My biggest adventure?"

"Or the biggest step outside your comfort zone?"

He hesitated. "I voted."

The wine Lori sipped burned when she started to laugh. When her eyes started to tear up, she took a drink of her water.

"Are you okay?" he asked.

"Voted? That's outside your wheelhouse?"

"Well, yeah, what if the guy I voted for won by one vote? What if he sucked or started a war? That's a lot of responsibility."

He was messing with her, but she liked to laugh.

"Ever been married?"

He nodded. "Once. You?"

"Once. I was really young. No kids. You?"

He opened his eyes wide. "Oh, no. I'd be a terrible dad."

Their salads arrived and they kept talking. "Sounds like I found something outside your comfort zone."

“What about you? You’re beautiful, and obviously have your life together, with trips to China and this.” He pointed around the room. “Why aren’t you married?”

“Not interested.” Which was only half-true. Romance had been stripped out of marriage with her profession. “I like being in control, and marriage feels like giving away half of that.”

Reed lifted his glass. “To the Not Interested Club.”

Seemed Lori was drinking to all kinds of clubs this week.

They’d finished the bottle of wine and shared a froufrou dessert.

Even though neither one of them talked about their daily life, they managed to carry on a conversation for two hours.

“Nightcap?” Reed suggested.

She placed a hand over her stomach. “I don’t think anything else is going to fit.”

“Let’s take a walk, then. I’m not ready to say good night.”

“And if I am?”

“You’re not.” He turned her toward the doors leading to the deck.

“How can you be so sure?”

The warm breeze caught her hair and started to pull it out of the clip she used to pull it off her face.

“Because if you wanted to end this night, you’d

have said so by now. My guess is you're trying to determine if you're going to sleep with me or not."

Her jaw dropped. Not because he was wrong, no, he was completely right about that. But that he'd said it aloud.

"I am not!"

"Not thinking about it, or not going to?" He leaned against the railing and charmed her with his smile.

"Neither."

"Liar."

"Oh my God. You're so full of yourself." She tried not to smile back at him and failed.

"Because I say what we're both thinking?"

"I am not—" Her denial died on her lips when Reed took one step closer.

"Let me change that."

His kiss silenced any protest she had. Goose-flesh rose on her arms, her neck . . . and butter-flies fluttered in her belly like she was a virgin tasting a man's lips for the first time. He reached for the back of her neck, held her like he wasn't going to let her get away. Nothing was further from her mind.

"Open for me," he whispered.

Reed's eyes were warm, his thumb traced the side of her neck.

Lori opened her mouth and reached for him. His tongue found hers and made itself at home.

She tasted the cinnamon that had laced their coffee.

Cinnamon and Reed. The two would forever be branded into her mind by this simple kiss.

Her fingers fanned over his chest, touching him through his shirt, and she closed her eyes.

Footsteps of someone walking by reminded her that they were standing on the deck of a ship and not somewhere private.

She pulled away.

Reed placed his thumb under her chin. “You’re even more stunning when you’re aroused.”

“I am not arou—”

He lifted both eyebrows.

“Okay, fine.”

“Glad we cleared that up. Now let me walk you to your room.”

Her eyes narrowed.

“To say good night. I think I’ve taken you past your comfort zone enough for one night.”

“That’s probably a good idea.”

At her door, he kissed her again. This time pushing her up against the wall, the weight of his body reminding her how long it had been since she’d welcomed a man into her bed. Then, before she could change her mind, Reed took the key from her hand, opened her door, and pushed her inside.

And then he left.

Chapter Eight

By the time the ship pulled into position for the day, Reed was up, showered, and logged in. He started with Shannon Redding-Wentworth. From mainstream media to gossip magazines, Shannon was everywhere. She came from a wealthy family, married Paul Wentworth while he was campaigning for the governor's office in California. He had brought himself up to speed on her story before he arrived on the ship. His client knew about the cruise but didn't have knowledge of who she was sailing with. Reed knew his client was looking for something scandalous by way of a romantic interlude with the former first lady and would be disappointed that wasn't the case.

Reed backtracked through her life by looking up the private details of the governor. He found a wedding photo of the couple, and then another few sprinkled in at the reception. He clipped them into a file and moved forward to the announcements of the divorce.

Public records determined irreconcilable differences caused the divorce, much like nearly all divorces in the state of California. No one had to take the blame for a marriage gone bad in a no-fault state. There was mention of a prenuptial agreement removing any ability for Shannon to ask for more during their divorce. None of this was new news.

He clicked around until he pulled up a statement from the attorney mediating the Wentworth divorce.

He smiled. The law office of Lori Cumberland gave the official press release in regards to the high profile divorce.

He found an image.

Lori wore her hair up, and the tight black skirt and office jacket with crisp lines were nothing like he'd seen her in since they met.

He followed the ball and searched for recent mentions and images of Lori Cumberland. The one that caught his eye he'd seen before, only it hadn't meant a thing to him until now.

Trina. The quiet beauty who hid behind massive Kardashian-style sunglasses was none other than Katrina Petrov. New York stood in the background of the picture he found, which had been taken less than a month earlier. Katrina in widow's black, at the cemetery where she buried her husband. At her side were Lori and another woman Reed took a second look at. He switched back to Shannon's wedding photos.

A petite woman with auburn hair was the same woman flanking Lori and Katrina at the funeral. Dark glasses, her hair pulled tight to her head.

Reed took a closer look. Designer red soled shoes, a dress that belonged on a fashion runway even if it was appropriate for a funeral.

Money.

Lots of money.

Why were Shannon and Trina vacationing with Lori? Were they simply friends, or was Lori there as their lawyer? So far, Lori had hovered over the three women as if they needed constant supervision for fear of saying the wrong thing. He couldn't help but think he was onto something there. Lori was reluctant to tell him what she did for a living . . . was that on purpose?

Something smelled funny. And while he might learn a thing or two about Paul Wentworth through his ex-wife, Reed didn't think getting Shannon to open up was possible.

Lori, on the other hand . . .

He saved the file, the pictures, and turned his computer off.

With his cell phone, wallet, and sunglasses, Reed left his room in search of his travel companions.

Lori should have woken rested and ready for the day. Unfortunately, she'd tossed and turned most of the night. She wondered what Reed's goal was. The man seemed to have one, and so far, keeping her attention on no one but him stood out. She hadn't so much as looked at another man since they'd met.

When she and the other women found Reed, Rogelio, and Miguel waiting on the dock in Naples, she wasn't surprised.

"Good morning, ladies."

Avery and her all telling grin slid into Rogelio's arms and kissed him like they'd been lovers for longer than one day. "*Hola*," she said to him.

He said something slow and sultry, and Avery giggled.

"Do I want to know what he just said?" Lori asked.

Trina and Miguel both said no at the same time.

"So what will it be today? A walking tour of the city? A trip to Pompeii? The catacombs underground?" Reed asked the group.

"Where is Antonio?" Shannon asked.

"He has friends here, said he'd see us back on the ship tonight," Reed said.

"I'm game for anything," Trina said.

"Careful with that statement, Trina. Reed will have us jumping out of planes if he had his way."

Trina lowered the sides of her big, floppy hat. "No way in the world I'm jumping out of a plane."

"Sounds like a challenge," said Reed.

"I was a flight attendant for years. Staying inside a pressurized cabin is the only place to be while in the sky."

Reed shook his head.

"You're outnumbered," Lori told him.

"I'm a patient man," he offered with a mischievous twinkle in his eye.

She was sure his statement had more than one meaning.

"Let's walk the city, drink wine, eat pizza, and save the touristy stuff for Rome," Shannon suggested.

"Sounds perfect."

"So no scuba diving?" Reed asked, a hopeful lift in his voice.

"Oh my God, where did you find this guy, Lori?"

"At the bar."

They walked into the center of the city and weaved their way through the steep hills and narrow streets. The stench of fish was everywhere, and merchants sold their wares from baskets on bicycles and folding tables.

Above their heads, clotheslines littered with laundry were strung between buildings. A woman who had to be in her sixties stood on a balcony screaming at a man below.

Lori stopped to watch. "What's going on?"

Trina started to laugh.

"She's saying something about today's fish."

The woman spoke with her hands.

The fisherman on the street yelled back, turned to walk away, and then back around.

Still complaining, the woman lowered a basket from her balcony with a long rope.

The fisherman removed the money from the basket, and for a moment Lori expected him to taste it with a quick bite to make sure it was real. Instead, he filled the basket with loosely wrapped fish.

Once the entire melodrama was over, Avery started to clap.

The Italian woman waved a hand in the air.

"I think she just told you off," Shannon said.

"Yep, she did!" Trina added.

Sometime before lunch, Reed reached for her hand and ran his finger along her palm.

Why handholding flipped her nerves, she didn't know. But it did. And for the rest of the day, he made a simple statement of ownership by holding her hand.

On one breath, she cautioned herself. On the other, she reminded herself that this was only a week of her life. Might as well enjoy it and not think too hard.

Buzzed on espresso, Lori and the others found lunch overlooking the sea. Hundreds of boats dotted the water as the midday sun warmed the ocean air. "Watered down wine and a five-course meal," Shannon said.

"Heaven," Avery added.

"Have you ever been here before?" Miguel asked them.

Lori lifted her hand. "I have."

Shannon chimed in, "I have, too."

"Not Naples, but I've been to Rome," Trina told them.

"First time in Italy." Avery sipped her wine. "Won't be my last."

Miguel glanced at Reed.

"First time for me too."

"Americans don't venture far from home, I've noticed," Miguel said.

"It's expensive for a lot of people."

"But not for you, ladies . . . eh?" Miguel questioned. "All of you in private penthouse rooms. Even on board most people share."

Lori felt the weight of Trina's eyes, hidden behind sunglasses, focused on her.

Avery came to the rescue. "We knocked over a liquor store for the travel funds. We're all on the run."

Shannon laughed.

Lori found Reed staring at her.

Rogelio said something to Avery in Spanish. Lori waited for Trina or Miguel to translate.

"He said he's delighted Avery had the funds to travel."

Avery animatedly batted her eyelashes.

Rogelio kissed her briefly.

"Do you two work together?" Lori asked them, doing her best to switch the subject of how the four of them could afford to travel the way they did.

"No, no. Friends from our school days, eh,

Rogelio?" Miguel translated again, Rogelio nodded, and the two spoke of their college days.

Lori caught Reed watching the two men closely, his expression unreadable.

He caught her staring and smiled. From under the table, he reached out with the back of his hand and brushed her thigh.

The Italians loved their carbs. Small plates of pastas, breads, and cheeses littered the table. They grazed their way through lunch and rolled out of the restaurant and back toward the ship.

At some point between lunch and returning to the ship, Reed reached for Lori's hand and held it. A teenage memory of a boy holding her hand in the halls of her high school surfaced and brought with it tiny butterflies in the pit of her stomach.

Some of the merchants were rolling up their wares for the day. The streets started to empty as the cruise ship filled.

"I need a nap," Avery told everyone as they took the stairs to their deck.

Rogelio said something and Trina nudged him. "I think she means to *sleep!*"

Rogelio pouted, and they laughed.

"Are we doing the Cirque show tonight?" Trina asked.

They discussed their evening options as a group. Somewhere between Barcelona and Naples, the group had become travel buddies.

"And dinner?" Miguel asked.

The women moaned and grabbed their full bellies.

"We'll meet up with you in the dance club."

"I could use the workout." The words left her mouth and Reed's smile spread.

"On the dance floor."

They turned the corner to their bank of rooms. "I'm with Avery, I need to rest before turning the next page of tonight's activities."

Reed held back when the others disappeared behind stateroom doors.

"Italy agrees with you." He brushed the side of her face with his index finger.

"Oh?"

"Yeah, you dropped your protective armor for a good hour today."

"I don't have protective armor."

Reed stared into her eyes. "You hover over these women like you're their mother."

"I-I . . ." She wanted to deny him. "Whatever."

Reed stepped aside when another passenger passed by them. "I'll see you at the club. Maybe by midnight you'll be ready for dinner."

"I can't eat another thing."

"Or we could just turn in early." His gaze lingered on her lips.

She laughed and pushed against his chest. "I'll see you tonight."

He didn't attempt to kiss her before walking

away. Once she slipped behind the door, she leaned against it and muttered, "You're wearing me down, Reed."

Lori glared at her dusty computer. Instead of dropping in bed for a much-needed nap, she made use of the proximity of land and higher speeds of the Internet and logged into her e-mail.

Over two hundred unread messages.

She moaned.

After skimming the names and the glimpse of the messages, she opened the one from her paralegal marked *urgent.*

> Lori
> I hate bothering you; however, the executor of Alice Petrov's will has contacted the office saying it was urgent that we speak with them. I made the call, explained you were out of the country.
> Yours,
> Vivian

Lori calculated the time back home and dialed her office. A quick platitude with her secretary and the call was transferred.

"Hey, Vivi."

"You received my e-mail."

"What's up?"

"The short answer?"

"Why say five words when two will do?" Her courtroom mantra.

"Alice Petrov met with her attorney one month before Fedor's death and changed her will."

"I'm listening."

"That's all I have. You have to call her lawyer and Trina needs to be at your side. I told him you'd videoconference so he can confirm Trina's identity."

These kinds of requests were always followed with a big punch, leaving Lori wary of what was coming. Lori wrote down his number and told her paralegal to let him know they'd be calling in the next ten minutes.

Lori knocked on the adjoining door to Trina's room. A dead bolt and a simple door lock later and Trina opened. "Missed me already?"

"Come in." Lori set her computer up for a video call. They needed to do this quickly or miss the window of time where reception would play a factor.

"What's wrong?"

"I'm not sure anything is *wrong*. My paralegal informed me about a change in Alice's will."

"What kind of change?"

"I'm not sure."

"What do I have to do with Alice's will?"

"Let's video call her attorney and gather the facts."

They both glanced in the mirror, smoothed back the day's mess in their hair.

"Whatever," Trina said. "It doesn't matter what I look like."

Lori set her computer up to where both of them would be seen in the picture.

Their image stared back at them until the office picked up their call. "Mr. Crockett?"

"Yes, hello."

"I'm Lori Cumberland, and this is Katrina Petrov."

"Good morning." The man staring back at them was in his early sixties with salt-and-pepper hair and a kind smile. He sat in an office decorated in dark wood and leather chairs. "Thank you for getting back to me so far away."

"We called as soon as we could."

"Getting away from such tragedy was a wise plan, Mrs. Petrov." Mr. Crockett spoke to Trina.

Trina fidgeted. "It's been a hard few months."

Mr. Crockett's lips pulled into a soft smile. "I've heard quite a bit about you. Let me start by saying I'm greatly sorry for your loss."

"Thank you."

"I attended Alice's funeral. She would have been pleased that you saw to all her requests."

"Alice was a lovely woman. I regret that I didn't know her longer."

Lori grasped Trina's hand and found it cold.

"She told me the same thing."

“Mr. Crockett, in an effort to keep this connection, the ship we are on will be pulling away from the mainland anytime, and I can’t guarantee it will last. My paralegal said it was urgent that we speak. I’m assuming since you requested Trina here, this has something to do with Alice’s estate.”

“Yes, yes . . . Alice specifically wanted her will read a month after her burial.”

“That would have been yesterday.”

“Correct. But since you’re out of the country, I had to hold off.”

“Why?”

Mr. Crockett ruffled through papers on his desk before removing his reading glasses and staring at the camera.

“As you know, Alice’s only child was Fedor. Who she cherished with all her heart.”

“They were very close. I don’t think he could have lived through her death.”

“Unfortunately you are right about that. Alice also knew that Ruslan would have done everything in his power to obtain her estate through Fedor.”

Trina nodded. “The man is evil.”

“I won’t argue that.”

Lori glanced out the balcony, noticed the shoreline moving.

“Mr. Crockett, the ship is pulling away . . .”

“Of course, Counselor. Trina . . .” He hesitated.

Trina squeezed Lori's hand.

"Alice left her estate to you and you alone."

Trina sat speechless.

"When exactly did this change in her will happen?" Lori asked.

"One month before Fedor took his own life."

"Did Fedor know?" Trina asked.

"Not unless Alice told him. Which I don't believe was her intention. We had a very lengthy conversation when she changed the will."

"I don't understand, Mr. Crockett. Why me?"

The screen started to sputter.

"I'll have my secretary arrange a time for us to come in when we return to the States."

"Of course. I wanted to let Trina know what she was coming home to," he told them. "We are talking in excess of three hundred and fifty million dollars, depending on the price of a barrel of crude oil."

"I'm gonna be sick."

"Thank you, Mr. Crockett."

Once Lori managed to redirect Trina to a shower, she called Sam.

"We have a problem." In a few sentences, she explained the change of events.

"How is Trina?"

"Shell-shocked." Lori glanced at the clock.

"How much money are we talking?"

"Three fifty."

"This is going to be a big story when it breaks."

"With lots of people seeping from the walls to try and get their share." Large estates drew out roaches, poaching off the wealthy.

"And here I thought she'd be able to find some normal when she returned," Sam said with a heavy sigh.

"We need our PI to look into the family, see if there are any players that are going to attack. Ruslan won't take this sitting down."

"And I'll have Neil arrange security for Trina in New York." The Alliance team was tight. Woven from family and lifelong friends. Neil and Rick worked security for Alliance and were physical roadblocks who brought their *A* game when it came to protecting their charges. "Outside of this, how is the trip?"

Lori instantly thought of Reed. Her smile wavered. "Avery is hooking up with a Spaniard by the name of Rogelio. Doesn't speak a word of English."

"Sounds like Avery."

"Trina is starting to smile. And Shannon . . . I'm worried about her."

"I feel responsible."

"We both do."

"Try and have fun. I'll let you know if anything is leaked to the media so you know what you're coming home to."

Chapter Nine

Reed watched her from across the crowded deck. Lori pulled Trina aside and they put their heads together.

Trina swayed, and Lori caught her arm and guided her to a chair.

Lori looked around the two of them and ducked her head close again.

Reed swept the deck with his eyes, wondered if anyone else noticed the tension between the two women.

From his periphery, he saw someone watching them. A woman, her back was to him. But her eyes followed Trina and Lori just as closely as Reed's. When she looked toward an upper balcony, Reed followed her gaze, saw the back of a man turning away.

Miguel?

He waited to see if Miguel was going to take the stairs and approach Lori and Trina, only he didn't. It was as if he was observing, just like Reed.

Just like Reed and the unknown woman.

Lori kept one eye on Trina, the other on the show.

"Is everything okay?" Avery leaned over and asked Lori.

Lori shook her head. Trina was understandably upset.

Finally Trina gave up on the show, stood without warning, and left the auditorium.

Lori followed. And right behind walked Shannon and Avery. Once they were in the bright lights of the ship, they surrounded Trina.

"I don't want this," she all but shouted to Lori.

"What's going on?" Avery asked.

"Didn't you tell them?" Trina asked.

"Of course not." She lowered her voice. "I'm your lawyer. It's not my news to share."

Trina turned to Shannon and Avery. "My mother-in-law left her estate to me."

Lori noticed someone walking by turn their way.

"What?"

"Oh my God," Shannon exclaimed.

"Let's go up to my room. We don't want to discuss this here."

Shannon put an arm around Trina as they wound their way to their suites.

Datu met them in the hall. "Good evening, ladies."

"Hello," Avery said.

Lori opened her door, ushered the others inside.

"Can I assist you tonight?" Datu asked.

"A bottle of red and a bottle of white. You pick," Lori told him.

"Yes, ma'am."

She winked and closed the door.

"She left you everything?" Shannon asked.

Trina stared at Lori. "Tell them."

Lori tossed her purse on the desk, moved to open the balcony door. "Everything. I'll learn the details when we get back."

"Why would she do that?"

Avery put her hand in the air. "Okay, someone bring me up to date."

"Alice, my mother-in-law, was from a prominent family big in oil. Her estate was always separate from her ex-husband's."

"That didn't mean that Ruslan wanted it that way," Lori said.

"Ruslan is your father-in-law?" Avery asked.

Trina nodded. "Before Fedor took the easy way out, he'd tell me that his father was working hard to get on his good side so when Alice died they could merge their money and build an empire."

"Daddy said it that way?" Avery asked.

"No, but there was a lot of manipulation on Ruslan's side. Fedor despised the man. Fedor felt that if he were married, not only would it help his mother pass peacefully, knowing he was taken care of, but Ruslan would ease off. And it worked. About a month after we married, Ruslan's calls were less frequent and Fedor was more relaxed."

"What did Alice think of her ex?" Shannon asked.

Trina stared at the ceiling. "She called him a manipulative bastard she was wise enough to fear."

"It sounds as if you had a healthy respect for the woman," Shannon said.

"I didn't know her long. But we did laugh and share a few moments."

"Do you think she guessed about your arrangement with Fedor?" Lori asked.

"I don't know. Fedor would hold my hand when we saw her. Put on a show of a loving marriage."

The women nodded. Each of them understood the need to pretend and pull out their best Oscar winning performances for their fake marriages.

"So how much money is this estate?" Avery asked.

She blew out a breath. "Three hundred and fifty . . . million."

Trina grew pale and Datu arrived with the wine.

He lost the woman on the stairwell between the fourteenth and fifteenth floors. Midlength dark hair, olive skin. He hadn't seen her face, not all of it. Unless she wore the same outfit again, he'd be hard-pressed to recognize her a second time. Was she a spy? Or did she recognize Trina?

And why was Miguel standing above them, watching so intently? How had the woman noticed Miguel? Were they working together?

A byproduct of being a private investigator was observing others around you and assuming they were PIs, too. Or had hidden agendas at the very least. If someone hired him to spy, it was safe to assume others were watching as well.

His initial investigative target had been Shannon, and Reed's attention landed on Lori, admittedly because of their attraction. And of all four of the women, Lori had been the most skittish, hovering . . . like she was hiding something. Yeah, it could be nothing more than the lawyer in her trying to keep her clients from unwanted attention while on vacation. But Reed wasn't buying that theory. It didn't sit well in his head.

Ever since seeing Miguel watching, spying . . . or whatever he was doing, Reed questioned the Spanish duo's chance meeting at the singles mixer the first night on the ship. Was that meeting as "chance" as Reed's?

Reed sat in the small bar in the center of the suites and waited.

"There you are." Miguel took a seat beside Reed. The Spaniard wore a full kilowatt smile. A man who never frowned couldn't be trusted in Reed's book.

He shook his hand. "Where is Rogelio?"

"Probably with Avery."

No, Reed had seen the women disappear into the crush of people enjoying the show.

"He might need to save his energy, the week is young."

Miguel patted Reed on the back and signaled the bartender. "Can I get you a drink?"

He shook his head. "Pacing myself."

"I don't know what that is." Still smiling, Miguel ordered a top-shelf whiskey. "You and Lori seem to be getting along well, eh?"

"I think so."

"The adventure of the chase," Miguel said. "Almost as sweet as the win, don't you think?"

"And Trina? How is that going?" Reed didn't think the woman was available, but perhaps he was mistaken.

"The quiet beauty. I will wear her down. I always do."

A strange need to protect the recent widow pulled at his collar. "She is guarded."

"Most are, but we have our ways to get what we want."

Reed suddenly felt the need for a straight shot of something. The smirk and the wink sat on the wrong side of his stomach. This man was a predator, Reed would bet his next paycheck on it. "What was it you did for a living?" Reed asked as if making conversation.

"Marketing." He muttered something in

Spanish as a woman wearing a skintight black dress sauntered by.

"Interesting. For what company?"

Miguel smiled. "Many. How do you say it . . . I work with many companies."

"Freelance?"

"*Sí* . . . yes. I freelance. And you? What is it that you do?"

"Data processing." The lie came easy.

Miguel narrowed his eyes, looked at Reed's hands. "Those look like fingers that work, not fingers that type."

"Things are not always as they seem."

Miguel's drink arrived and he toasted the air. "To the mirage, then."

"Cheers."

"Lori!"

She turned to find Reed fighting the flow of people leaving the ship for the day.

"Hey." He stopped in front of her. "Sorry about last night. We had a slight female emergency."

"Oh?" Reed looked concerned.

"Yeah, we drank too much wine and had a slumber party instead of hitting the club."

"So everything is okay?"

"Yeah." Well, no, but she wasn't going to gossip or talk to anyone about Trina other than the women. "Are you headed off the ship?"

He shrugged, looking a little lost. "Are you?"

The invitation to spend the day with him hung in the air. The desire to do just that was too hard to pass up.

"We're getting a slow start." She was going to do her best to get Trina off the ship and keep her mood light. The progress she'd made in the first few days was swept away with one phone call.

"I can wait if it means I can spend time with you."

Thoughts of Trina fled, and the girlie part that had been attracted to the man in front of her made her feel playful. She reached her hand out. "Give me your phone."

He reached into his back pocket and hesitated.

"I'm not going to steal it," she teased.

Reed handed it over.

She placed her number into his contacts and typed in a name before handing it back to him.

After glancing down, he said, "Hot chick on ship?"

She giggled. "Send me a text so I have your number, and I'll let you know when we're leaving." She turned to walk away. "Oh, have you seen Rogelio and Miguel? Avery was asking about them."

Reed hesitated. "No, actually."

Lori shrugged. "Probably for the best."

An hour and a half later, Lori texted Reed and suggested he meet them on the dock.

Trina left the ship reluctantly with the promise

of Shannon returning early with her if she couldn't take it.

On the dock, Reed stood alongside Antonio. Miguel and Rogelio were nowhere to be found. Much as Lori wanted Trina distracted, she didn't think an interest in a member of the opposite sex was the diversion she needed.

Antonio greeted all four of them with kisses on both cheeks. "How lucky are we, Reed, to escort these beautiful ladies around the city of love."

Avery rolled her eyes. "I thought that was Paris."

Antonio spat something in Italian before painting on a smile. "Paris has a tower . . . we have the Colosseum, where gladiators fought to the death."

"He has a point," Lori told her.

"What is more romantic than that?"

"More romantic than death?" Avery asked.

"She has a point," Reed told Antonio.

They boarded the ship's transportation to ride into the city. Lori smiled at a man dressed as a gladiator who escorted them onto the bus. Once inside she turned to Reed as he took the seat beside her. "You should get one of those outfits."

"You like playing dress up?" he whispered.

Her cheeks warmed.

"That's what I thought."

Lori glanced over to see Trina hiding behind massive sunglasses while talking to Avery, and Shannon kept a cordial smile as Antonio attempted to charm her.

She'd been to the Colosseum before but never failed to stop and stare at the massive, decaying structure that once held fights to the death. The macabre nature of it all fascinated and repulsed . . . and now it was simply a tourist attraction. Sure, there was history to learn, but tourists forked over money for that special trinket to mount on their wall at home or place on their fridge door. And the men dressed as gladiators were happy to let you take a photo so long as you paid them for their efforts.

Trina walked ahead with Avery and played tour guide. Antonio and Shannon lagged behind, leaving Reed and Lori in the middle.

"Do you know your Roman history?" she asked him.

"I know what they did here. Barbaric."

"Did you know there were female gladiators as well?"

Reed narrowed his eyes. "Seriously?"

"Not many, but that's what I was told the last time I visited. Sometimes they were told to fight dwarfs, and other times each other."

"Call me old-fashioned, but I don't like to see women fight."

"I don't like watching men do it either."

She looked down at the stage of the structure, imagining it filled with screaming, bloodthirsty

Romans. "I'd like to think that the human condition has grown from the times this arena was used, but I'd be lying to myself."

"How so?" Reed asked.

"From reality television where we thirst for the fight, to watching endless loops of violence on the evening news, we're completely desensitized to pain and suffering of other people. We turn off the TV, go to bed with our bowl of ice cream, and get up the next day, tuning out what we've witnessed the night before." She shook her head. "Makes me understand a little better how the Romans allowed the fighting here for so many years."

"You've given this some thought."

She was a lawyer; she fought all the time with words as her weapons. "Everyone fights. It's the how of the fight and how far they'll push their moral barometer that often determines the winner."

He leaned against the rail that kept people from walking farther down the crumbling path. "What about strength?"

"If you're talking a physical fight, yeah, strength comes into play, but often will and determination is what takes the win."

He stared at her for several seconds. "What do you do for a living?" he asked.

She thought of her office, shut her eyes. "I told you."

“Yeah, I don’t see the pole dancer in you.”

“Then you’re not using your imagination.” She took his hand and dragged him toward the others, who had all moved ahead of them.

“You didn’t answer your phone!”

Hours later, Reed stood in his room in nothing more than a towel as he prepared for the evening.

“I was preoccupied.”

“And what have you found out?”

“Ms. Cumberland is Ms. Redding’s divorce attorney.”

“That isn’t news.”

“They are vacationing together.”

“Hmmm, why?”

“Ms. Cumberland is also the attorney for one of her other companions on the ship.” And even though Reed knew Trina’s name, he wasn’t going to reveal that information quite yet.

“What is the significance?”

“I don’t know, yet,” Reed said.

“Has Shannon opened up at all about her ex?”

“Not yet. She either has nothing to say or has excellent control of keeping her emotions and opinions to herself.” Not that he’d prodded her overly much so far.

“Have I wasted my money sending you there, Reed?”

“No. There is something at work here, I just

haven't figured out what it is yet. And I'm not the only one on this ship watching them."

There was a long pause. "Are you sure?"

"Positive."

"Are they watching Shannon?"

"Hard to say, the women travel in a pack."

"Well then, we need to find out who this other person is and who they work for."

"What do you think I'm doing?"

"One never really knows, Reed."

He looked at his reflection in the mirror. "I'll be in touch. Don't call me."

"I'm paying you."

"And your calls interrupt my investigation."

"Find something."

Chapter Ten

The ship was like Vegas and New York City all rolled into one. Between the different nationalities and the party atmosphere, the cruise ship never slept. Reed had to remind himself he was working more than once.

Reed read Lori's text about going to the dance club they'd played in the first night and responded by showing up half an hour later. His eyes took some time to adjust to the scene because of the flashing lights on the dance floor. He considered his plan to arrive late a win until he reached the table she occupied with her friends to find Miguel and Rogelio whispering Spanish sweet bullshit into Avery's and Trina's ears.

Lori waved him over.

Her honey blonde hair was down. Something he wasn't used to seeing. So far their time in the Italian sun had her pulling her long strands away from her face in a clip or a band. But this, this soft look around her high cheekbones, he liked. Her blue eyes sparkled in the lights, the color of her skin from the Mediterranean sun offered a healthy glow that wasn't hidden by excessive makeup. She really was a beautiful woman. He might have fabricated a few things to get her attention, but his platitudes about her appearance were all from the heart. Or whatever organ it was that had created the warmth in his stomach.

He waved. "Hello," he said as he approached.

Trina smiled and Avery listened to whatever Miguel was saying.

Reed took the liberty of sliding a hand along Lori's waist and pressing his lips against her ear. "You look ravishing." Between the hair and the off the shoulder top that displayed enough creamy flesh to make his mouth water, Reed wanted to stare.

She smiled and mouthed the words *thank you.*

"Where is Shannon?" he asked, realizing she wasn't there.

Lori pointed to the dance floor.

The former first lady of California was spinning around with Antonio, who was putting his moves on. Harmless fun. The kind he didn't mind being a part of when he wasn't working.

He glanced at Lori.

Or even when he was working.

Trina laughed at something Rogelio said, and Miguel leaned over the women to translate to Avery.

At face value, it looked like any normal night in a club where two best friends were finding a couple of girls with whom to get naked. Only Reed picked up on Trina's tense shoulders and tight smile when Miguel pushed into her personal space.

"Miguel?" Reed directed his attention to him. "Where were you guys today? We missed you in Rome."

"I've seen the city many times and decided to rest my morning away to have my energy for tonight." He said something in Spanish and turned to Trina. "Let's dance."

"Oh, I don't—"

"You didn't come here just to drink. I won't bite."

Avery pulled Trina from the chair. "C'mon."

From where Reed sat, Trina seemed to reluctantly fall into the pressure of her friend and moved from the table to the floor.

Reed positioned himself on the other side of Lori so he could watch. "No slumber party tonight?" he asked.

"No. We wanted to get her out."

He looked around. "Trina, or Shannon?"

"Trina. She's had a hard few months."

He wanted to ask why but held back. "A week of nightclubs and dancing should help."

Lori didn't look convinced. "Why aren't you here with a friend?"

"I'm here with you."

"No, I mean on the ship? Seems a little strange that you're traveling alone."

"Actually, I planned on a buddy of mine

coming. But he got a job at the last minute and couldn't get away." His lie was easy. He'd used it before when asked why he was somewhere alone.

"That's too bad."

"Not really. I might not have latched on to you and your friends if we were one over the needed testosterone dose."

"Is your friend a nice guy?" Lori watched the dance floor closely.

"Yeah, unless he's watching football."

Lori smiled, turned her attention toward him.

"Are you a sports guy?"

"Take it or leave it. The big games are fun because of the party they create. You?"

"My younger brother was All-American in high school, played college football, but then tore his ACL and was out. We watch the games during the holidays, but that's about it."

"You're close with your brother?"

"Yeah. What about you? Brothers or sisters?"

"Two sisters." Which was the truth. "One older, she's married with two of her own, and then the baby in the family." Who was twenty-three. His parents had a whoops kid. The kid that surprised everyone when his mother announced she was pregnant. Reed was fourteen when his baby sister was born.

"I always wanted a sister," Lori confessed. "I guess that's why I have so many girlfriends."

He followed her gaze, found it landing on her friends.

"You'd have been the best older sister."

She grinned. "You saying I'm old?"

He didn't take the bait. "I'm saying you hover."

"You keep saying that."

He stopped a cocktail waitress and ordered a beer, asked Lori if she wanted something. She waved him off.

The music switched beat, and Trina and Miguel returned to the table.

Trina reached for her glass and finished what was in it.

"I'll get you another one."

"I'm good."

He ignored her and turned toward the bar.

"Having fun?" Reed asked.

Her eyes were glossy and her cheeks were pink. "I forgot how much I like to dance."

She moved to sit on the high stool and slipped a little. Reed reached out to catch her, but she found her balance using the table. "Did the ship move?"

Lori laughed. "No, you did."

"Geez, I didn't even have a lot to drink."

"You didn't eat much at dinner," Lori reminded her.

Miguel arrived with their drinks right as Rogelio and Avery were returning. Close behind were Shannon and Antonio.

"We're going to step out and get some air," Shannon told them.

Lori lifted an eyebrow.

Avery laughed. "You know what that means, right, Lori?"

Lori leveled a finger in the air in Avery's direction. "It means what happens in the Mediterranean—"

"Stays in the Mediterranean," Miguel finished for her.

Trina laughed a little easier, smiled a bit wider. Miguel took that as an invitation and put his arm over her shoulders.

When she didn't shrug him off, Reed put his beer down and decided maybe drinking wasn't a great idea tonight. He couldn't help but think of Miguel as a fox circling Trina's henhouse. And Trina was uncharacteristically intoxicated.

Miguel reacted to Reed's stare and lifted his chin.

"Hey Trina, what is it you do for a living?"

She closed her eyes and shook her head. "I was a . . . a flight attendant."

That's right, he thought he heard that fact earlier. "Was?"

Lori leaned in. "Now she's a pole dancer with me."

"Again with the pole dancing."

"And *I* own the strip joint." Avery joined the lie.

"Now this I want to see," Miguel said.

Trina stood on wobbly legs and pretended the stool was a large pole. Miguel licked his lips and Rogelio clapped.

"I think you might need to slow down." Avery patted Trina on the shoulder.

Trina blinked a few times, her smile a little too wide. "I'm fiiine."

"Let's take that on the dance floor."

Avery and Lori exchanged glances when Miguel kept Trina upright and walked her away.

Rogelio nodded at Avery, encouraging her to join his friend. She waved him off.

"Is she okay?" Avery asked Lori.

"I don't know. I've never seen her like this."

Miguel pulled Trina deeper on the dance floor, making it difficult for Reed to keep track of the couple. "How much has she had to drink?"

"Not much, we shared a bottle of wine at dinner, so maybe a glass then, and two drinks here. But over several hours."

That wasn't a woman with a high alcohol level, unless . . .

Reed glanced at the drink Trina left behind, picked it up, and sniffed. Some kind of vodka fruit combination, but he didn't smell anything suspicious. Not that it mattered. Most of the designer stuff had no taste and no smell.

"You don't think . . ." Lori's question hung in the air.

Rogelio tugged on Avery's arm.

She wasn't having it.

"I'm not comfortable with this," Lori said.

Neither was Reed.

"Dude! Not now!" Avery yelled at Rogelio.

His smile fell as well as his hand from her arm.

"I'm going to get her, take her back to the room."

Lori and Avery left the table in search of Trina.

Reed put the drink down, glared at Rogelio. "I really hope I'm wrong."

Rogelio stared, and a wave of recognition made him think that the Spaniard knew a little more English than he let on. "*Problema*?"

"Reed?" Lori pushed through the crowd. "They're not here."

With a final glare, Reed turned and followed Lori onto the dance floor. They split up and met in the entrance of the club.

"Where did they go?"

"My guess is Miguel's room or hers."

"Miguel is sharing a room with Rogelio," Avery told them.

Reed took over. "You take the back of the ship, Lori take the direct route, and I'll find the stairwell in the front. We'll meet at her room."

They didn't argue and took off in different directions.

Eyes wide open, Reed weaved through the crowds toward the forward stairwell and started the long climb. He hesitated when he reached the pool deck and those that allowed couples to enjoy a romantic walk in the moonlight, then veered off his path to the *maybe* route of two possible lovers. He searched the starboard side of the ship, then rounded onto the port. Reed had about given up when he heard a familiar laugh.

Trina.

Her back was to him. She and Miguel stood at the railing; Miguel's hand was behind her neck. The man was smiling.

Until he felt Reed's stare and looked over.

Miguel directed his attention to Trina, said something Reed couldn't hear.

Reed slowed his pace as he approached.

"I think perhaps tomorrow," Miguel said.

"There you are." Reed moved to Miguel's side, took a good look at Trina. She was hardly awake, her eyes half shut, her body upright only because of the railing she held on to and the man whose arm held her waist.

"Reed, my man. Perhaps you can help me. Seems our friend isn't feeling well."

His alarm shot high.

"I'm fiiine. Just a little dizzy."

"I bet," Reed said. "Trina?"

She blinked a few times, her hair fell in her face, and she batted it away like a child swatting a mosquito.

"Lori and Avery are searching for you."

She attempted to open her eyes wide, licked her lips. “M’kay.”

Reed weaved his arm under hers, took her weight.

“She said she needed air,” Miguel told him.

“I needed air.”

Miguel took her other side, and the two of them walked her up the remaining stairs toward her room.

Lori ran to them when they reached the hallway. “Is she okay?” Lori placed both hands on Trina’s face.

“I’m fiiine, just a li’l too much to driiink.”

“C’mon, we’re going to my room.”

“I’m okay.”

“Yep, sure you are.” Lori didn’t say anything further before opening the door to her room.

The suite had a separate sitting room and dining table. Through a set of doors, she pointed to her bed.

Miguel and Reed sat Trina down. Miguel placed her legs on the bed as Reed laid her back. Before he could stand, Trina was out cold.

Lori brushed Miguel off when he reached to remove Trina’s shoes. “I got that.”

Avery ran through the open door, past them, and to Lori’s side. “What happened?”

“I think someone drugged her,” Reed said, his eyes landing on Miguel.

“That would be my guess, too,” Miguel agreed.

What game are you playing? The question swam in Reed's head like water down a drain.

Lori reached for the phone by the bedside.

"What are you doing?" Avery sat beside Trina and wiped the hair that had fallen in her face.

"Calling the ship's doctor."

Miguel shifted from foot to foot. "You should turn her on her left side in case she becomes ill."

"Yes, this is Lori Cumberland in 1703. I need the physician right away." She paused. "No, I can't come down. My friend is out cold. Yes, yes, but not a lot. We think she's been drugged. No! That isn't the kind of person . . . okay, okay, thank you."

Lori walked around the bed, moved Miguel out of her way, and removed Trina's shoes.

"We'll step in the other room," Reed said.

"Don't leave," Lori told him.

"We're not going anywhere."

Away from the women, Miguel turned to Reed. "I know how this looks."

Reed kept silent.

"I didn't do it."

"I never said you did."

"Your eyes betray you."

The women were focused on their friend, none of them noticing the battle of wills between him and Miguel. The fact the other man wasn't running off might have suggested he wasn't guilty to the others, but Reed had met Miguel's type before. Guilty men who smiled into their lies and grieved openly for men they'd killed.

Miguel wasn't fooling Reed in the least.

Chapter Eleven

Lori, Shannon, and Avery opened the doors between their adjoining rooms and tag teamed sleep during the night. The ship's physician deemed Trina intoxicated with the chance of drugs in her system. Since that particular combination wasn't unheard of on the ship, and since with some effort he could wake her and her vital signs were stable, there wasn't a need to take her down to the infirmary. He did leave a cup for her urine sample so they could test her for drugs.

"I don't need that. I just had too much to drink," Trina protested the pee cup the next morning.

"But you didn't." Avery sat cross-legged on the bed where Trina sat holding her head.

"I feel like I did."

"What do you remember about last night?" Shannon had joined them shortly after the doctor left. Lori left a message in her room for her via Datu, and she camped out with the rest of them.

"We had dinner."

"We were at the club. Do you remember dancing?"

"Yes." She shook her head. "Kinda."

Lori thrust the cup toward Trina again. "Just pee in the damn thing."

"Stop, okay. I'm fine. Hungover, but otherwise fine." She stood, held her head. "You guys should go ashore. I'm sure there are better things for you to do than babysit me."

"Doesn't it worry you that Miguel might have slipped something in your drink to loosen you up?" Avery was starting to get pissed.

Trina's gaze scanned the three of them. She grabbed the cup from Lori's hand. "Fine." Then disappeared into the bathroom.

The three of them slipped from the bedroom and into the living room section of her suite. The balcony door was open, with the view of Florence in front of them.

"What is she worried about?" Avery asked.

Lori wondered the same thing.

"Let's shower and regroup for breakfast." Lori could use the time alone with Trina to pick her brain.

Shannon and Avery left her suite in search of their own. Lori waited for Trina to emerge from her bathroom. She glanced around the room.

"They went to their rooms to get ready for the day."

Trina sighed and sat in one of the chairs. "I'm sorry."

"What are you sorry for?"

"For ruining your night. All of you—"

"Please. Don't even go there. If someone spiked your drink, you didn't cause this."

Trina glanced at the bag in her hand.

"I've been, uhm . . . taking a mood stabilizer since Fedor. It says right on the bottle I shouldn't really be drinking while taking it."

"We've been drinking since we arrived in Spain."

"I know." Trina studied the floor.

"Have you been taking the medication the whole time?"

"Yeah. I guess I just hit the breaking point."

Lori wasn't a doctor, but she assumed that might have something to do with it.

"Let's let the doctor figure that out, shall we?"

"Seems a waste of his time."

"Maybe it is."

"I don't want you to think less of me because I'm taking pills. I didn't really want to, but my doctor thought it would help."

"Has it?"

She shrugged. "It hasn't hurt . . . until last night."

"Let's get to the bottom of it. As far as I can see, last night you had less to drink than the previous four. You haven't so much as been tipsy this entire cruise."

Trina opened her mouth.

Lori stopped her before she uttered a word. "I will never judge you for taking medication. I might blame myself for being a part of your marriage to Fedor, but I won't judge you."

Trina offered a fake smile. “No one forced me to marry Fedor.”

Lori agreed, but it didn’t ease her guilt at all. “Let’s visit the doctor, okay?”

Twenty minutes later she sat in the small waiting room while Trina spoke with the doctor. Her phone buzzed with a text from Reed.

> How is she this morning?

> Hung over. We’re in the infirmary now.

The dot, dot, dot had her waiting for his message to come through.

> Anything I can do?

It was nice of him to offer. No, go enjoy your vacation in Florence. I doubt we’ll get off the ship today. She had enough guilt knowing Trina had been reduced to taking drugs to get through her day, Lori didn’t want to take advantage of Reed’s goodwill.

> Would you ask me to help if you needed it?

She considered lying. I’m not used to asking anyone for help.

> I’m here if you change your mind.

The comfort of his words warmed her. Not that she would take him up on his offer.

The door to the exam room opened, and Trina stepped out.

"Well?"

"He suggested I stop taking my medication if I'm drinking."

Sound advice. "And?"

"And that there was a trace of something extra in my urine."

Lori felt her muscles tighten. "A trace?"

"He's sending the sample off the ship for further analysis. He said new designer stuff comes out all the time, and some of it is almost impossible to detect if there are other substances in the bloodstream, like the medication I've been taking."

It was Trina's turn to look guilty.

"How are you feeling?"

"I have a headache, but otherwise I'm good. A little hungry, even."

Lori nodded for the door. "Let's take care of that."

Outside the door, Trina stopped her. "Don't tell the others about all this . . . I don't want them to worry."

"They're going to worry anyway."

"About the drugs. I don't want them to know . . ."

"If you haven't already figured it out, I'm good

at keeping secrets. You tell them what you want them to know and I'll back you up. But Trina . . ."

"Yeah?"

"No more drinks handed to you by anyone other than the three of us."

"I don't have to be told twice. No liquor for me today at all. Maybe the rest of the week. The meds are going in my suitcase until I'm home, too. I don't like not knowing what I did last night."

"I don't like it either."

There were many things Reed was good at, and blending into a crowd was one of them.

He didn't see Miguel and Rogelio as art connoisseurs and found it surprising when they entered the Piazzale Michelangelo. Reed held back when the men he was following paused at the famous statue and studied it.

Reed tracked their gazes up to find the statue of David's goods right out there for everyone to see. Nothing quite like being mooned from the front, in marble, to make you appreciate your own package.

His targets moved, and David's chilled package was quickly forgotten. Reed followed them around the plaza, weaving in and out of crowds of people, and then lost them both when they slipped into the restroom.

Reed waited for ten minutes before going in,

only to find the space occupied by a half dozen others who were not Miguel or Rogelio.

"What the hell," he whispered to himself.

There wasn't a back door, and he'd only let his eyes off the restroom a few seconds at a time. He doubled his step to the door, scanned the people standing around.

On the other side of the street, a leggy brunette hidden behind large sunglasses looked away once he noticed her. He recognized her profile from the ship . . . the sunglasses. Had she bumped into him on the street? He wasn't quite sure.

Either way, he knew she was spying on Miguel and Rogelio. He also knew, as he looked around the sea of unfamiliar faces, that he'd lost them.

He reached for his cell phone inside of his jacket pocket.

"What the hell are you doing calling this early?"

"Cut the crap, Jenkins, I need a favor."

"At o-dark-hundred in the morning?"

"I'm in Italy. Are you going to help me or not?"

"Well aren't you going all James Bond on me. Of course. What's up?"

Jenkins was a good ten years younger than Reed, a decent private investigator who spent way too much time calling him to learn the trade. The man owed Reed a favor or two.

"I have a couple of names I need you to look up."

"That's easy."

"In Spain."

"Okay, maybe not so easy."

"I have faith in you." Reed gave him Miguel and Rogelio's names, or at least the ones they were using on the ship, and told Jenkins to watch his e-mail for pictures of the guys.

"So what are you working on?"

Reed scanned the crowd again. "Do you know what the word *private* means?"

"Someone's touchy."

"I haven't gotten much sleep. Dig a little, see if you can find anything."

"Any context you can share?"

"I'm not sure if these guys are opportunistic predators or real players of some sort."

Reed didn't prefer to work with partners, but in this case, where he was thousands of miles from home with no real danger of putting his partner at risk, he made the exception.

Reed considered the last time he'd worked with a partner and how that had panned out.

His mind wandered back to when he carried a badge. He was a cop then, and he and his partner, Luke, had been investigating a few amateur drug dealers and were on the path to finding their suppliers. A tip had come in about a warehouse. They were going in to plant surveillance to capture the brains who were beyond the simple dealers.

The two other cops that scoped out the scene with them said they did a pass of the location when they were planting bugs, but as it turned out, that team wasn't playing for the good guys. Reed and Luke had been ambushed. They didn't have time to be anything but reactive when they realized the danger they were in.

The trap cost Luke the full use of his right arm and two years of his life to learn to walk again after a bullet ripped through his spine.

Reed escaped with thirty tiny stitches along his jaw and a hole through his desire to carry a badge.

It took six months for Reed to learn the truth about the pair of bad cops. Six months of investigation he had to do on his own, since the force didn't believe Reed had a claim.

And when Reed went above his captain with the information, Reed had been the one to take the fall. One cover-up after another, and Reed ended up looking like the bad guy.

That's when he decided to back out.

All because he hadn't been proactive in his investigation of the drug-dealing thugs.

And what had he learned from all that? To distrust the system and work alone. Becoming a PI seemed the right move.

Still, it was hard to watch and not get involved when something bad was happening to someone good. Reed couldn't shake the feeling bad was about to come down on his new circle of friends.

Reed hung up without saying good-bye before making his way back to the ship.

He found Lori two hours later stretched out beside Shannon by the pool. Still wearing the jeans he roamed the city in, he was slightly out of place among those soaking in the sun.

Lori tracked his frame as he walked closer, a smile on her face. "Hey. How was Florence?"

He shrugged. "Lots of statues of naked people."

"Not your thing?" Shannon asked.

He couldn't stop his grin, or his eyes from landing on Lori. "I like naked as much as the next guy. It's the marble and brass thing that does nothing for me."

Lori's eyes narrowed, her smirk faint enough to show she heard him.

He tried to keep his eyes from traveling to the tops of her breasts.

He failed.

Lori's chest rose and fell a few times before he looked back into her eyes.

"Ha! Maybe I should leave you two alone." Shannon lifted her sunglasses from her eyes.

"Don't be ridiculous." Lori cleared her throat and patted the space on the lounger by her feet.

Reed took the invitation and sat. He rested his hand on Lori's calf and took her lack of pulling away as a positive step in the right direction.

"How is Trina?" he asked.

"Better. You just missed her. She has spent most of the day out here but thought a nap was a good idea."

"Did the doctor find anything?"

The women exchanged glances. Their body language answered before they opened their mouths. "A trace."

His smile wavered. "Of?"

"They don't know yet," Shannon told him. "They sent out a blood sample."

"Even if they do find something, chances are they won't make a big deal about it since nothing happened. Word getting out of spiked drinks on a cruise ship is going to hurt sales." The lawyer in Lori was coming out.

"Would that leave the ship open for liability?" he asked, knowing it would.

"Probably not, since Trina was drinking and ended up passed out in her stateroom with supervision. We found her before anything bad happened."

That didn't sound right to him.

When Lori didn't meet his eyes, he knew there was more to the story. And perhaps he needed to do a little more digging into Lori's circle of friends. He'd ask himself later if it was to find dirt for his client or collect information to keep them safe. Right now he justified all of his actions based on being a decent guy.

"Lessons learned," Shannon said as she picked up a magazine.

He turned his attention back to Lori. "Can I sneak you away tonight?"

Shannon didn't bother looking up from her riveting reading material when she replied. "Yes, please. Mother hen needs to let someone else helicopter for a while."

"I'm not a mother hen." Lori spoke first to Shannon, then turned to Reed. "I'm not."

He placed a hand on her ankle. "After dinner? Night diving off the back of the boat?"

She lost her smile, her eyes widened. "Do they do that?"

Shannon started laughing.

He laughed and shook his head.

"Man, Lori, for a lawyer you sure are gullible."

Reed knew if he stuck around these women long enough, one of them would reveal what Lori did for a living. So he smiled and pretended he was surprised. "A lawyer and a pole dancer. That must get complicated."

Lori slapped at Shannon's arm.

"Oops."

Lori rolled her eyes. "Whatever."

He let Lori believe he'd just learned the information about her true profession but didn't press for more. He'd do that later.

Timing was everything.

"So . . . tonight?"

Chapter Twelve

She couldn't remember the last time she went to the movies on a date. Dates for her had been dinner, talking, and deciding if the man was breakfast worthy. Reed offered a nice change.

She liked the man. He seemed genuinely interested in Trina's health, and concerned the night before when they couldn't find her. His chivalry came in the form of opening doors, listening without interruption, and remembering a blanket from the room. The fact that he was easy to look at was a bonus.

Lori wondered what he thought about her. She questioned what he saw in her that kept him coming back. It wasn't like he was pushing to get her into bed. Maybe he was turned on by intelligent conversation. Although Lori had never considered herself in that pool, she was starting to change her mind. Then again, she'd done most of the talking, clearly attracting him, while he was doing the manly things that shot her pulse on high.

"I hope you like popcorn." Reed walked up from behind her, a giant bucket in his hands. The smell alone had her mouth watering.

"Where's yours?" she asked with a straight face.

He hesitated, and then smiled before handing her the big tub of salt, butter, and carbs. "Careful, I'm always up for a challenge."

A wave of her hand encouraged him to sit. "Hot chocolate is coming."

"Perfect."

A jumbo screen was set up over the main pool, and the deck had been turned into an outside movie theater. The people around them were settling in, most had their eyes focused on the stars in the night sky. It reminded her of the Fourth of July right before the fireworks were due to blast off, and those who remembered the words belted out "The Star-Spangled Banner." She fisted a handful of popcorn and handed the tub to Reed once he sat down. "This is a fabulous idea."

"Inside your comfort zone?"

She nodded. "That doesn't make it boring."

"I imagine a lot of things with you would not be boring."

Her eyes lingered on the expanse of his chest before taking their time moving back to his face. "I can be fun."

"For an attorney?"

She moaned. Damn Shannon for letting that out of the bag. "It was much easier to convince you of my fun factor when I danced on a pole."

Reed handed her the popcorn and unfolded the blanket he'd brought out as he spoke. "The imagery of a stripper tanks that of sitting behind a desk."

"I wear heels," she defended herself.

"Platforms?"

"Oh, please. I can't walk into divorce court looking like a hooker."

He spread the blanket over the both of them and moved close enough for her to feel the heat of his body on the double chaise lounge chair.

"Divorce attorney, eh? That fits, I suppose."

"It does?"

"Sure. Shannon refers to you as the mother hen, seems to me like you've appointed yourself as the caregiver for the whole group."

"I am, in a way."

"Are they all your clients?"

She blinked a few times, felt a pull of responsibility for her client confidentiality. "They're my friends." Which was true.

"Nice diversion, Counselor." He winked. "I get it. Not my business."

The lights on the deck started to fade, and Reed skillfully placed his arm over her shoulders and tucked her into his personal space.

Her stomach twisted and her head felt light. When was the last time she'd been held while watching a movie? And why hadn't she actively tried to find someone to do so? The truth was, she hadn't met someone in a long time worthy of quiet movie moments.

He smelled fresh, his body was warm, and he kissed the side of her head once he settled. She could get used to this.

When the opening credits of the movie started to roll, she looked up at him. "Thanks for not pressing."

He brushed her arm with the backs of his fingers and turned his attention to the movie.

The movie ended and all but a few stayed behind to enjoy the quiet night outside. The ship glided over the ocean with almost unnoticeable movement, the breeze picking up as the night grew on.

"I say we paraglide tomorrow."

Lori had curled up on the lounger, Reed kept his arm around her and talked against her ear while they watched the stars.

"Jump off a cliff with a tent over my head?" she teased, but didn't seem as dead against high adrenaline activities as she had when they first met.

"How about off the back of a boat?"

She seemed to contemplate that image. "Over the water?"

"I don't think you can do it off a back of a boat that isn't over water."

She pushed at his feet with hers. "Smart-ass."

"C'mon. Push yourself."

"I can't tell if you're manipulating me or bullying me."

He should have been insulted. "You haven't said no."

Her lips pushed together. "I'm thinking about it."

"I bet Avery would do it."

"Avery is younger than I am."

"Oh, you're so old." His voice was rich with sarcasm.

"Plastic surgery and fillers. I do live in LA."

For half a second he found himself searching for telltale scars.

"Now who's gullible?"

"So I'll book us in the morning."

"I should ask the others if they want to join us."

"Is that a yes?"

"It isn't a firm no."

That's a start. "So you're in LA."

"Isn't everyone?" she asked.

"Feels like it at three in the afternoon on the freeway."

"I know, the traffic starts earlier and earlier."

"I'm in Santa Monica," he told her.

"House or condo?"

"Renting. I haven't decided if I'm going to stick there." Which wasn't completely true. But since his business was run out of a cell phone and a post office box, it was easy to stay mobile.

"I have a condo downtown."

"Loft space?"

"No, high-rise. I love it. Close to my office, close to the courts." She snuggled deeper in his blanket.

"I'd like to see how you live." While the line was one he'd used in the past to gather information, he said it now with an unwelcome wave of guilt. He pushed it aside.

She hesitated. "Do . . . do you think *this* can continue outside of a cruise ship?" she asked, tilting her head up to see his face.

"Honest answer?" he asked.

"Of course."

"I don't know. I haven't completely figured out what *this* is. Have you?"

Lori settled back in the crook of his arms. "Well, we're both adults."

"We are that." He held her closer, as if emphasizing their age.

"Neither of us are married or otherwise attached."

"True."

"It's safe to say there is some chemistry." She kept rattling off her list of obstacles they'd already overcome.

"I like the chemistry," he said against the lobe of her ear.

"We live in the same general area of the world. Which is a coincidence I'd question if I were somewhere other than a cruise ship in the Mediterranean."

"Maybe it's fate." He hoped she hadn't noticed his hand pause during her last comment.

"I'm not a big believer in fate. In my world, things happen on purpose, not accident."

It was his turn to twist this around on her. "So you've been stalking me and set us up to meet?"

She laughed, as he anticipated.

His gut twisted with a taste of guilt licking the edges of his psyche.

"No, that would be on you," she said.

"Guilty," he admitted. "Ever since I saw you at the bar that first day on board, I've been stalking you."

Her amusement leveled into something much deeper. His lines were working, he felt it in how her body relaxed against his, how when she looked up at him, her eyes peered deeper into his.

"To what end?" she slowly asked.

His hand that had been lingering on her arm took a long stroke up until the back of his fingers stroked the edges of one breast.

She shivered under his touch.

"I can think of a couple."

Lori lifted her chin and turned up toward him. "Only a couple?"

"You know of more?" he teased.

"Maybe." Her word sounded like sin.

He liked the banter.

Reed reached for her neck, ran his thumb along her jaw, and felt his erection spring to life.

Lori sighed and closed her eyes.

He lowered his lips.

"I have a question," she said before he could kiss her.

"Ask it," he said.

"Why are we sitting on this deck when we both have perfectly good private rooms?" She opened her eyes, stared at his lips.

"That is a very good question." And unless the ship started to take on water, he was taking his investigation to a dangerous level.

"Your room or mine?" she asked.

He lifted his frame from the lounge chair, reached a hand for her. "Mine. Your friends tend to show up in yours."

Once she was standing, Reed slipped a hand behind her back, pulled her body flush with his, and reached for her lips. He tasted cream as she melted against him. She kissed him back, open mouth and wanting.

Reed wanted her.

God help him.

Lori's palms started to sweat when Reed unlocked the door to his stateroom.

Was he serious about wanting to see if they could be something off the ship and home in LA, or was he handing her a line?

Did she care if it was a line?

Yes, she did. Against her better judgment.

She told herself to live in the moment and not worry about what she had no way of controlling.

Truth was she was the one who wanted Reed. Even if he was a sweet talker saying all the things she wanted to hear in order to get her naked and under him. She wanted that, too.

"Looks like we share the same decorator," she said, trying to hide her nerves. She entered his room and crossed to the drapes, which were open to the sea. "Same view."

She felt his eyes on her back and turned.

Reed leaned against his closed door, his hands casually in his pants pockets. "You're nervous."

"No," was her immediate reaction. She sighed. "I shouldn't be."

"We don't have to."

For a moment, it felt like he was backing out.

"Bite your tongue," she teased.

He pushed away from the door and approached her. "I'd rather you do that."

"Oh? You like pain?"

He shook his head before reaching for the back of hers. His kiss was an inferno in under a second. Unlike the ones they'd shared before, this one promised a much more satisfying end. Their tongues dueled until they were both breathless. He removed the clip that had held her hair back all evening, his fingers massaging the strands free of tangles as he continued to claim her lips, her neck.

She moaned. "Oh, you have that down."

"One of my talents," he said with a little growl.

Lori opened her eyes, found him watching as he kissed her. "Do you have more?"

His hands ran down her shoulders before falling to her waist. "You'll have to tell me."

She reached behind his neck and pulled his head back down to hers. He nibbled her lower lip before lifting her off her feet and carrying her the few feet it took to place her on the bed.

He followed her down, the weight of him the secure blanket of comfort she desired.

Lori wrapped a free leg around his, felt the vibrations of his low moan through their lips. He kissed, nibbled, and worked his way down her neck. He found a spot that made her shiver.

"There you are," he muttered. "Relax, I have you."

He cupped her breast through her clothes, teased her nipple through her bra.

Her body warmed, her limbs shivered. The sway of the ship lightened the cells in her head, and Reed blew them away with his touch.

Reed separated her legs with his knee, pushed against her fully.

"Too many clothes," she whispered, wanting.

He chuckled and reached under her shirt, the heat of his hand met her skin, electrifying her senses. Lori clawed at his shirt, slid her hand beneath the waistband of his pants, met the cool flesh of his hip.

Teeth met her breast through her shirt. "Take it off." She wanted it off . . . everything.

"Demanding." There was laughter in his voice.

"Please."

He huffed out a laugh and tugged her shirt over her head. Sitting up, she helped him out of his, was rewarded with a man who worked out and lived by the beach. Tan, muscular . . . and touching her.

Her nails ran down his chest, circled his nipples before reaching around his back.

Without warning, he shifted her around the bed until she was on top, straddling him.

Her hair fell around her face. Reed pulled it back and smiled up at her. "I like this look," he told her.

"Me on top?"

"No . . ." He traced her bottom lip with his thumb. "Aroused."

She traced his bare abs, ran her hands lower. "And what does that look like?"

"Sexy."

Something she couldn't identify crossed his face before he pulled her in to kiss.

Reed liked to play, his hands made quick work of the rest of her clothes, she helped him shed his.

He looked just as good out of his clothes as he

did in them. While she didn't have body image issues, Lord knew she wasn't as fit as she'd been in her early twenties.

Did he notice?

Did he care?

"Lori?"

His thumbs parted the folds of her sex.

"Yes . . ."

"You're beautiful."

"Are you reading my mind?"

He pulled her under him, kissed the top of one breast, moved to the other. "I am. One of my talents."

His tongue and teeth traveled lower.

"Oh?" She shivered.

"Top secret skill. I shouldn't be using it now."

It took every ounce of will to not push him lower. The heat of his words carried on his breath tickled her belly. "I won't tell anyone."

He licked the edge of her hip.

"You want more."

She lifted for him.

"You can just tell—"

"Stop! Talking!"

He laughed before he found her. A lick, a nibble, and a suck, and Lori was lost.

It didn't matter how skillful she was at completing certain tasks on her own, nothing took the place of a man's mouth on her sex. And Reed had skills.

She really hoped the walls of the ship were insulated when she called his name in her release.

Lori opened her eyes when air met her flesh.

Reed stared at her.

She hid under her arm.

"I'm doing that again," he told her.

"Now?" She wouldn't survive it.

"Later."

She flung her arm to her side. "Good."

He shifted over her, the heat of him pressed closer.

Lifting her legs over his hips, she invited him in. "Don't stop."

Reed placed a hand on the side of her face as he sank deep. Conversation ended, replaced with an effort to breathe while racing toward a common, satisfying goal.

He said something she didn't quite catch, not that it mattered, and her body shattered in delightful waves.

Chapter Thirteen

Lori was drunk on orgasms, Reed could see it in her face, could feel it in the lazy touch of her hands. If he were being honest with himself, he'd admit he was as loose as a doll made of string.

With her head tucked into the crook of his arm, Lori traced imaginary circles on his chest, which managed to arouse him more than once already, and it was only one in the morning.

"Have you always been in California?" Lori's pillow talk was a bit of a minefield. Reed had learned early on to give as many facts as he could without telling everything about himself.

"Mostly. Spent a little time in my twenties traveling around. How about you?"

"Born and raised. Did my undergrad in Chicago, froze my butt off for four years, then law school at Columbia."

Her leg was tucked up beside his, his hand rested on her naked thigh. He gave her butt a tiny slap. "Where you froze more of this off."

She laughed and wiggled her rear end. "I couldn't wait to get back to the sunshine."

"And traffic."

"Traffic is everywhere. Adding snow and ice makes it worse."

He knew that.

He also knew that now was a great time to probe her about her relationship with Shannon.

"You could be an attorney anywhere."

"Wealthy clients are in LA," she offered.

"Like Shannon?"

"Yeah."

"I guess that's good for you."

"Wealth doesn't make divorce any easier, it just makes it more lucrative for me."

"How so?"

"Best example is to compare a typical divorce from a middle income family in, say, Nebraska, to a high income family in Bel Air. The first couple have a home, two cars, a moderate savings. Nothing in ways of stocks, bonds, yada yada. Couple of kids, maybe a dog. For argument's sake, let's say the wife decided to be a stay-at-home mom. The marriage falls apart without too much fanfare. Maybe the house is sold, most likely the wife and kids will stay in the family home, ex-husband has to pay for home, for the kids . . . the wife needs to go back to work. There is no fighting over possessions, since what they had was minimal. He keeps his junk he kept gathered in the man cave garage and she keeps the Pier 1 Imports buys."

"It sounds like the wife is making out."

"Probably, but no more or less than what she had when she was married. But in a wealthy marriage, there are multiple houses, sometimes in different countries. Custody is an issue if the couples live in different places. Cars, assets, stocks, bonds; you name it. I had a couple fight over a collection of Montblanc pens."

"Are those expensive?" He was a Bic kind of guy.

She looked up at him. "Yes, very. Anyway, the rich take a long time to sort out their crap."

"And the longer they take, the more hours you can bill."

She placed her chin on his chest. "Yes. Which sounds awful, but I always warn my clients when they come in what it's going to cost if they can't come to some kind of resolution before going to court."

Questions about Shannon's divorce were on the tip of his tongue, but he swallowed them back. "I didn't have much when I divorced. I was barely twenty-three, and she had just reached the age to drink in a bar. It lasted less than a year, neither of us fought to keep the couch."

"That's smart."

"What about you? Was your own divorce simple?"

"Yes and no." Her smile fell.

"Oh?"

"We met in law school."

"You were both lawyers?"

"No. He was a year younger than me. I graduated, took the bar . . . passed. He graduated by a hair and failed the bar three times. I found my first position with a firm, and he was working as a paralegal and hating it."

"That sounds like a recipe for disaster."

"Or divorce, as it turned out. He had enough legal knowledge to hold on long enough that I cut him a check for alimony and he ended up with the condo."

Reed couldn't imagine any able-bodied man taking his young wife for that kind of payout.

"So where is the *yes* part of 'was your divorce simple?' Sounds like you got screwed."

"It was simple in that I didn't drag it out. My attorney's fees were nothing compared to what my clients pay me. I learned two very valuable lessons before I turned thirty."

He could probably guess, but he didn't try. "Which were?"

"Love is grand, but divorce is a hundred grand."

He grinned. "And the second?"

"Prenuptial agreements should be mandated before anyone enters into marriage."

Her eyes were fading, and she lay back down on his chest.

After a few seconds, he said, "Prenuptial sounds loveless."

She hummed, and her breathing slowed. "I refer to my previous statement."

Reed closed his eyes. "Love is grand . . ."

"Divorce is a hundred grand," she finished for him.

She went to sleep in Italy and woke up in France. To seal the morning up, Reed faked a French accent and woke her with indecent kisses all over. By the time she took her walk of shame to her cabin, she was floating on a sexual cloud with appropriate body aches from the previous night's exercise.

"Go spend the day in France with your friends," he had encouraged her.

"No skydiving?"

He laughed. "You're not ready."

She wasn't. "Dumping me already?"

"Not a chance. But I need to recharge, and I'm not sure how I can do that while staring at you all day. Besides, you're here with your friends."

His words reminded her of why she was on the cruise in the first place. Somehow, the trip for her clients had become her own personal *Love Boat* episode.

Lori left his stateroom after several steamy kisses, and slipped into hers. After enjoying a hot shower, she met the girls on the dock.

"Good-bye Italy," Shannon announced as if she were the tour director. "The country of high emotions, no toilet paper in the public restrooms, and more carbs than your personal trainer can ever melt off your ass, and welcome to France, home of coiffed poodles and croissants."

Trina took a long, deep breath through her nose. "Ahhh, yes. It smells like sex."

All three women stared directly at Lori.

She settled her sunglasses on the bridge of her nose and offered a smug smile.

"That would be Avery," she diverted.

"Ha!" Trina exclaimed.

"She has a point," Avery said.

"No, this is a new pheromone, laced with American male and sprinkled with a certain lawyer's perfume."

Shannon had a way with words.

Lori regarded them from over the rim of her sunglasses. "Well, he is *very* American . . . everywhere."

Trina wrapped her arm over Lori's shoulders. "Well, good! You needed it."

Did she ever. Only a few hours' sleep, and she still felt like she could run a marathon.

"So no male companions today?" Shannon asked.

"Not on my end," Avery said. "Outside of the sheets, Rogelio and I have very little to say to each other."

"It would help if you spoke Spanish," Trina teased.

"Whatever. He and Miguel are off our radar today."

"And Reed didn't want to impose."

"He isn't—"

"I know," Lori interrupted Shannon. "But this is *our* vacation. The chances of the four of us getting to France together again are slim."

"She has a point."

"Okay, then." Trina twisted toward the city. "Let's find those croissants!"

Reed perched himself off the ship and far enough away to avoid anyone from realizing he was stalking the passengers disembarking.

The unnamed woman watching Lori and Trina was on board. All he needed to do was stay in the obvious place she would show up and follow her.

Lori's group was easy to spot. She wore a wide smile he hoped he was responsible for putting on her face, and the other three scampered along in search of a French adventure.

Or maybe just wine and mild entertainment.

A good thirty minutes later, Miguel and Rogelio stepped off the ship.

He was half tempted to follow the men but didn't think he'd gain anything if he did.

She was there . . . long legs, brunette.

She wore a hat, one that stuck out and made those around her pay attention.

Her features were hidden by the massive sunglasses and wide brim.

Taking pace behind her, Reed felt the hair on the back of his neck start to prickle.

"Too easy," he muttered to himself an hour later.

She meandered, he followed.

An outdoor café beckoned with the scent of pastries and rich coffee. She chose a table under the shade of an umbrella. Once seated, she lifted her head and focused her attention directly at him.

I'm being played.

Instead of playing more cat and mouse, he took the direct route to her table and sat without invitation.

"Mr. Barlow." The thickness of her accent screamed Slavic. He didn't pretend to know which part of the region she was from.

"You have me at a disadvantage."

Olive skin, high cheekbones, her eyes still hidden by the sunglasses that couldn't conceal her beauty.

"Will a name make you feel better?"

"Any chance you'll give me a real one?"

Her bright red lips lifted. "As if Barlow is yours."

The waiter approached, spoke in French.

Miss Slavic responded in kind.

When the waiter looked at him, Reed shook his head. "I'm fine."

Unimpressed, the skinny man lifted his chin,

turned on his polished heel, and walked away.

"Who do you work for?"

"I was about to ask the same question."

He sat back, said nothing.

"Seems our conversation has already stalled."

"I'm sure you anticipated that."

She smiled.

"Why today?" he asked.

The waiter returned with coffee.

"Our travels are nearly over, are they not?"

What the hell is your deal? "And have you obtained the information you need?" he asked.

"I'm close."

"And talking with me today is bringing you closer?"

She shook her head, brought the cup to her lips. "No. I wanted to know what you're made of."

"Know your enemies?"

She set her cup down after taking a sip. "Are we enemies, Reed?"

"You tell me."

"I have no quarrel with you. I'm not entirely convinced we're after the same thing."

He kept his face blank. "Are you working with Miguel?"

She said something in a language he didn't understand. "I'm insulted. I make it a policy to avoid amateur thieves."

Which was half of Reed's conclusion about the man as well. "You're following him."

“Know your enemies,” she quoted him.

“Who the hell are you?” The bite in his question made her grin.

“Call me Sasha.” She stood.

“Who are you working for?”

She smiled, didn’t answer. “Until we meet again.”

Sasha left him with a sway of her hips . . . and the bill.

Chapter Fourteen

It was formal night on the ship, and Lori and the others decided fancy dresses and high heels were in order to accompany their dinner reservations at one of the fancier restaurants on the ship. That was until Trina pounded on her door and pulled her into Avery's room.

"Her jewelry is gone," Trina exclaimed once they were both hovering over Avery, who knelt by the open safe.

"What do you mean, gone?"

Avery looked up at Lori as if she were the ripe old age of three. "Ripped off. Someone stole my shit."

Lori knelt down in the slim-fitting formal dress and looked at the empty boxes inside Avery's in-suite safe. "For crying out loud." She stood. "Don't touch anything."

Minutes later, Lori stood outside of Avery's stateroom while security and some of the Italian brass on board asked Avery questions.

They were drawing a crowd.

Datu stood to the side, his face sheen white, his hands visibly shaking as his boss questioned him.

"Does she know how much the jewelry was worth?" Shannon asked.

"Somewhere around fifty."

Lori knew her share of rich women, and tossing fifty thousand dollars worth of jewelry into their bag while vacationing wasn't unheard of. Most wore that alone on their ring fingers.

Two plainclothes security guards brushed past the three of them and down the stairs.

"Hey?"

Lori heard Reed's voice from behind her and turned to see his questioning eyes.

"What's going on?" He peeked around the door, then back toward her.

"Someone stole Avery's jewelry."

His mouth opened. "You're kidding."

"We were getting ready for dinner, she went to find a pair of earrings, and hello . . . nothing left in her safe," Trina explained.

Reed looked over the banister separating the decks, then back. "Did someone break into the room?"

"The door wasn't broken down," Shannon said.

"You said she found the safe empty. Did she notice the safe was broken open?"

Lori stared at Reed, waiting for Trina's answer.

"No. In fact, we didn't notice anything at all. If she hadn't looked for the earrings, we might not have known they were missing."

"Ms. Cumberland?" One of the brass in the room called her.

"Yes?"

"Would you mind?" He stood to the side of the door, inviting her into the room.

Reed kept looking over the banister.

"Of course." Lori walked away from the others, past the living room of the suite, and into the bedroom, where she found Avery sitting on the edge of her bed while three other people searched the room and one sat in a chair, asking questions.

Lori took a seat beside her friend.

"I told them you're my lawyer."

"And why would you need your lawyer when you're the one victimized?" Lori asked. She turned her attention to the man asking questions.

"Ms. Cumberland, please accept my apologies. These are standard questions, I assure you."

"Who are you?"

"Joseph Bianchi, I advise the ship's staff."

"You're not the police?"

"The ship doesn't have police, Ms. Cumberland. We're a luxury liner subject to maritime law."

"What exactly does that mean?"

"That's what I asked," Avery said.

"Ms. Grant said she left with you and your companions today at nine in the morning."

"That's correct."

"My jewelry was in the safe when I left."

"You looked in your safe before you went ashore?" The uniformed man didn't sound convinced.

"Well, no. But it was the night before when I went to bed."

"With your companion?"

Avery glared. "I've told you this already. Rogelio left after midnight."

"Do you think Rogelio stole your stuff?" Lori asked her.

"He's never been alone in my room."

The officer said something to the remaining men in the room, and they quickly left.

Lori glanced around. "Aren't they going to look for fingerprints?"

"I assure you, we will investigate every lead."

"Your butler, Mr. Datu, says he has seen your companion in your stateroom many times."

Avery shrugged. "That's not a secret."

"You trust this man?"

"Well . . ." Doubt waved over her face as she looked at Lori. "Yeah. I mean . . ."

"Mr. Bianchi, if there is a question about Avery's friend, ask him a few questions, search his room."

"We plan on doing that. We just want to make sure Ms. Grant would like to stick with her statement."

"Why wouldn't she?"

His smile was meant to pacify. But only managed to tick her off. "Cruise ships are often the target of false claims."

"You think she's faking this?" Lori found her lawyer hat and pulled it down hard.

"I didn't say that. Perhaps Ms. Grant misplaced her belongings."

"Misplaced?" Avery stood.

"It has happened in the past. We hate to upset other passengers with false accusations—"

"I haven't accused anyone of anything. I'm telling you someone stole my shit."

Mr. Bianchi stood, placed his notebook in his pocket. "We will look into it."

"Do you have security cameras?" Lori asked.

"Some."

Avery rolled her eyes. "I can't believe this."

"I want to see them," Lori told the man.

"We will see what we can find. I suggest you enjoy your evening, ladies. I'm sorry for this unfortunate occurrence; however, there isn't much to do now but stand back and let us do our jobs."

"Unbelievable." Avery paced the room after the man left.

"Where is he going?" Shannon asked.

"Dinner, probably," Avery yelled.

"What?"

"I don't think they're taking this seriously."

"Why not?" Trina asked.

"Because they don't have to. They're not subject to American laws, and international waters have their own idea of what a crime is."

"Stealing someone else's stuff sounds criminal to me," Lori said.

"Yes, but you'll be leaving this ship in a couple of days, and the investigation will be left up to that guy." The Italian that wasn't a cop and wanted to rule out foul play by suggesting Avery *lost* her stuff.

Lori looked up when she heard a knock on the door. Reed stood listening. "I saw a few men from the ship hovering by Miguel and Rogelio's room."

"And?" Trina asked.

"I'm not sure. They were speaking in Italian."

"Was Rogelio there?" Avery asked.

"No. Neither of them."

"It's not like they went far," Shannon pointed out.

Avery sighed. "I can't imagine he'd do this."

Lori caught Reed's stare.

A stare that she was sure matched hers.

Their idea of a night of fancy food and entertainment squashed, they all returned to their rooms to dress down and look over the ship themselves to find Miguel and Rogelio to ask their own questions. Agreeing to meet back on the pool deck in an hour, they separated.

Reed took up space beside Lori.

"You think he did this," Lori said once they were alone.

He scanned the deck as they walked through.

"I wasn't happy with Miguel's answers when it came to Trina."

"But this is Rogelio."

"Right. Miguel's friend from school. Isn't that what he told us?"

She didn't remember.

"It could be random," she said.

Reed stopped her, touched her arm. "Really, Counselor? Most crimes are committed by someone you know."

"You sound like a cop."

"I watch a lot of *CSI.*" He pulled her along his side as they searched the deck.

Poolside, an hour later, none of them reported seeing the Spanish duo.

"I haven't gotten rid of Rogelio since we met, now he is nowhere to be seen," Avery complained.

"It's a big ship," Trina said with a hopeful smile.

"We should probably get something to eat, let the ship's authorities do their job," Lori said.

"I have a sick feeling about this." Avery slumped down in a poolside chair.

"Someone just jacked fifty thousand dollars worth of jewelry, of course you have a sick feeling," Lori said.

Avery waved both hands in the air. "No, it's not that. I don't care about the stuff, I have insurance . . . but if it was Rogelio . . . damn it. Am I that naive?"

Shannon took a seat beside her. "Hon, we all met the guy. He seems normal to me."

"Me too."

"I wouldn't have guessed. And I'm the cynic in the group."

Avery dropped her head in both her hands. "I knew it was too good to be true. A hot cruise fling, no strings. Just fun. After my year and a half of purgatory, I deserve some fun, right?"

"Think that was the point behind this trip," Trina said. "Have fun, slip out of purgatory."

Avery pinned Reed with a glare. "You're a dude, what do you think?"

"I think you're being too hard on yourself. If he is behind this, chances are he's done it before. That doesn't suggest you have an inability to judge character. It means he's a professional at manipulating. He had all of us fooled."

Avery's chest deflated. "Yeah, but I slept with the man."

"I bet he shows up by morning," Shannon offered.

Lori would bet her next paycheck he wouldn't.

Miguel and Rogelio never reboarded the ship after the stop in France.

Reed wasn't surprised.

Sasha, for lack of a real name, had labeled

Miguel as an amateur thief. Thief, yes . . . amateur? Well, that was left to interpretation. And if Reed had been anywhere other than on an assignment, he would have picked up on their game and called them out on it. But to do so would have brought attention to his own game.

The last stop of the cruise was on the island of Majorca, in the city of Palma.

Instead of any activity, the women decided to sit on the beach and drink rum by the buckets.

Reed made it a point to hand them water to keep them from getting sick from too much liquor. Keeping an eye on them had become his mission. Well, one of his missions, in any event.

They were being reckless in their scorn, and as much as he wanted them drunk enough to start talking about their connections, and possibly clue him in to something to bring back to the person paying him, he didn't want to see them hurt.

"Make sure we're back on that ship before it takes off," Avery charged him with the task.

"I have my watch set."

"You're not wearing a watch."

He smiled at Trina. "My phone. My phone is set to alarm us when we need to leave."

"I can't believe I fell for that asshole." Avery's statement was burned into Reed's mind. She'd been repeating it every fifteen minutes or so since they arrived on the beach. No, make that since they met before leaving the ship.

"All men are assholes," Shannon told her, and Trina agreed.

He looked at Lori, who was slightly less inebriated. "Should I be here?"

"You're fine." She offered a drunk smile.

"You know, things might not have ended that great, but I sure am glad we all came to Lori's little get-together."

"I'm glad you can find the bright side, Avery."

"I'm not looking forward to going home," Trina said.

Reed kept an ear on the conversation, his eyes in a spy thriller book he'd brought with him.

"We have some things to figure out, but you're going to be fine," Lori said.

"I don't even want to think about it."

"We have a long flight home to think," Shannon told her.

"Is Sam sending her jet?" Avery asked.

Reed followed the conversation, had to think about the name *Sam* for a moment.

"I spoke with Sam last night. The jet will be waiting when we arrive in Barcelona."

"Good, cuz I have a feeling I might not be up to playing nice on a commercial airline."

"That's because you're going to be hungover at this rate," Trina told Avery.

"Blame the asshole."

Reed glanced up to see Avery tipping her cocktail back. She reached for the pitcher they'd ordered, and he stopped her. "Uh, how about some water?"

She scowled but reached for the water instead.

He pretended to go back to his book.

"You're dropping me off in New York?" Trina asked.

"Yep. Your bodyguards are picking you up while we refuel."

Reed looked over the edge of his book. "Bodyguards?"

"Hey, maybe I should have one of them."

"Don't wish that on yourself," Shannon told Avery. "I always had guys around when I was married to Paul. It's overrated."

"I don't want to hear that," Trina said. "I like my privacy."

Lori set her drink down. "It's not that bad. Neil's team is the best. Discreet. You'll be fine."

"Hey?" Reed caught their attention all at once. "Why do you need a bodyguard?"

For a moment they all just stared at him like he was an idiot.

"Should we even be talking about this?" Avery, the drunkest of them all, asked the logical question.

Trina rolled her eyes. "I came into a little bit of money. And clearly there are people out there who think nothing of taking what isn't theirs."

"A little bit of money?"

Avery spread her hands wide and mouthed the words *a lot.*

"Huh . . . so maybe it's a good thing you cut Miguel off," Reed said.

Again, the women were all silent as they contemplated his words.

Avery broke the silence.

"I can't believe I fell for that asshole."

Then came the chorus.

Reed found himself joining in. "All men are assholes."

And he was one of the worst of them all.

He met Lori and the others after they cleared customs the next day.

Avery and Trina were huddled under the dark shades of their sunglasses, shielding their eyes as if the clouded sky burned their retinas. Shannon appeared slightly better, and Lori looked almost normal.

"I see you're all alive," he addressed them while a valet gathered their bags and put them in the back of a massive SUV.

"I probably have you to thank for that," Avery told him.

He grinned. "You're welcome, then."

She waved a hand in the air and moved toward the car. "I need to sit down."

Trina offered him a quick hug. "Thanks for watching over us."

Guilt sucker punched him. "Take care of yourself."

Shannon said her good-bye next. "Thanks for not bringing up the obvious."

He hugged her. "I didn't vote for him, if that makes you feel any better."

She sighed and got into the car.

Then there was Lori.

"I don't envy their flight home," he said.

"They'll be okay. Probably sleep most of the day."

He placed a hand on her shoulder. "And you?"

"I have a lot of work to catch up on."

"Back to business?"

"Yeah."

He took up position in her personal space and placed both hands on her cheeks. "I want to see you again." Which was true. They hadn't shared five carefree minutes alone since Italy.

"Do you think we can work back in LA?"

"Not sure, but it's worth trying."

She pressed her frame next to his. "You have my number."

He leaned in and kissed her, felt his chest tighten with guilt or pleasure, he wasn't sure. Probably a little of both.

He heard the trunk of the SUV shut and ended their kiss.

"Safe flight home, Counselor."

"Good-bye, Reed."

He waved as the car pulled away.

He turned back toward Barcelona . . . where he planned on finding out more about Miguel and Rogelio . . . the amateur thieving assholes who gave all men a bad name.

Chapter Fifteen

Jet lag was a combination of the hangover of a lifetime and receiving an injectable dose of caffeine at two in the morning.

Lori looked at her bedside clock as two in the morning turned into two thirty. She'd punched her pillow, turned it a few times to see if cooling her face would lure her to sleep.

Nothing worked. She had an early morning meeting followed by lunch with Sam to go over all the details of her trip, and at this point Lori was fairly certain she'd be dozing off in her soup.

Giving up, she switched on the dim bedroom lamp and grabbed her cell phone.

Was he thinking about her?

Did Reed toss and turn in his bed, close his eyes, and sense her beside him?

On the ship, she'd been inundated with responsibility and still managed a little romance. Now that she was home in bed . . . without the swaying of a ship reminding her that she had a job to do, her mind kept flashing back to Reed and his smile, the way he held her, kissed her.

The problem with the thoughts milling about in her head wasn't the lift she felt in her chest, or the schoolgirl excitement that made her smile, it was the possibility that she was alone in her joy. Was Reed a weeklong fling?

Would he call?

The clock slipped closer to three.

She opened up her text messages and found Reed's name. She reread his texts from the ship several times. Then, before she could talk herself out of it, she started typing.

> I can't sleep. My body is still in the Mediterranean.

She pressed "Send" and tapped her thumb against the side of her phone for ten minutes, willing Reed to respond with her mind.

Nothing.

At 3:10, she set her phone aside, turned off the light, and forced her eyes to close.

With one ear open to catch the buzz of a response from her phone, Lori finally fell asleep thirty minutes before she needed to get up to go to the office.

Reed timed it so he left his apartment after the morning traffic was done clogging up everything. Although, in LA it was always a crapshoot when you aimed your car toward a freeway, even at two in the morning.

He'd spent two days painting profiles of four women.

Shannon Redding-Wentworth, just about to turn thirty-two, had met and married the governor before his run for office. Then a year and a half into his four-year term, they filed for a divorce. Shannon walked away without fanfare, a tidy sum, and a house in Southern California. The divorced couple were still seen at the same functions at times, no bad publicity circulated in the gossip magazines that didn't appear completely fabricated. After meeting the woman and spending the better part of a week with her, he didn't believe for a minute that she'd been found with twenty-one-year-old twins at a seedy Hollywood club. The tabloids had a way of making a story where there wasn't one. So did politicians, like the one who hired him to find dirt. Any other case, Reed would have reported to his client that there wasn't anything there. Except he had the nagging feeling that something wasn't completely right. Then there was Sasha . . . who didn't seem to be following Shannon at all. No, she was watching Trina and Lori. Why?

The retired police officer in him had surfaced sometime between when he climbed into a crowded plane for a free trip to Europe and now.

And that hadn't happened in years. He'd reinvented himself as a PI void of emotion. He had gone through the motions of investigating, spying, gathering dirt for his clients, delivering it, and walking away with enough money to pay his rent and have a few nice things. No emotion, no involvement . . .

Until Lori.

He found her text when he forced his eyes open at eight in the morning. The irony was he'd been up thirty minutes before she'd sent her message, and desired to send one himself.

He didn't, not wanting to wake her . . . and more, not wanting to come off as an infatuated lover.

Even though that was exactly what he was.

Instead, he sent her a text after nine, made a crack about her inability to sleep because of him.

Lori flirted back with a crack about his ego.

He shook his thoughts about her aside and thought about the case he was forming in his head.

Avery Grant, just turned thirty, newly divorced from a man nearly twice her age. It took some searching, but he found enough information about her divorce to know she'd also walked away with a tidy sum from her rich, hedge funding husband. No nasty tabloid bits about their marriage, but keeping with the theme he'd seen on the ship, Avery didn't wait to cut loose. He didn't know divorce parties were a thing, but someone managed to take pictures that were printed in a tabloid the week after her divorce was final.

Trina Petrov . . . now there was a woman with some seriously bad mojo. He found pictures of her late husband and her . . . they didn't match. She was stunning, and he had been less than mediocre. Then again, that happened sometimes, like the supertall woman with the man scratching at five four with a two-inch boot. Still, they'd been married for just under a year when hubby offed himself. The financials of what was left to her weren't disclosed, but he was still digging. Follow the money and you'll have a case . . . or so he had learned when he was on the force. He could only imagine the kind of wealth the man had. He was a grandson to a prominent oil family, a businessman with his own multimillion-dollar company.

Trina's face was in plenty of tabloids with the death of her husband and mother-in-law all in the same month.

She was a woman torn. He'd seen her with barely a smile on her face, and he'd seen her stumbling drunk and dancing. Sure, there was a high probability of someone drugging her, but still. Would a widow who loved her late husband even be on that ship in the first place? There was something missing in this link.

And then there was Lori. The divorce attorney who said they were all friends simply traveling together.

Avery and Shannon's divorces were highly publicized, and Lori was mentioned both times. Trina didn't count, since her husband was dead.

Or did she? There was something he was missing, yet he knew it was right there if he just looked close enough to see it.

Lori's office was a posh little affair sitting in ambiguous office space in one of the many high-rises in Los Angeles. She didn't work for a firm and didn't have several partners of her own. Which told him that she didn't need their financial help in keeping office space or staff. That didn't mean she had a tiny footprint, however. Her office screamed money nearly as much as the clientele that walked through the door.

A little over a week after he'd left her in Spain, Reed walked through the thick wooden door of Lori Cumberland, Attorney at Law, and into a reception area large enough to keep two feuding parties far enough apart to avoid Armageddon.

He stepped up to the empty reception desk and looked around.

Lori's business card, along with one for her paralegal, sat in a small basket. He picked up Lori's and ran his thumb over the silver embossed lettering.

"Can I help you?"

The voice belonged to a woman in her late forties.

"Is Lori in?"

"Do you have an appointment, Mr. . . . ?"

"Barlow, and no, I don't. If you can tell Lori that Reed is here."

"Ms. Cumberland isn't back from lunch yet." The secretary took a seat in one of those ergonomic chairs and placed a set of reading glasses on the bridge of her nose. "She's extremely busy this afternoon. I can schedule an appointment."

Reed leaned against the high reception desk, offered a smile reserved for charming answers out of women.

"I'm not in need of a divorce."

The secretary smiled, her eyes questioning him before she asked, "Are you writing up a prenuptial agreement?"

"No, I am not."

"Then what is it that you need Ms. Cumberland's service for?"

He couldn't stop the image of Lori's face as he kissed her from taking firm hold in his head.

"It's personal."

"I'm sure it is, Mr. Barlow, but I'd still need to make an appointment in Ms. Cumberland's schedule to accommodate you."

The office door opened from behind.

Business Lori wore a tight pencil skirt, heels that weren't too tall. Her silk blouse covered the creamy skin of her chest but accentuated the curve of her breasts. Her hair was partially held back in a loose bun that probably took her way too long to put up.

She made it two steps into the office with an

auburn haired petite woman at her side before she recognized him.

"Reed?"

"Hello, Lori." He dropped his voice.

She blushed.

"What are you doing here?"

"I was in the neighborhood." Via a few freeways and with no other destination in mind.

"I was encouraging Mr. Barlow to make an appointment," Lori's secretary said from behind the desk.

"It's okay, Liana. Reed's a friend."

The redhead cleared her throat with an amused smile.

"I'm sorry. Sam Harrison, this is Reed Barlow."

Ah, yes . . . the woman from the papers.

He held out his hand.

"Lori and I met in Barcelona."

Sam shook with the grip of a woman in business and not one only used to entertaining guests from her country club. "Is that right? How come you didn't tell me about *him?*" she asked Lori.

Lori opened her mouth, closed it, and turned to Reed. "I wanted to keep him to myself."

Sam choked on a laugh.

"I guess I messed that up," he said, grinning.

Lori rolled her eyes and stepped close. He took her advance as an opportunity to kiss her cheek in greeting.

"It looks like we will have more to talk

about at dinner on Sunday," Samantha told Lori.

"Should I be worried?" Reed teased.

"Probably," Sam said. "Lori's always welcome to bring a plus one . . ."

Reed wanted to jump at the invitation; instead, he looked to Lori for direction.

She wasn't jumping.

"Maybe next time," he told Lori's friend.

"Perhaps. Lori?" Sam turned to her friend. "I'll see you this weekend. Call me after New York."

The two women hugged briefly before Sam turned and left.

"Liana, when is my next client?"

"Twenty minutes."

Lori gave a quick nod into the depths of the office. "That's all the time I have," she told him.

"I'll take it."

He followed her down a short hall, past a conference room, around a small kitchen, and past an open office. From there, she welcomed him into her office space.

It wasn't cluttered with papers all over a desk or useless knickknacks. It was clean lines and professional decor mixed with just enough elegance to say the space was occupied by a woman.

She closed the door behind them and walked around her desk.

He followed her.

"What are you—"

He didn't let her finish her question before he

grasped her slim hips, turned her around to face him, and lifted her until her butt was on her desk.

Lori sucked in a breath but didn't push him away.

"I missed you."

She bit her lower lip, and he replaced her teeth with his kiss.

He tasted her surprise, followed quickly by acceptance.

Lori kissed back with a fevered pitch. Her hand traveled down his back and over his ass before she dug her fingertips in.

All his brain cells traveled down in a mad rush to fill his cock with heat.

Danger zone, Reed.

He attempted to pull back, but she didn't let him. Lips open, tongue demanding, Lori moaned until she started to squirm.

Reed gently grasped her groping hands and weaved his fingers together with hers. "Greedy woman," he whispered when he forced their kiss to end.

"You started it."

He took one of their clasped hands and rubbed the back of hers against his erection.

"Have an itch?" she asked, teasing.

"Yes. And only a high-powered divorce attorney by the name of Lori can scratch it."

She licked her lips. "I have to work."

"Tonight . . . for dinner."

"Can't. Dinner meeting with a client."

He narrowed his eyes. "Tomorrow?"

She gripped his hands tighter. "I have a late appointment. But maybe."

"Seven?"

Her eyes narrowed.

He rubbed himself with her hand again.

She smiled. "Fine. My place, but you can't stay the night. I have an early flight to New York."

"You just got home."

"Can't be helped. Trina needs me."

Yep, yep . . . more to the Trina story.

"Okay. I'll leave by midnight."

"Eleven."

Was this a negotiation?

"Eleven thirty, and I'll bring wine."

She smiled. "Deal."

Chapter Sixteen

Lori counted the hours until her date with Reed.

Okay, maybe it wasn't a date so much as a prescheduled booty call. But hey, she bought a few things to go with the wine he was bringing, so it could double as an actual dinner date.

With her hands loaded with bags from the store, Lori exited the elevator to her condo and fished her keys out of her purse.

She fiddled with the door twice before managing to unlock the thing. Two steps inside she heard someone in her kitchen.

Her first thought was Reed . . . not that he could have gotten in or that they'd gotten to the point where he would just appear without invitation.

Lori hesitated when she saw Avery ducking into her wine fridge.

"You don't have chardonnay."

She dropped her bags on the counter.

"Ah, hello, Avery."

"You don't like white? I can do red, if that's all you have."

Lori dropped her purse, looked at the clock on the wall.

"There are a few pinot grigios in there."

Avery ducked back in, pulled out a white. She

moved to a drawer, pulled it open . . . didn't find what she wanted and moved to another. After obtaining a corkscrew, she found two glasses and continued opening the bottle. "You're home kinda late."

"Business meeting." She looked at the clock. *And a date.*

"Hope you don't mind me letting myself in. I begged the concierge to let me in and they agreed. They know you and I are traveling together. I was pacing the walls upstairs."

"Uhm—"

"I was talking to Trina earlier today. She's bouncing off the walls, too."

"It's called jet lag."

Avery laughed, popped the cork. "Post-vacation . . . postmarriage . . . prechapter in what the hell do we do next. That's what it's called."

Lori knew Avery moving into a condo in the same building was probably a bad idea.

"Uhm . . . Avery . . ."

"Did you want white? I can open a red if you'd like."

"I'm good with white," Lori found herself saying. How the hell was she going to get Avery out of there before Reed showed up? He was due in less than half an hour.

"Did Trina tell you what the security guards found in her house?"

"She didn't call me about anything."

"That's surprising."

"I'm flying to New York in the morning. What did they find?"

"Bugs."

The first thing Lori thought of was an insect. Then her mind shifted. "You mean spy crap?"

"Yeah. They didn't think it was there long, but they found several all over the house."

"Holy cow." Lori fished her cell out of her pocket and sent a quick text to Sam.

> Do you know what is going on with the bugs in Trina's house?

"Explains why she's bouncing off the walls. My question is why would someone be spying on Trina? I don't get it."

"She's worth a lot of money."

"She's also squeaky-clean, a virtual saint compared to me."

Lori didn't argue.

Her phone buzzed.

> No details, just that Neil's guys found them. You're leaving tomorrow, right?

Avery poured the wine.

> Yes.

> Let me know what you find out.

Lori sipped the wine, put her phone down.

"Was Fedor in trouble with the law or anything?" Avery asked.

Lori shook her head. "No. Nothing like that." Her eyes settled on the bags containing the groceries she'd bought for her date.

Shit . . . her date.

Six forty-five.

"I wonder if we'll ever hear from the cruise line about Rogelio and Miguel."

"I somehow doubt it will be anything we want to hear."

"Still can't believe I fell for that. What is wrong with me that I'm so ready to fall like that?"

Lori felt like she'd been answering this question for the better part of two weeks.

"He was the schmuck, not you. You had your guard down. On vacation in the sun halfway across the world. He'd obviously done this before."

"I'm such an asshole." Avery sucked down half her glass right as the bell at Lori's door rang.

"Uhm . . ."

"Who could that be? It's kinda late."

"Well—"

Avery stared for a second before her eyes opened wider. "Wait . . . did you have something going on?"

"Kinda."

Lori looked in her hallway mirror, rolled her

eyes at the day-old appearance that stared back at her.

"Why didn't you say something?" Avery called from the kitchen.

Lori smoothed a hand down her skirt and opened the door.

Her jaw dropped. "Danny? What are you—"

"Oh, *hello* . . . who are you?" Avery asked from behind Lori.

Danny's devilish smile and charm swept over Avery before settling on her. "Hey, sis."

Danny had a bag slung over his shoulder as he passed through her threshold. "Did I know you were coming?"

"We talked about late summer."

Yeah, last Christmas. Not a word since.

"Uhm . . ."

Danny pushed past her, dropped his bag in her foyer, and extended a hand to Avery with a flirty smile. "I'm Lori's much younger brother."

"I'm Avery." Avery's voice dropped an octave, as if she were in a smoky bar, sizing up a man offering to buy her a drink. She turned to Lori. "Did I know you had a brother?"

"No."

"And here I thought you had a date."

Lori ducked around the corner, past the two who were saying way too much with their eyes, to see the clock. "I *do* have a date."

"Do you live with my sister?" Danny asked, completely ignoring Lori.

"No. I have my own place upstairs."

"It's nice to have neighbors."

Lori closed her eyes. "This is sooo not going to happen!" She put a hand between her brother and her client and waved them apart as if that was possible.

"You always were so bossy, sis." Danny leaned in and kissed Lori's cheek. "How is that death job you have? Shuffling papers and making calls?"

She wanted to call her brother out on his lack of job but held her comments back.

"C'mon in, Danny. We just opened a bottle of wine."

Lori squeezed her hands tight. How had her quiet naked night with Reed become so crowded?

She started to follow the others when there was a knock on her door.

Reed stood with a jacket and a bottle of red wine.

"Who's that?" Avery called from the kitchen.

Reed's smile dropped.

Lori shook her head and pulled him inside. She lifted both hands in the air. "I'm sorry in advance."

"You have company?"

"I didn't—"

Avery walked around the corner. "Reed? I didn't expect to see you here."

Lori shook her head. "I told you I had plans."

"Oh, well." Avery took the wine from Reed's hand. "Let me open this for you."

Lori wanted to crawl in a corner and hide.

Reed peeked around the corner. "Are we having a party?"

She moved close and whispered, "I came in and Avery was making herself at home . . . then my brother showed up unannounced."

He tilted his head. "Your brother is here?"

"Should we Uber in some food?" Avery asked from the kitchen.

Lori stepped close to Reed and rested her forehead on his shoulder. "I'm sorry."

The strength of his arms circled her back. "Don't be."

". . . and then Lori stood up, grabbed the largest knife on the table, and proceeded to hack the turkey right down the middle. She grabbed her plate once she'd managed to butcher the poor, dead bird, shoved as much of it as she could on one tiny plate, and then damn near threw it at Uncle Joe and said, 'There ya go, half for you, half for Dad, carve the damn thing the way you want!' "

Lori buried her head in her hands. "It wasn't one of my finer moments."

Danny talked around the forkful of food he'd just shoved into his mouth. "The best part—"

"Oh, God."

Danny ignored his sister and kept going.

". . . was when she pulled off one of the turkey legs with her bare hand, waved it in the air, and told the men to grow up before stomping out of the dining room."

Reed tried to picture her waving poultry at her arguing family.

"There hasn't been a holiday dinner since where Lori doesn't have a turkey leg on her plate."

The red in Lori's face was priceless. "I don't even like dark meat."

Danny shoved his sister's shoulder with his. "Serious props. Uncle Joe and Dad never bitch about who does a better job at carving a turkey anymore."

"They were being ridiculous."

"And you reacted with poise and grace?" Avery asked.

"I'm an attorney. I cut it down the middle. Seemed appropriate at the time."

"My family dinners are full of 'pass the salt' and 'how are your roses growing this year, Adeline?' I have the most boring family ever," Avery exclaimed.

"That isn't always a bad thing," Lori told her.

"One of these days I'm going to have to do something outrageous just to have something to talk about every year."

"You just divorced a millionaire. I'm sure that will keep the gossip going for a while."

Avery had already given the skinny to Danny about her recent divorce and how she knew Lori. Information that Reed knew but now felt free to talk about.

"My family half expected it."

"Oh?" Danny questioned.

"Yeah, Bernie was exactly what my family wanted me to be with. Most of them whispered that it wouldn't last."

Danny looked genuinely bothered by her statement. "That sucks."

"Whatever. It didn't last." Avery flipped her hair and turned on her smile. "So, Danny, how long are you staying in town?"

Lori leaned in. "Yeah, how long are you sleeping on my couch?"

"Don't you have a guest room?" he asked.

"Depends on how long you're staying."

Danny narrowed his eyes at his sister. "I know you love me, sis. Don't even try and deny me."

"I love you for two weeks in my guest room or three weeks on my couch . . . four and you're sleeping on the floor."

Danny placed a hand over his chest. "You wound me."

"Danny . . ."

"Two weeks. I'm actually on my way south of

the border. I hear there's some great fishing off Cabo."

"You're a fisherman?" Avery asked.

He shook his head. "No, I'm just allergic to work, and fishing is a great way to tan, eat, and make a few bucks."

Reed soaked in Lori's body language.

If he was reading her right, she wasn't kidding when she suggested her brother sleep on the floor if he planned on staying longer than he was welcome.

Avery tipped the last of the second bottle of white wine into her glass. It was empty. She reached for the red, shook the half an inch in the bottom of the bottle. "Should we open another one?"

Lori looked up at a clock on the wall. "I have to get some sleep. I have an early flight in the morning."

"But I just got here," Danny said.

"And if you had called, I would have told you to wait a few days."

"You know I hate phones."

Lori glanced at Reed. "He doesn't have a cell phone."

"How is that possible?" Avery asked.

"He makes collect calls."

"As in he calls an operator to make a call?" Reed knew there was doubt in his voice.

"He . . ." Danny said as he pointed to his chest.

"Is sitting right here. And yes, it's much cheaper than a cell phone."

"For you!" Lori told him.

Danny worked her like a violin. "I'm worth it."

Lori directed her unamused glare toward Reed. "See what I have to deal with?"

Yeah, he saw it. Danny was a couch surfer, and this month he was landing on Lori's. Something he guessed had happened before. The question was if Danny took full advantage or not. He seemed like a decent enough guy.

Avery was certainly charmed.

"I hate to be the buzzkill—"

"Since when?" Danny asked his sister.

Lori glared. "But I gotta get some sleep."

"You're going to see Trina, right?" Avery asked as she stood and grabbed some of the empty boxes of Chinese food they'd ordered.

"Yeah. The estate attorney is meeting us at two tomorrow."

"Sounds boring," Danny said.

Not to Reed. He was quite interested in what Lori and Avery were muttering about. He picked up their plates and followed them into the kitchen.

"I'm worried about her," Avery told Lori. "She said something about someone spying on her."

Reed stacked the dishes by the sink. "Why

would someone be spying on Trina?" he asked.

"I don't know. Her bodyguard people found bugs in her house when she arrived home from Spain," Avery told him.

Lori smiled but didn't add anything.

"Trina didn't seem like a woman who holds secrets."

Avery blinked a few times, glanced at Lori, and said, "I was thinking about going to her place for a while. I think she can use a friend."

Lori released a breath she seemed to be holding. "That's a great idea. I'd love to know that she has someone close that she can talk to."

Avery glanced toward the dining room table, where Danny was collecting empty wineglasses. "He's a bad idea . . . isn't he?" she whispered to Lori.

"He's my *brother!*"

"Okay, okay . . . when are you flying home?"

"Saturday morning."

"I'll fly out Friday. Can you water my plants while I'm gone?"

Lori narrowed her eyes. "Do you have plants?"

Avery laughed. "No."

Lori nudged her. "I'll let you know if the building catches fire."

"Perfect."

Lori turned her attention to Reed.

He nodded toward the living room.

She followed.

He placed a hand on her waist and pulled her close until he could circle her with his arms. "You take care of everyone, don't you?"

"You noticed."

There was a tension in her frame, in her eyes. "Who takes care of you?" he whispered.

Her strangled smile fell. "I'm good."

"Everyone needs someone to look out for them once in a while."

"I've been taking care of myself for a long time."

Laughter from the kitchen had them both looking back.

"Sorry about tonight," she told him.

"You know . . . for a strong, independent woman, you sure do apologize a lot for things you can't control."

"I do?"

"Yes. You do." He kissed the tip of her nose. "Call me when you land in New York."

"Why?"

Yeah, why had he told her to do that? Then it dawned on him. "I want to know you arrived safely."

For the first time since they'd met, doubt crossed her face.

"Okay?" he asked.

"The chance of a plane dropping from the sky is less likely than me biting it in the car on the way to the airport."

God, she was adorable when she went all lawyer on him.

“Then text me when you get to the airport, and then call when you land in New York.”

She blinked several times. “Fine. I’ll do that.”

“Did that hurt?” he asked.

Lori started to shake her head before she turned that shake into a nod. “Yes.”

“Good.”

Chapter Seventeen

Lori stepped away from her priority seat on the commercial airline slightly frazzled. The hour delay on her flight gave her very little time to commute into Manhattan for her two o'clock meeting with Mr. Crockett and Trina. Thankfully, she didn't need to stick around the airport for luggage since she only had a carry-on.

"I'm late," she told the driver she'd hired to pick her up from the airport. The second he closed the door and settled behind the wheel, she said, "I'll pay for your speeding ticket."

He glanced at her from the rearview mirror and sped off.

Gotta love New York. Hand gestures and horns, the drivers took a "hold no prisoner" approach to driving in order to get where they wanted. How any of the cars there survived was a mystery.

Lori fingered through the files on Alice Petrov and her estimated wealth that she'd obtained before Trina married Fedor. During her flight, she'd spent the first hour reading before lingering jet lag knocked her out. When she woke, she had barely an hour to refresh her memory about the Petrov players. Who was going to be happy with

Alice's decision to leave her estate to Trina, and who was going to fight?

Up until the last months of Alice's life, she was an active member on the board of the oil company her family had founded. She was the eldest of three girls, all of whom were given equal shares of the company upon their father's death.

Lori placed a hand against the seat to keep from toppling over when the driver cut off a horn-blaring car.

She turned the page of her document, skimmed the next page of Alice's bio, the part where she took a philanthropic role in many organizations: Women's Health United, Women for Women, Empowering Girls, Battered but Not Broken, Federation of the United . . . and finally, Girl Scouts.

A corner of Lori's brain started to itch. Something, or some chain of events, must have prompted this path of philanthropy.

Her body lurched forward as her driver pulled to an abrupt stop before the high-rise on Forty-Second.

She looked at her watch.

One fifty.

"You're good." She pulled a hundred-dollar bill from her wallet, added that to predetermined fare.

He handed her his card. "Anytime you're in the city."

"I'll keep you in mind."

He jumped out, but she was already one foot out the door before he could open it for her.

Cars honked behind his double-parked effort, not that he seemed to care.

Before she reached the doors of the building, her phone rang.

She answered without looking at who called. "I'm on my way in right now."

"Hey."

The voice threw her. She was expecting Trina on the other end.

"You didn't call me when you landed."

She damn near tripped as she hustled through the glass doors. "Reed?"

"Were you expecting someone else?"

His call was so unexpected she stopped walking when she should be running. "My flight was late, I fell asleep . . ."

"I was worried."

The wind in her lungs rushed out.

She started walking again and found herself flat in the middle of a massive chest.

Looking up, her heart beat for entirely different reasons. "Mr. Petrov." She took a giant step back.

"Ms. Cumberland. I was hoping to speak with you."

Behind Trina's father-in-law were his two cronies. Massive men who screamed *Don't fuck with me* in multicolor.

"I'm late for a meeting." She attempted to walk around him.

He blocked her.

"Lori?" The voice came from the phone.

"I won't take but a moment," Ruslan told her.

"You can make an appointment with my secretary," she told him.

He laughed. "I make my own appointments."

She stepped to the side.

One of his musclemen blocked her.

Squaring her shoulders, she lifted her chin and straightened her arm that was holding the phone to her head.

Although the hair on her neck was straining, she looked around and noticed several meandering people close by. New York was a good many things, but it wasn't full of wimps. If she found herself being dragged out of this building screaming, someone would jump in.

"I have nothing to—"

He lifted a finger to her lips, touched her.

She backed away.

"My dear Alice wasn't thinking right when she passed."

She opened her mouth.

He lifted a finger to it again.

Lori jerked her head aside.

"I'd hate to see everything you've built collapse because of my poor, sick wife."

Her teeth grew cold. "Ex. Wife."

"In the eyes of God, we are still married."

"What do you know of God, Mr. Petrov?"

His smile unsettled her.

"I know which one of us will see him first."

Keeping her face neutral was one of the hardest things she'd ever done.

"Is that a threat?"

He looked her up and down . . . slowly. "I'm clairvoyant."

"No," she told him. "You're just an asshole."

Both his hit men stepped around her.

Ruslan stopped them with a hand in the air.

He leaned in.

She held her ground until his lips were close to her ear. "We will speak again."

Ice ran down her spine.

Ruslan Petrov brushed past her and out the door.

She took a step forward, felt her knees shaking as adrenaline dumped into her system.

"Lori? Talk to me, damn it. Lori!"

She glanced at the phone in her hand, confused. Then she realized that she'd been on the phone. "Reed?"

"What the hell is going on?"

"Did you hear all that?"

"I heard enough. Where are you?"

"I'm fine. I'm headed into my meeting. I have to go."

"Did that man threaten you?" Reed's frantic voice matched the pulse under her chest.

"It's not the first time that's happened," she lied. The elevator doors opened. "I've got to go."

"I don't like this."

"We can talk later."

"How long is your meeting?"

She started to answer when her phone lost the call as the elevator shot to a higher floor.

His skin itched, and not in a good way.

Reed scrambled through papers on his desk until he found a blank notebook.

The tone of the man Lori was speaking with meant business. Russian accent. Reed heard the name Petrov.

And that man had threatened Lori with her life.

That, Reed heard loud and clear.

What kind of man did that?

Reed typed in *Katrina Petrov* and started his search all over again.

Lori had caught her breath by the time she reached Mr. Crockett's office . . . five minutes late.

The secretary walked her back to the office, where Trina sat on the other side of a desk, hands folded in her lap.

"My apologies," Lori said as she walked in. "My flight was delayed."

Mr. Crockett stood and rounded the desk, extending his hand. "It happens. Glad you could be here in person."

Lori turned her attention to Trina, who sat wide-eyed and fidgeting. She kissed her cheek. "Where is your security?" Lori asked.

"In the garage with the car."

"Ladies, we should get started," Mr. Crockett interrupted them.

Lori lifted a hand, stopping him.

"I just had a rather uncomfortable confrontation with your father-in-law in the lobby. I'd like to see your security by your side at all times when you're out of the house."

Trina's face lost color.

"Call your guy, ask him to wait in the lobby up here."

"Is everything okay?" Mr. Crockett asked.

"Trina needs a little more protection these days, all things considered."

"Of course. Would you like to use my phone?" He lifted the receiver.

Trina removed her cell phone, sent a text. "I have it."

"Shall we get started?"

Lori drew in a fortifying breath, pushing Ruslan Petrov from her head. She opened a legal notebook and readied her pen.

He started by opening the document containing Alice's will. The usual rhetoric of what the document was, all the right words put in the right places to appease anyone questioning whether Alice was of sound mind while writing it were in place.

"It is my will that my estate, after the above-mentioned stipends for my staff, is bequeathed solely to Katrina Petrov. My controlling interest in Everson Oil is bequeathed solely to Katrina Petrov, where she will be welcome to take my place on the board with the guidance of my sisters and their advisers. If it is not in her interest to do so, she can waive said right and hold that position for her future."

Trina interrupted. "I don't know the first thing about being on any board."

Mr. Crockett put the papers down. "Alice wanted to give you the option and an occupation. She wasn't the kind of woman that liked to see others in the shadows of their husbands."

"Like she was with hers," Lori said.

"Exactly."

He tapped the papers. "Everything is spelled out in detail. What to do if the oil company needed to disband. How and who you could sell your shares to. The reality was Alice wanted her share of the company to stay in her family."

"So why didn't she leave it to Fedor?"

Mr. Crockett blinked silently. "She worried that it would pass to Ruslan one way or another. Giving everything to you ensured it wouldn't."

Lori reached over, grasped Trina's hand. "If the estate had passed to Fedor, and something happened to him, Daddy would have jumped in and protested."

"They were divorced."

"That wouldn't stop the man," said Mr. Crockett. "Now that the estate is in your hands, he has no choice but to accept it."

Lori shivered. "I somehow doubt that is going to be the case."

"Outside of him finding the gun Fedor used with your fingerprints on it, Ruslan doesn't have a case."

Trina's jaw dropped. "I . . . God almighty, would he try and pin that on me?"

Lori turned to Trina. "What Mr. Crockett is trying to say"—she glared at the other attorney before swinging back to her friend—"is that outside of murder, he has nothing." Lori took charge of the conversation. "Is there anything in Alice's will addressing Trina directly?"

"Several things."

Lori lifted her eyebrows in question.

"None of which she directed me to deliver yet."

Trina sat up in her chair. "What does that mean?"

"It means that Alice wrote a series of letters for you to receive in time."

"You're kidding?" Lori asked.

"No. Alice was very specific. As executor of her will and wishes, I will honor them to the best of my ability." Mr. Crockett sat back in his chair and folded his hands in his lap.

"Do you know what the letters say?"

He shook his head. “No. She wrote them herself, sealed them.”

Trina looked around the office.

“They aren’t here, Mrs. Petrov.”

“I’m supposed to sit back and wait until some letter fairy drops information?”

Lori squeezed her eyes shut momentarily. “That’s the nature of a will. Whoever writes it has final say in everything regarding it.”

“But why?”

“I assure you, Alice had her reasons. I’m sure whatever she has to say to you will make sense once you hear everything.”

Trina stood and started to pace. “I don’t like this, any of this. I didn’t ask for her money. I don’t want her money. I don’t need Ruslan Petrov breathing down my neck.” She turned to Lori. “Or yours! This is stupid. All of it.”

“Mrs. Petrov,” Mr. Crockett interrupted. “There is something you need to know.”

“What?” Trina snapped. “Do I need to stand on one foot and sing ‘Dixie’ now?”

Lori let Trina rant. She would, too, if someone or two someones had taken control of her life the way Fedor’s selfish death and Alice’s choices had.

“Alice’s estate belongs to you. No changes can be made for a minimum of twelve months, or until all the letters that Alice has for you have been received and read.”

Trina held her hands at her sides, fists clenched.

"Is there anything in that stack of papers that will need explanation?" Lori asked him.

"Much of the same. All my *t*'s crossed and *i*'s dotted. We thought of every contingency that may have come up."

Lori's eyes narrowed. "Including Fedor's death?"

Mr. Crockett's eyes lowered. "No. I don't believe Fedor's death was anticipated. Unless she says so in her letters to Trina, there is nothing here."

Trina spun in a circle, grabbed her purse. "I have to get out of here."

Lori stood, walked Trina to the door.

Outside, a man doubled in size by either steroids or a millennium in the gym pushed to his feet.

"You work with Neil?" Lori asked as Trina started to storm past him.

"I do."

"Don't leave her side."

He pivoted and followed his assignment.

Lori turned back into Mr. Crockett's office.

"She's had a hard couple of months."

He indicated the chair and returned to his seat. "The fact that she's not jumping at this estate says a lot about her character."

Lori leaned forward. "What was Alice thinking, Dwight?"

"I'm not completely sure. I tried to talk to her about the concerns of leaving her estate to her daughter-in-law. What happened if she and Fedor split . . . what happens to the estate then? She didn't listen."

"Is there anything in the will regarding a possible divorce?"

"There is. If a divorce occurred at any time, half of whatever the estate was worth at the time of the divorce went to Trina, the other half was split between her sisters and Fedor."

"So she did consider all the possibilities."

"Damn near. I haven't found any loophole yet. And I'm looking, since I don't trust Ruslan not to toss this into court, contesting Alice's sanity in the end."

Lori leveled her eyes. "Is there any question of that?"

Dwight rubbed the bridge of his nose. "I've known Alice for thirty years. That woman was sharp as a tack. Smart beyond her years and pulled away way too soon. But I made sure to have a doctor back up my own knowledge with an evaluation the day after she changed her will."

"All clean, I'm assuming."

"Squeaky. Alice did this on purpose. Tell your client to hold tight. She doesn't have to do anything with Alice's estate anytime soon. The houses she owns are all being maintained by the money set aside in the estate to do so until Trina takes control."

"Houses? How many?"

"A few. It's all spelled out in here." He removed a second copy of the will and handed it to Lori.

Lori stood, placed the stack of papers in her briefcase. "I'll be in touch."

He stopped her before she walked out of the office. "Lori?" She turned. "Ruslan Petrov is a dangerous man. If he is cornering you in my office building, he sees you as a threat."

"I figured that out."

"And he despises strong women."

Lori lifted her chin. "Then he is bound to hate me."

"Be careful."

She smiled. "Thank you, Dwight."

Chapter Eighteen

Lori called the driver from the morning's commute to drive her to Trina's estate.

Within a half an hour, she was en route out of the city and on the phone.

"Our client's father-in-law cornered me," she told Sam from the back seat.

"Explain 'cornered.' "

Lori told her about Ruslan's actions. "I'm not going to lie, he rattled me."

"I don't like this, Lori."

"I'm not exactly a fan either." She watched the city disappear behind them as they entered the tunnel and left Manhattan.

"Extra security for you."

"I don't have anything the man wants."

"If that's true, why did he approach you in the first place?"

Lori hesitated.

"I'm calling Neil."

"Sam!"

"You can argue, but you're not going to win. Where are you now?"

"On my way to Trina's."

"You're staying with her?"

"I am."

"Okay. I'll make sure there's a shadow for you when you land back in LA."

Lori groaned.

"Get over yourself. I've had a shadow forever."

"You're married to a duke," Lori reminded her.

"As if anyone cares about that kind of thing these days."

Lori shrugged. "It impresses people I name-drop on."

Sam laughed. "Text me your flight information."

There was no use arguing with the woman.

Besides, she was right.

Once Lori hung up, she flipped around in her cell phone until she located her flight information and forwarded it to Sam. Daytime security only. My brother is staying at my place for a couple weeks.

We'll see. was Sam's reply.

When Lori pulled up into the gates of Trina's estate, security met her at the door by name. Trina was still bouncing off the walls.

"I don't even want this house," she yelled after Lori explained a few more details of Alice's will.

"In a year you can sell them all."

"It's all a massive responsibility. And now Ruslan is threatening you."

"Men like Ruslan intimidate through fear. You take away that control by keeping your cool and not letting him see you sweat."

Trina glared. “Are you telling me you didn’t sweat?”

“I said don’t let them *see* you sweat. Ruslan is massive and his bodyguards make him look small. Does the man miss a meal?”

Trina smiled for the first time all day. “Why is he bugging you?”

Lori circled the sitting room they were talking in and opened the curtains wide. “Because he can’t get to you. Maybe he thinks I have some say over any of this.”

“Watch yourself. He’s mean.”

“Don’t worry about me. I’ll be fine. Did Avery call you?”

“Yes, she’s coming tomorrow. I can’t tell you how happy that makes me.”

“Avery’s a handful,” Lori reminded her.

“She’s also self-confident and headstrong. Two things I could really use right about now.”

“In the meantime, we need to draft a plan for you.”

“Plan? What kind of plan?”

“Your estate.”

It took a full minute for Trina to speak. “A will.”

“You’re worth a ton of money. The sooner you have something, anything, in writing the better.”

“I’m young and not ill.”

“It doesn’t have to be extensive. Just the bare

minimum. Who you want the estate to go to if something happened. We can amend and add at any time. Think of it this way . . . if the plane crashes, everything that has landed in your lap will now be tossed into probate and most likely end up with the likes of Ruslan. If you're okay with that, fine. If not, let's jot a few things down, have it notarized, and done. I have a colleague who specializes in estate planning and wills. When you want to add more details, we'll bring him in. Or you can go to him directly. Whatever you want."

Trina lifted her hand, palm up. "Let me read Alice's will."

When someone with as much money as Alice Petrov dies, the world knows about it. About the time Reed found the numbers and information on his own, the media in all the financial magazines and websites took little time announcing the findings in Alice's last will and testament.

Katrina Petrov was now worth in excess of $383 million and some change. With Everson Oil investing in pipelines and solar, the diversity and growth in the company was up 15 percent in the last quarter alone.

Reed dug up information on Ruslan Petrov, which included pictures.

The thought of this man towering over Lori and threatening her had him seeing red. Men who used their bulk in preying on women needed a few minutes alone in a dark alley alongside someone twice their size. While not twice the man's size, Reed wouldn't hold back if given a chance to even the threatening score.

Now the big question was, what had set Ruslan Petrov's sights on Lori in the first place?

It was well after two in the morning, and Reed was on his third pot of coffee. His computers smoked from use and his eyes blurred.

A massive tackboard flanked an entire hidden wall in his office. An image of Lori sat center, with strings to the women he'd met on the cruise. His client, the one paying him to search for hidden information, sat beside Shannon with a string. Next to Shannon was her ex-husband's picture.

Lori represented the women in their divorces.

Only Trina didn't divorce. So how was she linked?

By two thirty, Reed found an article about Fedor's death in the financial pages. His estate wasn't left to his brand-new bride. It wasn't left to his mother, who he knew was dying. No. His minimal shares in the oil company were spread among his aunts and their families. The bulk of his estate went to a multitude of charities. His wife . . . Trina . . . was left their residence and the financial ability to keep the home going for five years after his death.

According to the *Wall Street Journal*, Trina Petrov was willed the amount of money specified in their prenuptial agreement. Five million dollars and any gifts bequeathed to her during their marriage.

Five million dollars from an estate worth well over one hundred million.

Reed followed the bouncing ball and found Lori's name as the attorney that set up the agreement between husband and wife, premarriage.

A sticky note went next to Trina's picture with *five million* written on it.

Then he looked up Avery's divorce settlement. Five million and a condo.

Shannon . . . seven million and the house in Southern California.

Reed scribbled *a house* next to Trina's five million.

He stood looking at the board, arms folded over his chest.

He knew how all these marriages ended. And since he met Lori with these women, it's safe to say they all had the same lawyer, and the same general plan. The numbers were big, but not shocking when you considered the worth of the players. All these women were young. Their marriages brief.

His skin tickled his brain, or maybe that was the caffeine.

He backtracked Trina's marriage. She had been

married less than a year before Fedor's death.

He searched Shannon . . . two years from *I do* to divorced.

Avery . . . eighteen months.

No smoking guns, outside of Fedor.

No one caught cheating or falling in love with someone else. All the marriages appeared normal, including pictures of the couples at charity events, holiday functions. Then done!

At four in the morning, Reed had printed out four wedding photos from each couple. Shannon and Paul seemed to fit each other. Avery and her ex looked as if she was the gold digger and he was the rich old man looking for arm candy. Trina and Fedor were a bit better matched, but the man didn't stand close enough or smile wide enough for someone who'd managed to catch a woman as exotically beautiful as Katrina.

He found images of Lori at every wedding.

And one other woman.

Reed placed a picture next to Lori's.

Samantha Harrison.

"How do you fit?"

It was after noon on Saturday when Lori stepped off the plane and found the bodyguard Sam had insisted on waiting by baggage claim. Not that Lori had any luggage.

"Cooper, right?" Lori asked. She'd seen him many times before. The security surrounding the clients of Alliance and the Harrison family were the same net of men.

"I'm flattered." The man had a charming smile, his eyes hidden behind dark sunglasses that should have stuck out since he was inside a building. They didn't. "Luggage?"

She glanced at the small rolling bag in her hand. "This is it."

He took it from her and led her out the door.

"Neil briefed me on the threat," he said when she was in the back of the car and he'd pulled away from his parking space.

"Sounds very cloak-and-dagger," she teased.

"Ruslan Petrov is loosely linked to the disappearance of three businessmen in his country, one of whom was a lawyer representing his late ex-wife during her divorce. He's a dangerous man."

She stopped smiling.

Cooper glanced at her through the rearview mirror.

"Knowing your enemy, and what they are capable of, empowers you. I'm not trying to scare you, Ms. Cumberland."

"You did a fine job without trying."

"Neil told me you were a reluctant charge."

"Let me guess, Neil drafted your little speech."

Cooper looked over his shoulder as he pulled onto the 405 freeway. "No, Neil told me to say

'Tell her if she wants to be dead, then go ahead and dismiss you.' "

She glanced at the passing cars. "Sounds like Neil."

"Subtle as a heart attack, that one."

Lori removed her cell phone from her purse. "Well, thanks for making it sound like I'd just go missing and not end up dead."

Cooper looked over the rim of his sunglasses. "You look smarter than that."

"I am." She pulled up Reed's number, sent a quick text. Landed. On my way home.

It took a minute for him to reply.

Welcome home.

Chapter Nineteen

Reed arrived at Lori's condominium complex before she did. The doorman wasn't the same man as when he was there several days before. Reed made sure to make eye contact and smile as he moved past the doors and to the concierge desk.

The petite African American woman behind the desk smiled as he approached.

"Good afternoon," she greeted him.

"Hello. Reed Barlow for Ms. Cumberland in 1208."

She glanced at the computer. "There you are. I see that Ms. Cumberland is out of town until this afternoon. It's our policy to advise guests to call on our residents when they are home, Mr. Barlow."

Good, they didn't just let people in.

"Lori's on the way from the airport now."

She kept smiling. "You understand that we need to have you wait for her down here unless she advises us otherwise."

"Perfectly acceptable," he told her. He removed a photograph from his back pocket, slid it across the desk. "Have you seen this man, by any chance?"

"I don't believe so."

"He's made threats toward Ms. Cumberland."

The woman's smile fell slightly.

"If you see this man lingering about, please call Lori and warn her."

She took the picture. "Can I keep this?"

"Of course."

"I'll inform security."

"Thank you. I appreciate it." He turned away and moved to one of the many chairs dotting the lobby.

Not ten minutes later, he saw Lori being led through the door.

The man at her side scanned the lobby, his eyes landed on Reed. He positioned his frame between them. He said something Reed couldn't hear, and Lori looked up.

She smiled. "Reed."

She opened her arms to him, and he moved in, folded her close.

"What are you doing here?" she asked.

"I needed to see you."

"I was just here."

"That was one death threat ago."

She pulled back, leveled her gaze with his. "Not you, too."

The man who walked Lori in stood a few feet back, his eyes moving around the lobby.

"Who is he?"

"A bodyguard. Sam insisted."

"Sam?"

Lori shook her head. "She worries."

Yeah, there was a whole lot more to the Sam story. Instead of questioning her in the lobby, he closed the distance between himself and her bodyguard and extended a hand. "I'm Reed."

The man's grip was firm. His shoulders wide. The jacket screamed concealed weapon. "Cooper."

"Thank you in advance for watching over her."

A nod was Cooper's only comment. "Lori, I need you to introduce me to the staff, clear the way."

Lori left Reed's side and slipped to the concierge.

Afterward, they all rode up the elevator together. "Is Danny still here?"

"I assume so. I haven't spoken with him since I left. I told Sam I didn't need a babysitter at night."

Cooper smiled from under his sunglasses. "Good thing I don't babysit."

"You know what I mean."

"We'll figure out an acceptable arrangement," he told her.

Music met them at the door. Lori let them in with a key.

Danny wasn't in sight.

Cooper walked around the room.

"Danny?"

"In here."

She picked up a remote, turned the volume of the stereo down.

"Hey, I like that song!" he complained.

"I don't think my neighbors like it quite as much." She dropped her bag in the middle of the room, tossed her keys on the coffee table.

Reed watched Cooper's assessment of the space. It was obvious he'd never been there before. He looked out a window, opened one, and stuck his head through. "Any balconies or other points of entry?" he asked.

"No," Lori answered.

Reed corrected her. "There's a rooftop lounge, and an open pool level on the fifteenth floor. But the units don't have balcony space."

"Oh, yeah . . . that's right. I never have time to use the pool." Lori paused, stared at Reed. "Wait, how do you know about my building?"

Reed's mind scrambled for a logical answer other than he'd been spying on her.

Cooper moved away from the window. "I'm sure you don't mind if I look around."

"Make yourself at home."

Danny walked from around the corner in shorts and a T-shirt from a rock band popular in the nineties. "Hello."

Reed nodded. "Hey, Danny." Reed used the distraction of Lori's brother to avoid her question.

Danny's gaze moved to Cooper.

"Cooper, this is my brother."

Danny held out a hand.

They shook and Cooper moved along.

"Who is he?" Danny whispered once Cooper left the room.

Lori hesitated. "A friend."

Reed corrected her. "A bodyguard."

The jovial smile Reed had grown accustomed to seeing on Danny's face slipped. "Excuse me?"

"It's overkill and stupid. Lawyers are threatened all the time. Sam's just being overprotective."

"First, who threatened you . . . and second, who is Sam? How many men do you have in your life?"

"Sam is a woman, someone I work with . . . a friend."

"And the threat?"

"No one. It's stupid."

It was Reed's turn to talk. "Ruslan Petrov, ultrabig Russian with his own set of bodyguards twice the size of Cooper."

Lori narrowed her eyes. "Someone doing his homework?" she asked.

Reed took a deep breath. "When the woman I'm seeing is threatened, I'm going to know who that threat is."

"What did he say?" Danny asked.

Reed waited to see if Lori would be truthful or if she'd downplay his words.

She replayed the conversation for her brother.

"What the hell, Lori."

"Lawyers aren't popular to the opposing half of the legal equation. Making enemies isn't hard."

Cooper worked his way back into the room. And for the first time he removed his sunglasses and set them on the counter. Next, he removed his jacket. Sure enough, the shoulder harness housed what looked like a 9 mm at his side.

Danny stared at it, and Lori sucked in a breath.

Reed observed.

"You don't have a security system," Cooper said.

"I live in a high-rise with security and a concierge service."

"Let me repeat myself: you don't have a security system."

Lori pinched her lips together.

Cooper glanced at Danny, then back to Lori. "We both have our priorities, Lori. I've been told to assess the situation and make my recommendations."

"Which are?"

"Security system with monitoring. Personal armed bodyguard until the threat is neutralized."

"For crying out loud, you sound like there's a hit on me."

Cooper lifted an eyebrow.

"Holy crap, sis."

Lori placed both hands on the counter. "Security system, fine."

"With monitoring," Cooper added.

"Fine. But I don't need any armed anything around here all the time. Danny is here for a couple of weeks." She glanced at Reed.

"I'll be around."

She attempted a smile. "See. I'm covered."

"I'll call the crew."

She shook her head and turned toward her room. "I need a minute."

Once she left the room, Danny turned toward him. "How bad is this guy?"

"Nasty," Reed said.

"They don't get worse," Cooper added.

"How soon can you get a system in place?" Reed asked.

Cooper lifted his phone to his ear. "Two hours."

This Reed wanted to see.

Dressed in a simple pair of blue jeans and a sweater, Lori had her hair pulled back and her sleeves up. Bringing her condo up to speed on security was something she'd considered doing off and on throughout the years she'd been there, but as each one moseyed on through without any crime, she hadn't bothered. Besides, being in complete control of her own world and space had been a priority. Asking for help, even if it was an alarm system, felt as if she was relinquishing some of that control. Only now it would be unintelligent to pretend she could hold back the likes of Ruslan if the man entered her space.

Cooper brought in a team of four men armed with wires, monitors, sensors, speakers, and cameras.

Danny had left to visit a local friend since there were plenty of men around to keep her safe. Reed shadowed Cooper for a while, asking questions.

As each hole was cut into the ceiling or drilled into a window casing, Lori felt her privacy slipping away.

"What kind of service monitors all this?" she heard Reed ask Cooper.

"It's a private company."

"Armed response, I assume."

Cooper smirked. "Showing up with a baseball bat is useless, don't you think?"

Lori appreciated the sarcasm, which made light of the absurdity of it all. Much as she'd have liked to slip into her office for a couple of hours and finish some work, that wasn't possible with the pounding and drilling going on all around her.

"So what branch of the service were you in?" Reed asked Cooper.

"Marines. What about you?"

Reed shook his head. "Didn't serve."

Cooper looked him up and down. "I pegged you for the Army."

"No, no."

Cooper watched a monitor as one of the technicians aimed a camera in the far corner of the room. He flipped a switch and another camera from the hall came into view.

"Nothing in my bedroom," Lori told him.

"Main living spaces only. Nothing in the bathrooms or the bedrooms."

"Good." She sucked on her water bottle. "Guess there won't be any wild dining room sex," she muttered to Reed as he walked by.

He placed a hand on her hip and nuzzled her neck from behind.

"We can make up for it," he whispered.

She turned into his arms. "How was your week? We always seem to be talking about my world."

"Mine is boring."

"I'll take a little of that right about now."

"I bet. How was Trina?"

"Frazzled."

Reed rubbed her shoulders as they chatted. "Her name popped up online when I was reading the news yesterday. Is her estate what's causing all of this?"

"Ruslan Petrov has no dealings with me outside of Trina. I was as shocked as Trina when we learned she inherited everything."

"Which made her father-in-law mad."

"I guess. He's blowing smoke."

Reed looked over her shoulder. "Smoke that has gotten the attention of some influential people, apparently. How is it you have these kinds of connections?"

Lori followed his gaze with her head. “Oh, this isn’t me. This is all Sam.”

“The lady from the other day.”

“Yes, my overprotective friend. She knows everyone.”

“Apparently.”

“This will all blow over, I’m sure.”

He wrapped his arms around her, kissed the side of her head. “You’re a strong woman, Lori.”

She leaned into him, happy to have him holding her. Strong or not, it was nice to have his support.

Reed stared up at Lori’s ceiling. She’d finally fallen asleep, her hand under her cheek as it rested on his chest. Her mouth was open slightly, each breath a tiny whisper across his skin.

The crew left her house and Cooper lingered until Danny arrived, with the promise to return at dawn.

Lori argued, but Cooper told her that he didn’t take his orders from her. He apologized for it but made no excuses for his plans to invade her life.

The entire situation struck a raw chord inside of Reed. There was big money, big guns, and serious manpower behind the security team Cooper spoke of. And while Sam might be behind it, how was it she had pull over Lori?

He was dangerously close to coming right out

and asking Lori a few questions to get him closer to the truth. If he was just a guy who flittered into her life on accident, he would have asked already.

But that wasn't the case.

He had to be careful. Cooper had questioned him with more than just a look while he was following the man around. He'd pegged Reed's profession . . . well, his previous one, by a hair. He wasn't a military guy, but he had gone through the police academy and worked as a cop for over a decade.

Reed lifted his arm that wasn't holding Lori and rubbed the scar on the left side of his jaw. One nasty case and the battle scars to go with it, and he'd left the force. Falling into the world of private investigation was easy. He knew the law and how to avoid breaking it all while doing his job. He had a small pension from the force and didn't take on many cases unless they paid well. In short, he was doing okay.

He hated seeing shitty things happen to good people. Up until he spent any time with Lori, he was under the impression that all lawyers were assholes. In his experience, the stereotype was true.

Since his client was once a lawyer, he assumed this case was a product of two shitheads crapping on each other, except that Lori hadn't been his target when all of this started. And his opinion of the profession had vastly changed in just a few short weeks.

Lori muttered something in her sleep, snuggled closer, and something that felt suspiciously like a conscience stirred in his chest.

Chapter Twenty

"I need more information from you," Reed told his client the following Monday.

"What kind of information?"

"You want to discredit Wentworth."

"If you say it a little louder, the whole world will hear you."

Reed put his phone to his other ear and stared at his wall while he spoke. "One politician slinging mud at another isn't news. It's expected. Besides, my line is secure."

"Yes, Reed. I've told you this."

"And you're looking at his ex-wife to find something."

"Most ex-wives are pissed enough to let something out."

Except Shannon wasn't pissed . . . she was hurt. "If she's ticked, she's not showing it."

"Wentworth is way too clean. The state was charmed enough by his whirlwind wedding and delightful bride to elect him. Even their divorce barely put a dent in his armor. No one is that spotless."

Reed agreed, but he didn't see a victim here. The public at large wasn't unhappy with the current governor, nor had they been overly distraught when the man divorced. In fact, there seemed to be plenty of women lining up to be the next Mrs. Wentworth.

He paused. "Whirlwind?"

"What?"

"Whirlwind? What do you mean by that?"

"Jesus, Reed, don't you watch the news?"

Not if he didn't have to. Depressing hour on TV, if you asked him. "No."

"We all knew Paul was going to run, but he hadn't announced his candidacy yet. Right before he did, he met Shannon at some fundraiser, and within a month, they were married. There was some gossip that they'd met before, but they'd never been seen in the same place. The chances of him winning the seat in Sacramento were slim until he settled down."

"How does a man who is running for office have time to woo a wife?"

"Good question. Convenient, don't you think?"

"Who planned the wedding?" The pictures Reed had come across looked as if the plans were in place for some time. Quick weddings . . . divorces that were all neat and tidy. It was all too perfect.

"How the hell do I know? Who cares . . . are you getting married?"

No, but he knew who to go to for the divorce. His eyes landed on Lori's picture again.

• • •

"Trina and I are going to Texas," Avery announced later in the week over Skype.

Lori looked at both women on her screen. "Both of you?"

"Alice's sisters want to meet with me as well as the other members of the board."

"I told this one that we needed to tell you." Avery waved her thumb at Trina.

"Tell me, I need to be there. Give me twenty-four hours to clear my schedule, and I'll join you." Lori couldn't let Trina go alone. Who knew what she was walking into?

"I told you," Avery said to Trina.

"I can take care of it. I don't think anyone will be hostile there."

Lori leaned closer to the screen. "How well do you know Alice's sisters?"

"I met them at the wedding."

Lori attempted to look menacing on-screen to have Trina take the meeting more seriously. She was fairly certain it didn't work. "And the board, have you met them?"

"No."

"Any of them stand to lose something since you are stepping into Alice's shoes?"

"I don't know."

"Anyone there ready to discredit you just on principle?"

"What principle?"

“The fact you know nothing about this business, know nothing about the company, yet you have a third share in something worth over a billion dollars.”

Trina went silent.

Avery spoke up. “I told you she needed to come.”

After hanging up, Lori made a few calls, shuffled a client, and thanked her luck that she wasn’t due in court until the following Monday.

It was after six when Cooper poked his head into her office. “Just letting you know I’m here whenever you’re ready to leave.”

Lori pulled a stack of papers for her Monday case and piled them on her desk. “Might as well make yourself some coffee. I have a couple more hours to kill here.”

“Will do.”

He walked off as she tucked behind the desk and opened the file.

Cooper . . . how did he fit in with going to Texas?

Chances were someone would shadow Trina and Avery.

Lori set aside her case and called Sam.

“Okay, Mrs. Royalty. I’m not used to this bodyguard and attempting to live my life and conduct my business thing.”

“What are you complaining about?” Sam teased.

Lori smiled. "I'm meeting Trina and Avery in Texas. Do I buy a ticket for Cooper or just meet with whoever is with Trina and Avery at the airport? Keep in mind, nothing has happened since New York."

"Let me call Neil. I'll call you right back."

"Fine. I'm at the office."

Sam hung up and Lori dived into her case and didn't look up until her phone rang. She waited two rings before she remembered that everyone had left for the day.

"Lori Cumberland's office."

"It's Sam. So here's the deal. Neil already told Trina's detail that he was sending the plane to them. We can charter another one for you, no problem."

"That's stupid. Using a jet you have just lying around is one thing," she joked. There was no such thing as a jet just sitting around. Between fuel and the pilots, it wasn't a cheap trip no matter how you spun that bottle. "I'll take a commercial flight."

"I can see if Eliza and Carter's plane is available."

"You do realize we aren't talking about borrowing a Volvo."

"At the risk of sounding horrible, it is to us."

"Well, it isn't to me. I'll fly commercial. Can Cooper fly armed?"

"No."

"Then there is no point in him going. I'll just wait until I land and meet up with the others. I'm sure I'll be fine."

"Cooper is just as lethal unarmed."

Lori grunted.

"Neil's words, not mine."

"I hate this."

"So take Danny."

"I love my brother, but he's a lover, not a fighter."

"Then take Reed. Cooper seems to like the guy, says he could probably hold his own if he needed to. He only has to fill in until you land."

"I don't know."

"Or we book two rooms with adjoining doors, or Cooper sleeps on the couch in your hotel room."

"This is absurd."

"Hey, we both did the research; we know how nasty Ruslan can be. Now that he has nothing to lose, he's that much more dangerous."

"Okay, okay . . . let me call Reed, see if he likes big hats and barbeque." She disconnected the call more than a little frustrated that she needed to call in a favor from Reed, yet excited at the possibility of spending time with him.

"I appreciate you coming with me," Lori told Reed as they moved through the TSA precheck line. "If I thought I would win the argument with

Sam about flying alone, I wouldn't have drug you along."

Reed removed his cell phone, tucked it into one of the bowls provided, and waited to walk through the metal detector.

"You make it sound like Sam is your boss." Which was true, and his way of nudging more information than Lori might want to give.

"Nothing like that. We sometimes work together."

"She's not an attorney."

"No. It's a . . . it's complicated." And Lori started to stutter.

"It's a three-hour flight."

Lori walked through the detector first before they waved her past and him in.

"The bottom line is in her life, she's had her share of . . ." Lori's voice trailed off.

"Share of what?"

Lori placed her hand in the air, closed up, and removed her laptop case from the X-ray machine.

Reed followed up by collecting his wallet and tucking it into his back pocket. Once they were away from the airport gatekeepers, she continued, "Sam's had her share of security issues."

"Like?"

"Let's see . . . first, her father was the original Bernie Madoff."

"Really?" He had looked that up just the night before.

"Yep. It's public knowledge. And, of course, she's married to an incredibly wealthy man."

"Which has put her in danger?"

Lori moved around a family who had stopped in the middle of the walk lane to discipline a child.

"Yes. But Blake has always had an exceptional security team."

"The same guys that are at your place?"

"Yep. Neil, that's the name of the man who runs the whole thing, he's quite the roadblock. He served in the Marines."

"Like Cooper."

"Right. He recruits a lot of guys from the service. Men who didn't want to make a career out of the service but still like the adrenaline of the job."

"I would imagine babysitting adults would still get boring after a while," Reed said.

They stepped onto a people mover and stopped walking. "Except Neil's team has an impressive list of clients."

Reed stepped aside as two people rushed by.

"How impressive?" Reed waited for the name-dropping.

"Movie stars, politicians. Eliza Billings is Sam's best friend."

"Billings . . . why does that sound familiar?"

"Carter Billings is Eliza's husband."

The skin on his arms prickled. "The former governor."

"That would be him."

All his time in front of the computer in the past week couldn't trump the information he'd managed to obtain while walking through an airport.

They stepped off the people mover and continued toward their gate.

"I guess you can say Sam has witnessed enough crazy to assume that crazy always happens. And since Petrov is a wealthy man scorned and looking for a scapegoat, I'm saddled with bodyguards and alarm systems."

Reed placed a hand on the small of her back and ushered her through the first-class lounge of the airline they were using. "It's better to be safe than sorry, as they say."

Lori found a table for two that looked out over the tarmac. "For what it's worth. But look . . . here we are in an airport, and no one is trying to take me out."

She made light of it, but Reed felt the weight of her words.

"Can you get me a glass of champagne?" she asked. "I need to make a quick call."

He didn't bother sitting, instead moved to the full-service bar free for members. "Two glasses of champagne, please."

The bartender turned to fill the glasses.

Reed sensed eyes watching him.

He turned his head slowly, toward the heat.

Dark hair, dark skin, massive sunglasses, and red lips.

Sasha.

Lori didn't expect Reed to take his position of stand-in bodyguard so seriously. But apparently he liked channeling his inner superhero. He looked over his shoulder more than Cooper had when he'd gone with her to the supermarket. Only Cooper had suggested she shop online and have her bread and milk delivered. Which she promptly refused to do.

She took the window seat in the first-class cabin, and still Reed scanned the crowd as they boarded the plane.

"If you ever get bored with that data processing thing, maybe Neil can use you," Lori teased.

He lowered his voice, put his lips to her ear. "I have one job right now."

She grinned. He sounded so serious. "There isn't enough privacy on a commercial flight for that."

There was his smile. "Careful . . . that sounds like a challenge."

"Outside of my wheelhouse, Reed."

"That sounds like a fun wheelhouse."

Her body warmed at the thought of him doing anything intimate while on a crowded plane.

She crossed her legs, ignored the heat pooling in her belly. She leaned in, whispered in his ear,

"I think sex on an airplane is a little more distracting than a glass of wine."

"You on an airplane wiggling your tiny ass in that chair is distraction enough," he told her.

She suddenly had a strong desire to request a blanket and see just how distracted she could make him.

Reed stared, eyes wide, as if reading her mind.

He leaned close to her ear, but instead of whispering, he bit the tender lobe.

Not meaning to, she crossed her legs a second time. Lori made a mental note to take Sam up on the use of her private jet at her earliest convenience. The man had a way of turning her hormones into overdrive.

She liked this part . . . when a man was still playful and easily turned on. Where the conversation flowed and discovering each other met with genuine concern.

The flight attendant returned with her wine, which she happily tipped back.

The relationship with Reed was working out well. Almost too well. At the risk of jinxing anything, she wondered how long things could last. Would he get tired of her lifestyle or playing bodyguard? Not that she'd need one for long.

"See, I didn't need a bodyguard."

Reed looked over his shoulder.

She followed his gaze but only saw the tops of passengers' heads.

"You never know who is watching you," he told her.

"Ruslan's men are hard to miss."

"He could have sent a woman after you," he muttered.

Lori laughed, looked around again. She noticed a middle-aged housewifeish woman, another one in her seventies, and two women who looked like they were in college. That was the extent of the first-class passengers. Beyond the curtain that separated the cabins, Lori couldn't see. "I think I'm safe."

Reed's expression shifted for a second. "I think your friends are right about keeping your guard up."

"Oh? Why do you think that?"

"Because I looked up your dear friend Mr. Petrov, remember?"

"Ah, you do care."

He leaned back, the line in his jaw hardened. "Did you think I didn't?"

Oh, wow . . . she'd hurt him. "I was just teasing."

"Of course I care, Lori."

She reached over and clasped his palm in hers. "I kinda like you a little bit, too."

He squeezed her hand, the expression on his face softened.

Chapter Twenty-One

Humidity hit them as soon as they exited the airport. "I could never live here," Lori muttered as Reed placed their luggage in the back of the rental car.

"I spent a summer here when I was a kid, swore I'd never do it again," he said, keeping small talk going while he kept an eye on the people walking around.

Sasha had walked right through first class before sneaking just out of the first cabin and settling two rows back in coach. The back of Reed's head burned the entire flight.

Lori slid into the passenger seat, and he took one more look around before taking the wheel.

"If it wasn't so hot, I wouldn't mind traveling here more often. The people seem to take life a little easier."

"Nothing slows down in LA."

She pulled her shirt away from her chest a few times, and he twisted the fan on high. "Okay, copilot. Where am I going?" Reed asked.

"The hotel. I'll touch base with Trina, and then we have dinner with Alice's sisters. Tomorrow we face the board."

Reed removed his phone and looked up the

address of the hotel. "Might as well relax, it's going to take us close to an hour to get there."

Lori placed her purse in the back seat and relaxed. "Gotta love Texas."

He pulled out of the rental parking lot and onto a frontage road to the highway. Sunglasses became his cloak as his eyes worked overtime, scanning the traffic around them.

Would Sasha follow them, or did she already know the destination of the hotel? "How long have Trina and Avery been here?"

"They flew in last night."

And if Sasha managed a plane ticket, on the same plane as Lori's, chances were she knew where they were headed.

Reed picked up speed on the highway, kept an eye on the rearview mirror.

"Have I said thank you for being here?" Lori asked.

"You did, and you don't have to thank me. I'm glad you asked."

She reached over, ran her hand along his arm. "I'm glad I asked, too. Even though I need a bodyguard about as much as you do."

A tiny bit of his soul was buying a round in hell right at that moment. Not only did she need a bodyguard, she needed a new boyfriend. Right now, he sucked at being both.

"You got awfully quiet over there," Lori said.

He grasped her hand in his free one. “Just enjoying the drive without traffic.”

She squeezed his fingers and laid her head back. “You do that. I’m going to try and nap. I haven’t been sleeping all that well since the monitors went in.”

“Are they making noise at night?” He hadn’t noticed the night he spent sleeping in her bed.

“Nothing like that. I’m just wondering who is listening to hear if I snore.”

Reed kissed the back of her hand. “You don’t snore.”

“You wouldn’t tell me if I did,” she said with her eyes closed. “Those kinds of things only come out when couples argue.”

Couples? Had they become that?

He looked over to see her staring. “Not that I’m suggesting we’re a couple.”

“I suppose it’s a little early to use that definition, but I understood what you meant.”

She still looked as if she’d said something wrong.

“It’s all good, Lori. Close your eyes and snore away. I’ll wake you when we get there.”

She closed her eyes and said, “I don’t snore.”

Lori met Trina and Avery in their adjoining room to chat privately before dinner.

“We have a few things to go over before we

meet with Alice's sisters. Are you okay with Avery being here?" she asked Trina.

"Oh, please. I trust Avery as much as I trust you and Sam. So hurry up with the legal garbage so we can get all the details about your new bodyguard."

Lori felt the heat in her cheeks growing. "The legal *garbage,* as you call it, is why I'm here."

"Yes, I know . . . and we will be knee-deep in all that tomorrow. So skim it for tonight."

"Okay, here is the gist. You know how politicians say a lot without saying anything?"

Trina and Avery both nodded.

"That's you tonight. You can talk about your struggles surrounding Fedor's death, your genuine shock when you learned of Alice's will. But keep everything on the surface. If I interrupt you, it's not because I'm rude, it's because you're probably saying too much."

"When I spoke with Alice's sisters on the phone, I didn't think they were out to find me inept."

"You don't know what they want. And since we're talking about so much money, it's safe to assume there are people that we're going to meet either tonight or tomorrow that aren't happy it's going to you. If they ask you a question you're not sure you should answer, look at me. I'll nod if I think you're safe, or chime in if I don't."

"Okay, got it."

"And no overdrinking tonight."

Avery glanced at Trina. "Is it me, or does she sound like a mom?"

"She does, but I have to agree."

Lori smiled. "That goes for you, too, Avery."

"But I'm not inheriting anything."

"No, but you know more about the personal stuff than anyone. Gotta keep a lid on a few things. Remember, people will look right at you and pretend they're your friends while they are plotting behind your back. This is business."

Trina frowned. "I hate that people can't be trusted."

"We'll figure out who are the ones you can, but chances are we won't do this in one visit. This meeting will help me get the right person on your legal team to help cover this end for you."

"Why can't that be you?" Trina asked.

"My specialty is divorce. I can advise you now because of the circumstances."

"But I trust you."

"You can trust those I send your way, too. But remember, the one thing you should never speak of to your new representation was the intention of your marriage."

"Aren't they legally obligated to keep that secret?"

"They are and probably would. But those aren't chances Sam and I like to take. Consider the what-ifs of your current situation if something leaked about you and Fedor."

Trina shook her head. “I don’t even like the current situation, let alone the what-ifs of something different.”

“Good. We’re all on the same page.”

“So do we do the pinky First Wives handshake, or what?” Avery teased.

Lori rolled her eyes and looked at the ceiling.

“So Reed is your stand-in bodyguard, eh?”

“He just needed an excuse to sit next to me on an airplane and sleep in my bed,” she told them.

“I don’t know, he was very professional looking when you both walked into the lobby. He’s big enough and has a perfect resting bitch face for the job.”

“Can guys have a resting bitch face?” she asked Avery. “I thought that was only women.”

“Not sure, but he had one. Don’t you think?”

Lori sat back and listened to the debate about men and their facial expressions until the conversation wavered.

“Okay, so we’re meeting Alice’s sisters, Diane and Andrea, at the restaurant in an hour. I’ve been instructed that we need to take two cars for security reasons.”

“How very Secret Service of us,” Avery said. “Security for Trina I totally get. For me, not so much.”

Trina’s playful grin fell. “Petrov didn’t threaten me.”

“Yes, he did. Remember he shook his fist at

you? I wouldn't put it past him to threaten you again."

"Aren't you just a ball of positive," Avery prodded.

"Realistic. Even if it's negative. You can't ever accuse me of bullshitting you just to make the circumstances look better than they are. Even before you both signed contracts for your marriages, it was me who sat you down and talked about the pitfalls."

"Which totally didn't apply for me," Avery said.

"They didn't apply for me either," Trina added.

Lori pointed to Avery. "You haven't gotten out of the honeymoon stage of your divorce. Give it a few months." Then again, Avery didn't seem to let anything in, so having the reputation of a gold digging woman might not faze her at all. "And as for you . . ." She pointed to Trina. "No one foresaw Fedor taking himself out. Still bugs the garbage out of me that we didn't pick up on that in our research on the man."

"Don't blame yourself or Alliance. I was living with the man the last several months of his life, and I didn't clue in."

"Still . . ."

"Fine, beat yourself up. But do it in your room, I need to get ready for dinner." Trina stood and shooed them both out.

The bodyguard keeping tabs on Trina sat at the

end of the hall. He looked up as Lori and Avery stepped out of the room.

Lori kept her voice low. "You're good for her," she told Avery.

"We're two women who would never have met outside of you and Sam. I'm grateful."

"I am, too."

Avery spun in a circle, then laughed. "Why did I walk out of the room?"

"Divorce brain."

"What's that?"

"It's your mindset once your marriage is over and you have to do everything by yourself again. It leaves you walking in circles."

"I thought maybe it was early Alzheimer's."

Lori knocked on Trina's door.

When she answered, Avery pushed through. "Left my key in my room."

"Goofball."

Steak in Texas . . . nothing beat it. Though having too much was like having a bad potato in Idaho, or nasty cheese in Wisconsin—it just shouldn't happen. Lori attempted to avoid feeling drunk on red meat and one glass of wine. Like Avery and Trina, she wasn't going to overdrink and lose her edge during this trip.

But the steak threatened to cut the ice off her bones. Not to mention Diane and Andrea were some of the loveliest women she'd met in her life. Considering her job, Lori had met many, but these two were either Oscar worthy in their acting abilities, or they genuinely embraced what their late sister had put into motion.

Diane Hall and Andrea Upton had left their husbands and their children at home. Much as Lori hated booting Reed to the side, this dinner was about Trina. So Reed and Trina's bodyguard were at a table directly across from them . . . visible, but not listening or part of the conversation.

It had taken a bottle of wine and two bites of steak before everyone at the table relaxed enough to talk.

Andrea was the youngest of the three sisters at forty-eight. Diane was fifty, and Alice had been fifty-three when she passed.

"She was too young." Andrea cut into her steak. "If she'd still been married to that son-of-a—"

"Andi!" Diane cut her off.

"Ruslan was the worst thing to ever happen to this family."

"Fedor didn't like his father. You're not offending me by speaking your mind," Trina told them.

Andrea continued, "If Alice had still been connected to that man, I would swear he had something to do with her death."

"Cancer isn't something you can pass along like a cold," Diane told her.

"That man never got along with anyone, ever."

Lori sipped her water. "How long were they married?"

"Nine years. Nine brutal years." Diane poured more wine into her glass.

"Brutal?" Avery asked.

Andrea and Diane exchanged glances.

"She's dead, Diane. It's not like we're spreading gossip."

Lori glanced at Trina and Avery.

Diane finally spoke. "Alice never went public with anything."

Lori felt her appetite waning.

"Alice was a strong woman," Andrea exclaimed.

"She always struck me as a woman who didn't put up with a lot," Trina told them.

"But . . . she wasn't always. When she and Ruslan first started dating, it was all wine and roses and stupid tokens men think turn heads."

"It worked," Diane reminded her sister.

"Yeah, until they were married. Then those trinkets became demands."

Lori sat forward. "What kind of demands?"

"Ruslan wanted to take her place on the board. But no matter what he said or did, that wasn't ever going to happen," Andrea said.

"Why?"

"Because Daddy wouldn't let it."

"Your father is gone." Lori knew the Everson

estate enough to know the oil company went to the daughters.

"Gone, but reached beyond the grave to demand that his daughters stayed on the board as long as they were alive. Not their husbands, and not their children so long as we were sane and alive."

"Which our sister was both right up to a few weeks before she passed," Diane added.

"Daddy didn't want any man marrying one of us and taking over."

"But Ruslan didn't get the memo," Lori concluded out loud.

"Exactly," Andrea told her.

Trina finished her glass of wine off. "That still doesn't explain why Alice left me anything."

"It didn't shock us," Andrea told them.

Trina leaned forward. "Then explain it to me, please. I knew your sister for less than a year of her life. Yes, Fedor and I were married—"

Lori felt the lawyer in her kick in. "Trina."

Trina didn't listen to the plea in her voice and continued. "Yes, we were married, but the honeymoon wasn't even over. Why me?"

Diane released a long-suffering sigh. "Because Ruslan couldn't get to you."

Trina lifted her hands in the air. "Okay, so don't give it to her son, who none of us saw doing what he did . . . but why not just leave it to one of you . . . or both of you?"

Andrea and Diane looked at each other before

the younger sister answered for both of them. "We've asked ourselves that more than once. We're not entirely sure."

Lori felt her spine tickle. "But you have a theory."

Silence spread over the table like fog.

"Two . . . neither of which you want to hear."

Trina pushed her uneaten steak aside. "Enlighten me. I've been through too much in the past three months to have shock take me out now."

"We don't think Alice ever considered the possibility of Fedor passing before her. If she gave you the estate, it would encourage him to stay married to you."

Trina put on her game face. "Was that a question?"

Diane diverted her gaze to her plate. "She thought it was awfully convenient that you and Fedor married so quickly after you met."

Lori kept an eye on Trina, ready to jump in with one stray word.

"We didn't see a need to wait."

"Because of Alice?" Andrea asked, her eyes honed in.

Trina sucked in a deep breath, let it out slowly. "Fedor loved his mother. He wanted to see her at peace. Waiting to get married would only have prevented her from attending the wedding. That would have been cruel for everyone involved."

A look of acceptance washed over Andrea's face, an expression that told Lori the woman read through the lines and walked away with respect for the woman delivering it.

"So Alice wasn't convinced their marriage would last," Avery spoke when everyone had stopped talking. "So leave the whole damn thing to Trina?"

Diane laughed. "Yeah . . ."

"To keep it away from her ex-husband."

"Yep. Fedor protected his mother from his father. We think she wanted Fedor to continue protecting women until he learned to protect himself."

"Fedor wasn't that weak," Trina defended.

"Perhaps." Andrea and Diane exchanged glances.

Lori noticed when Avery reached over and grasped Trina's hand. "What is your second theory?" Lori asked.

"Alice wanted the target off her son . . . and us." Diane looked beyond her shoulder to the table where Reed and Trina's bodyguards were sitting. "If Fedor was still alive, there wouldn't be a threat, but with his death . . ."

Lori shivered. "Trina is Ruslan's target."

Andrea turned to Lori, smiled. "But . . . and here is where I hope all of you listen and don't ask too many questions."

"I'm an attorney, I always ask questions."

Diane laughed, drank the rest of her wine.

Andrea spoke for the both of them. “A mother as wealthy and wise as our dear sister Alice always did her homework. She knew the reach of her daughter-in-law’s friends. And knew, ultimately, that Trina would be safe.”

“And considering there are two very large and I’m sure very armed men sitting behind us, she wasn’t wrong,” Diane added.

Chapter Twenty-Two

Reed caught the whites of Sasha's eyes as they walked into the lobby of the hotel. She slipped into the hotel bar while he and Carl, Trina's bodyguard, walked the women up to Trina's suite.

Lori had made it clear she needed to talk with Trina alone before the meeting with the board. Once the three of them were in the room, he made his excuses and made his way to the hotel bar.

"Here to buy me a drink?" Sasha asked, tipping her amber-filled glass in his direction.

Reed waited until the bartender moved away to get him his beer. Watered down liquor was a better idea than anything hard he might be tempted to slam. "You work for Petrov." It wasn't a question.

Her sigh might be seductive to a man who didn't already feel the need to protect another one.

"I work for the highest bidder, just like you."

"I'm not like you."

"Which is why you're down here talking to me instead of watching over your woman."

His back teeth started to strain under the

pressure he placed on them. “The man hiring you is a murderer.” Or so his research pointed to.

“You assume too much. And even if the man you believe I’m working for is in fact a person who reduces the population by one or two, remember, politicians start wars. So please, leave your self-righteousness at the door.”

He hated that she might be right about that. Hated even more that this woman knew who had hired him. “Why are you here?”

“Same reason you are.”

He doubted that.

She leaned in. “The difference is, I have what I need.” Sasha lifted her glass. “Cheers.” After finishing her drink, she offered a half smile, placed money on the counter, and walked out of the bar.

He finished his drink and reached into his pocket.

The electronic skimmer captured her credit card. “Gotcha.”

Lori leaned over him, fully dressed.

Reed lay under the sheets, completely naked, and grabbed a handful of her butt as she kissed him good-bye. “You sure you don’t need me to go with you?” he asked.

“Carl is driving, and there is plenty of security in the Everson offices.”

If he didn’t have a goal for when she was gone,

he wouldn't allow her to blow him off. "Is Avery going with you?"

"Yeah. She is going to try her hand at a little spying."

He stiffened. "Oh?"

Lori gave him a quick kiss as she lifted her blanketing frame from his. "She's going to try and score a tour of the offices and talk to some of the employees to gauge morale."

He had a hard time seeing Avery doing anything other than flirting with the sexier members of the male staff. "Is there a question about morale?"

"Anytime management shifts in any way, people worry."

He wanted to ask if Lori thought Trina would take a role in the company but decided to wait for that information. "I suppose that's true." He shifted up in bed. Lori's gaze traveled to where the sheet rested against his hips.

His cock twitched.

She turned on a heel with a groan.

Someone knocked on the door.

"Saved by the bell," she said, laughing.

"I can wait right here, like this, until you get back."

Two steps and she was back over him, her lips on his, her hand resting quite comfortably in his lap.

The knock sounded again, with Carl calling her name.

Reed bit her tongue before breaking off their kiss. “Go to work, woman.”

She wiped her smiling lips before walking out of the room.

The second the door closed, he tossed back the sheets, pulled on his shorts, and went to work.

Okay you Russian spy, where did you hide the bug?

In silence, he started at the window and systematically searched. A tiny set of tools helped him open up vents, disassemble lamps, the back of the TV.

Nothing.

Leaving the “Do Not Disturb” sign on the door, he took his tools, crossed the hall, and picked the lock of Trina’s room.

Without saying a word, he started his search again. Only this time he started with where he’d place a bug and worked out. He was putting a lamp back together when his eyes landed on the sculptured art on the wall. Texans loved their cowboys, and the art in Trina’s room had a three-dimensional scene with a cowboy roping cattle on the wall across from the bed.

Reed ran his hand along the back of the metal art, and then found it.

The tiny little device with a mic shoved between the neck of one artsy cow and a rope.

Instead of destroying the device, Reed took his time and searched the rest of the room, and then moved into Avery's and started again. It was close to noon before he slipped out of Avery's room and back into his own.

If there was one thing Trina felt she deserved an *A* in over the past year, it was in her ability to pretend she belonged where she knew damn well she didn't.

Andrea walked them around the executive offices, introducing her to a few people as they passed by.

Several offered their condolences on Fedor as well as Alice. Both of which infused a level of guilt in Trina's gut. It didn't feel right to have people feeling sorry for her when she and Fedor were never destined for a long and happy marriage.

Instead of dwelling on the facts, Trina accepted the sympathy and channeled it toward the genuine heartbreak she did feel about the entire situation. The reality was, the life she'd been leading before Fedor's death was now completely gone. While she might be able to start her own company to help out her fellow flight attendants like she'd planned, the chances of her ever waiting on anyone, in the air or on the ground, weren't likely.

"How active was Alice in the company?" Trina asked as they settled into the boardroom an hour before the meeting's scheduled time.

"She was here several times a month before she became ill."

Diane had joined them and sat across from Trina and Lori. They'd dropped Avery off with an executive secretary who didn't seem to mind babysitting her. It helped that the secretary was six two and looked like he could bench-press her.

"What did she do?" Lori asked.

"A little of everything. She spent time in meetings with the engineers, marketing, public relations, you name it. She wanted to know a little about everything."

"And she did," Diane finished for her sister.

"Do either of you have a role in the day-to-day operations here?" Trina asked.

"We don't sit at desks and crunch numbers or decide where we should be selling the oil, if that's what you're asking."

"So what is your role? I know I'm probably sounding naive."

"The company belongs to us. Collectively, we are the CEOs of Everson Oil. And now you hold one-third of that. The three of us make the final decisions in the hiring or firing of the executives. We only need a majority, so two out of the three of us can make the decisions, which is probably why Alice felt it wasn't a bad company decision to leave this to you."

"So you could stop me from becoming a

part of this if you wanted to?” Trina asked.

Andrea and Diane looked at each other. “Voting out the third CEO is not possible,” Diane told her.

“This keeps the company moving forward if in fact one of us had a different goal.”

“That makes perfect sense,” Lori chimed in. She turned toward Trina. “Companies that have been in existence as long as Everson Oil have many contingencies to keep any one person from destroying it.”

“Everson Oil is responsible for the livelihood of thousands of families, both here in Texas and scattered throughout the States. Our father understood that and took the responsibility for our employees to heart.” Andrea tapped her chest. “I spend my time here talking with the different department heads and our staff from all levels. I will often know of a problem brewing before it’s brought up in a board meeting.”

“And I have spent the last few years working with the lobbyists and politicians about pipelines and alternative fuel.”

“Like solar?” Trina asked.

“Solar, wind, methane . . . we have so many renewable resources to tap into in the United States that go underutilized, it’s staggering,” Diane said.

“Foreign oil isn’t needed in our country, but there is so much political pull tugging on all ends we may never see a day when we're completely independent."

"Is that the goal of Everson Oil?" Trina asked.

"The goal of every company is to make money and increase shareholder value."

"And who are the shareholders?"

Lori grinned. "You three."

"Oh."

"It's not a public company," Diane said. "But some of the companies we've spun off are partially."

Trina's head was going to explode. "You have spin-off companies?"

"Everson Solar, Everson Turbines. The three of us hold controlling interest, but we've made the companies partially public to offer incentives to our employees."

"Which keeps our employees invested in the greater good of the overall operations."

Trina blinked a few times. "I'm not afraid of saying I'm overwhelmed."

Andrea reached out and patted her hand. "It's a lot to fall into."

"Like a rabbit hole," Trina sighed.

"Which is why you can do as much, or as little, as you want to do with the company. Andrea and I can make decisions without you. We don't expect that you have any idea about what we do here."

Trina leaned back and looked around the room.

"For the first time in weeks, I've been able to talk about Fedor and Alice without feeling like my stomach was going to drop through my feet."

Diane had Alice's smile. "Concentrating on what you can control, and not the things you can't, has a way of keeping us focused and moving forward."

"That sounds like something Alice would have said," Trina told her.

"She stole that line from me," Diane confessed with a wink. Her eyes glossed over with an unshed tear.

It was time for Trina to reach out and comfort the sisters.

"Truth is," Andrea started, "teaching you the ropes might be exactly what we need to move forward, too."

"You can stay in Alice's house, check things out . . . see if this is something you want to do," Diane suggested.

Trina cocked her head to the side, looked at Lori. "Is there a house in Texas?"

"If you want to call it a house. I seem to remember something about twenty-five acres and several horses."

"Holy cow."

"No cows," Andrea teased.

"Our sister didn't care for New York. She only went there in the end to be close to Fedor."

Andrea lightened the mood. "The weather

here sucks, not gonna lie. But hey, we have air conditioning."

"And when the power goes out," Diane continued, "we have all the resources needed to power it back up." She spread her arms wide, as if the company singlehandedly took care of all the coolness they'd need to survive the heat.

Suddenly the world didn't feel so dim. "I need to close up the house in New York."

Andrea and Diane chuckled.

"So you're in?"

Trina glanced at Lori. "I don't see any reason for you to walk the dark halls of Fedor's estate if you don't."

And just like that, Trina changed her life once again. "I'm in."

Diane stood. "Great. Let me invite the rest of the board in."

"Oh, God."

Andrea patted her on the back. "Most of them are Texans. Treating women with respect is way high on their priority list."

Trina's stomach rolled. "You better not be lying to me."

Diane opened the door, and the room flooded with boots, hats, and a whole lot of testosterone.

Chapter Twenty-Three

"Change of plans," Lori announced when she walked into the room at the hotel.

"You finally decided to try skydiving?" Reed teased. He was sitting by the window, his laptop open.

"You wish. No . . . but horseback riding might come into play." She moved to the closet and removed her suitcase.

He closed his computer. "Horses include luggage?"

"You're a funny guy."

Reed moved behind her and wrapped his arms around her. "I crack myself up all the time." He kissed her neck.

Her spine chilled. "None of that. We're going to Trina's."

"Across the hall?"

"That would be a bit crowded. No . . ." Lori rolled out of his arms and into the bathroom to gather her toiletries. "Alice left a ranch to Trina."

Reed moved to the doorway, leaned against it. "Let me guess, one of those houses is right here in Texas."

She picked up her makeup bag and patted

Reed's cheek as she walked by. "Funny and wise."

"I take it today's visit to the oil company went well."

"It did. Trina is finally starting to absorb all of this and has decided to spend the next few months here to see if she wants a part of Everson Oil."

Reed continued to watch her as she bounced around the room, packing.

"What does Trina know about oil?"

"Nothing. But she'll learn."

"You sound very sure of her talents."

She paused. "I think anyone who has been through as much as she has this year and isn't rocking to the voices in her head in a corner somewhere is capable of just about anything." Lori zipped up her suitcase, turned, and placed her hands on her hips. "What are you just standing there for? Pack."

Reed moved to the table where he'd placed his laptop and grabbed his suitcase from the closet. "Ready."

An hour later, they descended upon Alice Everson-Petrov's miniranch.

The humidity slapped Lori's face once again as they exited the car. Only this time, instead of looking over a parking lot or a tarmac, she had something better to take her mind off the uncomfortable heat. The rolling landscape of the ranch was as green as the hills in Southern California were brown. The single-story ranch home sprawled behind a circular driveway. A huge barn sat to one side and beyond that appeared to be a guesthouse.

The twenty-five acres that surrounded Alice's ranch appeared larger in person than on a map. Acres of adjacent properties buffered one home from the next.

Lori watched Trina as she tossed her head back and opened her arms. "It's so quiet."

"Peaceful," Avery echoed.

Carl stood to the side of Trina and moved when she did.

The front door opened and a woman in her late sixties walked out. "Mrs. Petrov?"

Avery swung her arm around Trina and walked her up the steps.

Lori hung back with Reed. "This is a little crazy, even for us."

"What do you mean by that? Even for us?"

"I have some wealthy friends, but this landing in Trina's lap is beyond imagination."

Reed narrowed his eyes. "She had to know she married into a wealthy family."

"Yeah, she knew . . . we all knew. But just because you marry wealth doesn't mean you're going to *be* wealthy."

"I'm missing something."

"Trina married a wealthy man, but she wasn't."

"They were married, it became theirs."

"Nope. Remember, prenuptial agreement. Compared to what she made as a flight attendant, that agreement made her wealthy, but not *this* rich. *This* would set Trina back her entire paycheck."

"Paycheck?" He laughed.

"Divorce settlement." How had she let that slip? "You know what I mean," she backpedaled. "What I mean is *this . . . this* is wealth."

Reed looked around. "Which is why security for Trina is paramount."

"Yeah." Lori's smile faded. "I should probably call Sam."

Reed was starting to see the connections inside Lori's head. Security and secrecy were Sam's role. Legal was Lori's.

He shadowed Carl as they walked around the house.

Lori slipped away to make a call while Trina and Avery were given a grand tour.

Carl was close to Reed's age, had the military haircut that men who have been in the service either embrace or run the opposite way from. "Didn't I hear Lori say something about Trina's home in New York being bugged?"

"That's what I was told."

Reed ran his hand along the frame of a massive window that overlooked the back of the property. Fences housed several horses that grazed on the grass growing in the field. “Might be a good idea to see if there are any here, don’t you think?”

Carl shrugged. “Mrs. Petrov lives in New York, her place was an expected target.”

“Yeah, that’s true, but her trip to Texas would have been a likely event, given she inherited a portion of the company.”

Carl chewed on that for a few minutes.

“And considering Alice Petrov’s ex-husband is the reason for your service, and that man knows about Alice’s assets . . . I don’t know. Seems like if he had the New York house bugged, he might have gone through the trouble of bugging anything that Trina now owns.”

Instead of agreeing or disagreeing, Carl turned and worked his way back to Trina’s side. “Mrs. Petrov, a minute, please.”

Reed watched from a distance as Carl spoke to Trina in hushed tones.

“Really? How likely is that?”

Reed stepped closer, pulled out his phone, and opened up a Google page.

“I’ll bring in a team to sweep the place just to make sure.”

“This is ridiculous.”

“What’s ridiculous?” Lori asked when she walked into the room.

“Carl seems to think he needs to look for bugs.”

The housekeeper overheard her and gasped. “I keep a clean house.”

"He means microphones. Spy stuff." Avery lowered her voice as if it were a joke.

The older woman squinted. "Why would someone spy on us?"

"Have you had any work done recently on the house? Any maintenance from outside companies?" Carl asked.

"It's a home, we have our share of problems. The Internet could always be better."

"Service people coming in the house?" Reed asked.

"Of course. We know horses here, not technical stuff."

Lori turned to Carl. "It won't hurt to look."

He took that as his green light and picked up his cell phone.

"In the meantime," Lori looked between Trina and Avery, "private conversations should be taken outside."

Which was what Reed would have suggested had he been given the chance.

The question was, how many private conversations had taken place in the hotel before he'd found the bug?

And what had Sasha learned?

"I know it's not skydiving, but hey . . . horses." Lori leaned over and patted the mare's neck.

It was close to dusk, and the temperature had dropped a good fifteen degrees, making the ride pleasurable instead of a sweaty mess for the horses and the riders.

"I haven't been on the back of a horse since I was a kid," Reed told her. He stood in the saddle and repositioned himself. "I'm not sure I'm going to be of any use to you when we get back."

Lori glanced over and giggled. "Ah, are you having a hard time there?"

"Tease me now . . . go ahead."

She licked her lips. "I'm sure I can manage to make it all better."

He groaned. The only thing harder than riding a horse when you had a dick was riding one with a hard-on.

"Are you sure it's okay that you're here? Your boss isn't going to be upset with the time off you've been taking?"

The tangling of the web he'd been weaving was starting to thicken up. "I get paid by the task, not by the hour. I'm good. Don't you have enough to worry about other than my job?"

"I do. But I'd feel terrible if something happened between you and your boss."

He really hoped the guilt down his spine wasn't showing on his face. "Nothing is going to happen. I promise."

They'd turned the horses back toward the ranch house and had to keep them from running home.

"If you ever wanted to change professions,

Avery seems to think you have the perfect fit for a bodyguard."

"And what does Avery know about bodyguards?"

"She said you have the perfect resting bitch face."

"Was that a compliment?"

"Not sure. Probably."

His horse tossed her head. "I wanted to be a cop, once." A half-truth was the best he could give her without more questions.

Lori tilted her head. "What happened to that dream?"

The memory of blood running down his neck from the slash in his cheek while he watched his partner struggling to breathe flashed. "It didn't work out."

"I think you would make a great cop."

As if he'd ever go back. Just thinking about it made the faded scar on his chin itch.

Reed glanced at Lori's bouncing boobs as she bobbed around on the back of her horse. He'd gotten so far off his investigation surrounding Shannon and overwhelmed with everything Lori and Trina, he would have lost his job if he were still on the force.

He reminded himself that there was still a connection between Shannon and the others to warrant his interest, but he'd be lying to himself if he said he was doing his job as a PI.

What had Sasha learned? Was she working for Ruslan?

"Someone got quiet." Lori pulled him out of his thoughts.

"I was just thinking." He scrambled to come up with something distracting from the subject.

"About?"

"How I would have been a sucky cop, but a pair of handcuffs might have come in handy."

Lori's eyes widened.

And when she didn't immediately deny that fantasy, he said, "Time to step out of your sexual wheelhouse, Counselor?"

Once again, she didn't say no.

And Reed finished the rest of their ride with a raging hard-on.

"So you finally let Reed take a day off." Danny moved around her kitchen as if he'd lived there for months rather than two weeks.

"He doesn't live here."

"Tell him that."

Lori washed the tomatoes and pulled out her cutting board. "He goes home."

Danny placed a hand on her hip, making her move so he could throw away the box that once held the spicy rice he was preparing on the stove.

"What's the story with him, anyway?"

"We're dating." As if that wasn't obvious.

"Dating exclusively?"

"There isn't anyone else on my speed dial right now."

"And his?"

Lori moved from one tomato to another. "I don't think so. We haven't really discussed it."

"Not that you give him any time to play with someone else. *Oh, Reed . . . I need a bodyguard, wanna step up?*"

"I don't talk like that!" But hearing her brother talk in a high octave, attempting to mimic her, made her laugh.

"What is it he said he does for a living?"

Lori tossed the end bits of the tomatoes into the garbage disposal and moved to the carrots. "Data processing . . . of some kind."

"You don't know?"

"He doesn't talk about it."

"Huh." Danny stood over the stove, stirring the rice. Inside the oven was the chicken he'd marinated most of the day. "It doesn't fit his personality."

Lori sliced the carrots, concentrating hard to miss her fingers. Nobody liked bloody salad. "What doesn't fit?"

"Data anything. He seems like the kind of guy who works with his hands."

"Isn't data processing working with your hands?"

"You know what I mean." Danny removed two plates from the cupboard.

Carrots are done . . . what dressing? Lori opened the refrigerator and found vinaigrette and a pear. "Do I have walnuts?"

"What?"

She opened her pantry door to look. "Never mind."

"I'm just saying . . . it doesn't really fit."

Along with the chocolate chips she'd bought a good six months before, when she was on a baking kick, she found the walnuts. The expiration date was still one month out. "Score."

"Are you listening to me?"

"Yes." She looked up and couldn't for the life of her remember the last thing Danny had said. "No . . . what were you saying?"

"Reed. He doesn't completely measure up."

The walnuts in her hands forgotten, she paused. "Measure up to what?"

"Where did you two meet?"

"On the cruise in Barcelona."

Danny leaned against the counter, arms folded over his chest. "Barcelona . . . as in Spain?"

"Yeah, I know . . . crazy, right? What are the chances of that?"

"Probably like point a zillion zeros to one."

"That's what I thought. But you never know."

Danny had that look in his eye that reminded her of their father. The one that made her sit back and wonder what she'd said wrong. "What?"

He shook his head. “So, am I sleeping on the couch now, or can I keep the guest room?”

She grinned. “Has it been two weeks?”

“Yeah, not that you’d know it. I’ve been here more than you have.”

“When are you due to hit the fisherman sea of Mexico?”

“When I get there.” Danny pushed off the counter, leaned forward, and kissed her cheek. “Your choice, guest room or couch. But I need to crash here a little longer.”

“What do you mean by *need?*”

“Do I really need to spell it out for you?” Danny stared her down.

“I can take care of myself.”

“Never said you couldn’t.”

When had her brother grown up enough to put someone else before himself?

“My couch is meant for sitting . . . not sleeping.”

He smiled and walked away.

Later that night, while staring at the ceiling and hearing the snores of her brother in the other room, Lori closed her eyes and thought about Reed’s hands. Rough, working hands. She thought of her own in comparison. Soft hands of a woman who worked with paper and a computer. Reed didn’t talk about his work at all. Or maybe she wasn’t being a reciprocating girlfriend who asked enough questions. Either way, rough hands usually equated to harder work, not data processing.

Falling asleep didn't come easy, and when she woke in the morning, she'd almost forgotten what had kept her awake.

Chapter Twenty-Four

Reed rolled his special pen in his hand while he glared at the flash drive microphone sitting on his desk. What the hell was he doing?

Was this how good cops turned bad?

One case? One twist of ethics that turned them into douchebags playing for the wrong team?

At some point in this investigation he'd sold a tiny bit of his soul. Because the more he learned about Lori and her gaggle of rich and lonely friends, the more he felt for them. And who would have thought that was possible?

God, what the hell was wrong with him?

He knew sleeping with her had been a bad idea the first time he'd done it. He couldn't help himself. And now . . . he didn't want to help himself. He felt like an addict every time he drove to the city. One last time, he'd chant. Plant the bug, make his excuses . . . then she'd smile and the lawyer in her would stop at the door and the flirt wearing a thong would come out.

Yeah, he wasn't going anywhere.

Because Ruslan was gunning for her.

And Sasha was on to her . . . and him by now.

Instead of trying to investigate a way to nail

Wentworth with information gathered from Lori and her gaggle of friends, Reed was trying to figure out how to keep their secrets that he had yet to learn.

He closed his eyes and cussed the universe.

It didn't matter what side of the political fence the public servant sat on, they all did one thing very, very well . . . they raised money.

Wearing a slim-fitting black cocktail dress with an expensive pair of red-bottom shoes that Sam had bought her for her last birthday, Lori stood with Gabi and Hunter Blackwell, wineglasses in their hands. Most of the time Sam, and sometimes her husband, would attend these events with her, but Sam and Blake were in Europe. So tonight, Gabi, a recruiter for Alliance, and Lori were there in support of Shannon.

Paul Wentworth was working toward his second term as governor, and he was helping the rich part with their money.

He'd asked Shannon to attend the event to show the world that there weren't any hard feelings between him and his ex-wife.

"This can't be easy for her," Gabi whispered while watching Shannon speak with a few members of Paul's staff.

"She didn't have to say yes."

"That isn't the kind of person she is," Gabi said. "Is she pursuing her photography at all?"

"I don't think so. She still has her studio and storefront, but she's never there."

"I understand taking time after the divorce, let things settle, but it's time to move on."

Hunter leaned in, kept his voice low. "Maybe she needs a few blind dates."

"I can't imagine she's hurting for invitations to dinner," Gabi told her husband.

Hunter slid a hand around his wife's waist and kissed the top of her head. "A lot of men are intimidated by beauty and success." He lowered his voice so only they could hear. "Maybe your marriage service should have a sideline dating service."

"Isn't the Internet full of those?" Gabi asked.

Hunter looked above many of the heads in the room. "I doubt there are very many people in this room on Tinder outside of those serving food."

Lori swept the room with her gaze. She liked the idea. Out of the ashes of Alliance marriages, there was a need to acclimate the women, and a few good men, to the dating world.

Lori's eyes flittered to Hunter, who lifted his eyebrows as if to say, *hey, my idea has merit.*

"I guess we know why you're so rich," Lori teased him.

He waved his hand in the air. "I won't even ask for a finder's fee."

Shannon looked up, met Lori's eyes with a silent plea.

She set her drink down. “Looks like I’m needed.”

Lori approached her friend with purpose. Go in, extract, keep it polite.

Shannon stood among three men and one woman, people Lori didn’t know.

Lori walked up to Shannon, placed a hand on her arm. “I’m sorry to interrupt. Shannon, you wanted to speak with the Blackwells before they left, right?”

The conversation she’d interrupted dissipated.

“That’s right. Thank you so much. I’m sorry.”

The shortest of the three men spoke up. “I’d still like to know how you feel about—”

“Lovely chatting with you,” were Shannon’s parting words.

“Thank you,” Shannon said under her breath as they walked away.

“That bad?”

“Some people gossip more than the tabloids.”

They approached Gabi and Hunter, and Shannon made a show of hugging Gabi and accepting a kiss to the cheek from Hunter.

“How are you holding up?” Gabi asked.

“I’m all right. I miss some of these people.”

“And the ones you don’t?” Hunter asked.

Shannon smiled. “I don’t have to talk to them anymore.”

“There is always a bright side,” Gabi said.

Hunter stopped a waiter walking by and handed

Shannon a glass of wine. "Now tell me, why are you doing this alone? I know a lot of men who would love to be by your side . . ."

"I don't—"

"Even if it's just for show," he whispered with a wink. "Probably put lots of wagging tongues and inappropriate questions in their place."

"I . . ." Shannon glanced over to where her ex-husband was standing. "Maybe next time."

Hunter laughed. "Check with these ladies, I'm sure by the time you're ready, they'll have a pool of men prepared to help." With that, Hunter made an excuse and left the three women there to talk in his wake.

"What was that all about?" Shannon asked.

"I think he's trying to find more work for us," Gabi said.

"I really like the idea," Lori told her.

"What idea?" Shannon asked.

"A dating service."

"Don't you already do that?"

Lori found her glass and tipped it in Shannon's direction. "You know the answer to that."

"Well, not for me. I don't want to date anytime soon."

"And how would tonight have looked if you had someone hanging on your arm willing to say the right things to those who ask?" If nothing else, Lori would like to see if Paul had any emotions when it came to his ex-wife. As long as Shannon wasn't getting on with her life, there was no way of really knowing if Paul ever had a thing for her. If he didn't, fine . . . but if he did . . .

"Hmmm . . ."

Lori's smile met Shannon's.

"Heads up, ladies. Incoming," Gabi announced.

Paul, in his perfectly polished suit and shined shoes, took a spot behind Shannon. "Thank you for coming," he said to her.

Lori saw her draw a fortifying breath before she turned to him with a practiced smile. "Hello, Paul."

He kept an appropriate distance, his smile wasn't cold, but it wasn't full of warmth either.

"How are you doing?"

"I'm doing well."

There were people watching the two of them, and the noise around them came to a low murmur.

"Would you tell me if you weren't?" he asked quietly.

"I'm not your responsibility any longer, Paul." Shannon's reply was spoken softly.

His jaw tightened and the next words he uttered were close to Shannon's ear and only heard by her.

Her attempt at a smile was weak as he turned and walked away.

Oh, damn, was that moisture in Shannon's eyes? "My brother cleans up really well. Next time, we come armed."

Shannon cracked a smile.

"Only a few more minutes and we can get you out of this room. Just hold your head up," Gabi coached Shannon.

"It's been two years. This should have been easy."

"Men never make things easy."

"This from a happily married woman living the dream."

Gabi rolled her eyes. "That man *never* makes my life easy."

"Yeah, but he makes it worthwhile," Lori chimed in.

Gabi blushed.

Noise around them said people were starting to move around again.

Gabi tugged Shannon away.

"I'll meet up with you." Lori needed a quick word with the governor.

As the other women worked their way to the ladies' room, Lori squared her shoulders and started toward the man who had upset her friend.

"Excuse me?"

A woman she'd never seen before cut off Lori's path. Tall, dark hair, with high cheekbones and full lips. "I'm sorry, do I know you?" Lori asked.

The woman looked at the ground. "No, I'm sorry . . . are you Lori Cumberland?"

"Yes, and you are?"

"I'm Susan."

Out of habit, Lori glanced at Susan's left hand to see if there was a ring molding on her finger. When approached at these events, most of the time it was a referral.

"Can I help you, Susan?"

"Maybe." Susan lowered her head and voice. "I heard from a dear friend that you might be able to help me."

"You're in need of a divorce?"

"No." Susan smiled. "I need a husband."

At first, Lori wondered if maybe Hunter was working the room, drumming up clients for the nonexistent dating service.

"Uhm . . ."

"You know, a temporary one. I was told Alliance could help."

Light shone as the pieces fell into place. "Oh."

"Are my resources correct?"

"Maybe. But I'm not the one to talk to. Do you have a card? I can have someone call you."

The woman blew out a sigh. "Oh, thank goodness." With long, red fingernails, she picked out a card in her handbag and gave it to Lori.

The name Susan Wilson was printed on plain gray cardstock with a phone number.

"This is you?"

"Yes . . . and no. I have to explain in private." Susan looked around them. "I'm sure you understand."

Lori smiled, tucked the card away. “Of course. Someone will get back to you.”

With a nod, Susan walked away.

When Lori looked up, Paul was no longer in sight.

Chapter Twenty-Five

When another week passed without so much as one sighting of Ruslan and his men, Lori shooed off the bodyguard.

"Neil isn't going to be pleased," Cooper told her as he tried to talk her into changing her mind.

"Good thing Neil's opinion isn't needed here. I might feel a little guilty if I thought you'd be out of work, but I know that isn't the case."

"The Harrisons will be back in a week. I can hang until then."

Lori felt the need to pack Cooper a lunch to send him on his way. "And I'll talk to Sam in a week. Sooner if I need to. Now c'mon . . . you're a young guy. I'm sure there's some hottie out there waiting to spend time with you."

Lori stood behind her desk and checked the time. Her next client was in five minutes. She'd scheduled the time to buzz Cooper off between clients to avoid argument.

It wasn't working.

"Just because everything is silent doesn't mean there aren't things in play."

"That may be, but my life has been interrupted enough because of one man's weak threats."

The intercom on her phone buzzed. "Your nine o'clock is here."

"Thank you."

"Lori—"

"No. I appreciate your concern, but the truth is, you're not needed. I'm either here or at home, or with Reed. I don't need a driver or someone hovering over me like I'm some kind of head of state. I'm a divorce attorney with a few high profile clients. That's it. Ruslan Petrov has no real beef with me." Or so she'd been telling herself for the past week. The last straw was when she went to the nail salon to have her fingers and toes painted and her regular girl kept eyeing Cooper at the door.

Lori could never be one to marry one of these rich men with all their rich problems and security.

"Call Neil, do what you have to, but no more."

Cooper held his hands up. "Fine. But if anything changes. You feel the hair on your neck stand up, you call me!"

Lori grinned. "You're a good guy, Cooper. Now go find your hottie you've been neglecting and make it up to her."

The slight gleam in his eye told her she'd hit a nerve.

He walked out of her office, his cell phone already to his ear.

She pressed the intercom on her desk. "Okay, Liana, send Mrs. Maghakian in."

Lori opened a legal pad and waited for her new client.

Wearing a dark blue pantsuit and a simple pair of pumps that complemented the Prada purse, the woman walked in with dark sunglasses hiding most of her face, her hair disguising the rest.

Lori walked around her desk, extended her hand.

The closer she got to the woman, the more makeup Lori noticed. "Mrs. Maghakian, it's a pleasure to meet you."

"Thank you for seeing me on such short notice." The woman's voice was as weak as her handshake.

"Can we get you something to drink, coffee? Water?"

"No, your secretary already offered. I'm fine."

With that, Liana left the office.

"Please, sit. Or if you'd like, we can talk over here." Lori indicated a couch and chair setup she'd placed in her office to help her clients relax. She'd learned long ago that half her job was being a therapist to her clients. Many, like the skittish one in front of her, often needed time to open up about their marital problems. Even if they'd spent time on a marriage counselor's couch, things took a turn when you were sitting across from an attorney to discuss ending your failed marriage.

Mrs. Maghakian turned toward the couch and sat.

Lori gave her the minutes she needed before taking a seat across from her.

Back rod-straight, the woman looked everywhere in the office except toward Lori. For a moment, Lori wondered if she'd say anything at all before bolting out the door.

Then, with a lift of her chin, Mrs. Maghakian removed her sunglasses, revealing the reason for all the cosmetics. Makeup might have covered up the color of the bruise, but the swelling and broken capillaries in her left eye required more than powder and paste.

"I need to leave him before he kills me."

Lori's blood chilled.

"Or I kill him." Mrs. Maghakian leveled her gaze to Lori's.

Lori took her work home with her all the time. It was part of the job. There were only so many hours in the day, and then you had face-to-face meetings and days spent in court. The paperwork she needed to go over alone was more time-consuming than any typical day job. Her paralegal secretary was one of the best, and flagged what needed her attention first and what could wait. When a case like Ana Maghakian's walked through the door, Lori was reminded why she chose the law as her profession.

All day Lori thought about Ana's side of the story. The story that manifested in bruises on her face, arms, and thighs.

Vivi poked her head through the door at five. "I'm outta here."

"I'm right behind you."

"I left the files for the Charleston case on top. You have court in Van Nuys at eight in the morning."

"I got it." Lori grabbed the files, which measured two inches thick but would end up thick enough to be dragged in using a small handcart by the time the Charlestons were officially divorced. "I'll see you in the afternoon."

Vivi left with a wave and Lori moved around her office gathering the files needed for the morning as well as the one she'd started on Maghakian vs. Maghakian. As far as everything else was concerned, it could wait.

She turned off the light in her office, closed the door, and then paused when she saw Reed sitting in her lobby with a magazine in his hands, one ankle crossed over one knee.

"What are you doing here?"

Reed dropped the magazine and smiled. "Hello, Counselor."

"Reed?" She looked around.

He stood, took two steps, and took her briefcase from her hand. "Cooper called me."

She squeezed her eyes shut and shook her head. "He shouldn't have."

"He said you fired him."

"I told him I didn't need him anymore."

"Because Ruslan Petrov has been silent, yeah, I heard."

"You don't agree."

"Did it ever occur to you that Ruslan is just waiting for you to tire of the bodyguards and surveillance to make his move?"

Lori grabbed her briefcase from him. "Not you, too." She started for the door.

"You know I'm right."

"No, I know I'm right. Trina is closing up the New York house this week and moving to Texas. Ruslan is in Germany, according to my resources."

"And do you think he would be the one to come after you? The man is smarter than that."

"Is he?" Lori was more than a little irritated. "And how would you know that?"

Reed opened his mouth and promptly closed it.

"Exactly. I'm fine, Reed."

"You're upset."

"Of course I'm upset. I don't like people telling me how I need to live my life."

"Even those people that care about you?"

Reed took her briefcase from her a second time and stepped into her personal space. "I care, Lori. And unless you want to fire me, too, I'm going to make sure you get home safely."

"In separate cars?"

He kissed her lips in the briefest peck. "I dropped my car at your place and Ubered over."

It was hard to be mad at him when he'd gone through so much effort just to drive her home.

He nodded toward the door to the office. "C'mon. I'll drive so you can relax."

"I am relaxed!" she snapped.

Reed tossed both hands in the air. "If you insist. I'll drive because I value my—"

She glared at him.

"Because you have work to do, and you can do it on the five-mile drive home," he teased.

Her glare softened.

"Fine," she said as she marched by him and waited at the door to lock it. Once she did, she handed him her keys and kept pace until she reached the elevators.

Reed brushed against her as other people in the building piled into the small space, but he didn't say any more.

She was a mixture of ticked, touched, and strangely turned on.

He cared. Said it out loud as if it was a dedication of some sort. Those words, along with the fact that he hadn't asked permission but just showed up to stand in for the bodyguard she'd told to go home, said something more than any man before him.

They walked through the parking lot in silence.

Reed unlocked the doors to her Mercedes.

Lori climbed into the passenger seat, put her belt on, and stared out the window.

She needed to start taking some control back in her life. The morning had started out with that in mind. Let Cooper go, find out what Petrov was looking for, and turn the tables by finding out where he was. She'd learned he was in Germany an hour before Reed showed up.

Reed climbed behind the wheel and pulled out of the parking spot.

He took her lead and kept quiet.

Lori found herself staring at his hands on the wheel of her car. Large hands, capable hands. She shifted in her seat and sucked in a breath through her nose.

Aftershave. Something unique to him that had her licking her lips.

He concentrated on driving, not at all realizing she was tapping her toes against the floor of the car and wishing he'd drive just a little faster.

Did he really think she was incapable of taking care of herself? Was it a macho thing, or was it some kind of *you silly girl* thing?

I care, Lori.

It wasn't an admission of love or promise for tomorrow, but it was more than she'd had an hour before.

The final light and around the corner they pulled into the parking garage and got out.

Reed reversed his earlier movements and brought out her briefcase and rode up to her condo in silence.

It was quiet, and dark.

Danny must be out.

"Do you want me to leave?" he asked after dropping her case on the foyer table.

She turned on him, pushed him against the closed door, and latched on to his lips.

A few stunned seconds went by before Reed clued in and kissed her back.

Those capable hands reached into her hair and pulled enough to make her break off the kiss. Her reward was his lips on her neck and the grazing of his teeth on her collarbone.

"I want you."

He filled his hand with her breast and squeezed hard. "I couldn't tell."

Lori filled her hand with his cock through his pants. "Liar."

Reed turned them around, shoved her against the door, and pushed his hips into hers.

She lifted one leg until he grabbed a hold of her thigh, then she tightened every muscle she had, used the door as leverage, and wrapped her legs around his hips.

Reed repositioned himself, her skirt rode high, exposing her panties to the cool air.

Their tongues fought for dominance, her hips grinding against the bulge in his pants.

One hand around his neck to help hold her in place, Lori reached for him. "Now."

"Here?"

She couldn't talk, instead she tugged at the zipper of his pants.

"The cameras," he reminded her.

"Don't care." And she didn't. Only one thought ran through her head. Reed, inside her, right then, right now.

"Okay, baby. I'm setting you down."

She held tighter.

"Just for a second."

He placed her legs on the floor, her head buried in his neck, her teeth marking him behind his ear.

Reed kicked his pants away and lifted her skirt until it was on her hips. Instead of removing her thong, he moved it aside and buried a finger in her slick center. "Jesus, Lori."

She bucked against him. "Please, Reed."

He chuckled and lifted one of her legs to his hip again, his erection already teasing her. "I hope we can do this without a trip to the ER."

With her grip on his shoulders, she wrapped her other leg around his waist, forcing his cock deep inside her. "Yes."

"Hold on, Lori."

She did, and he did all the work. The depth, the angle, the fact he was taking her with her clothes still on against the door. All of it hit several sexual fantasies all at once. Even the thought of someone possibly watching on the other end of those cameras all over her home added to the excitement.

Everything contracted inside her, and Reed cussed.

She pulled his lips back to hers and he thrust harder, faster, until she couldn't breathe. So close, so very close.

"Come for me," he breathed in her ear.

Her head fell back, her body arched. "Now, let go, Reed."

He did, right then, and together they reached that place they fought hard to find. As they floated down, Lori's body spasmed and took more than Reed willingly gave the first time.

Lori wilted. One leg dropped before Reed recovered enough to capture the other.

He swung her into his arms and walked her to her bedroom, followed her down as he laid her on the bed.

"I feel so much better," she muttered.

He collapsed to her side. "I think you killed me."

Something in her back hurt more than a little. The molding on the door probably left a mark. It didn't matter, she'd do it again if given the chance. "That was fabulous."

"Outside your wheelhouse?" he asked, teasing.

"So far outside I don't recognize me."

"I like this version of you."

She opened her eyes to find him staring at her. "I like it, too."

"Next time I'll make it last longer. Maybe I'll take you against that big glass window of yours."

"At night, with the lights below."

Reed shook his head. "Broad daylight, for everyone to see."

God help her.

"Ohhh, Lori likes that."

She ran her hand down his hip, dragged her fingernails along his thigh, felt him twitch. "You like it, too."

"I can be convinced."

"Convinced? And what kind of prodding am I going to have to do to achieve that?"

He turned away, lay on his back. "I'm sure you can come up with something."

Leaning up on her forearms, she unbuttoned the rest of her shirt and tossed it away.

His eyes watched and his cock swelled as she pulled her skirt down and off . . . panties, along with her bra, were next.

One leg over his hips and she straddled him, taking the lead and doing all the work.

Three mind-numbing orgasms and they hadn't had dinner. It was like Lori was on a sexual high and he was a vessel for her pleasure. Not that he was complaining. If this was what picking her up from work was going to result in, he'd happily play chauffeur.

Lying to his side, her arm thrown over her head, Lori was working on catching her breath.

"Good God, I needed that."

"You might have killed me," he teased. He looked down. "Yep, it's dead."

Lori started chuckling. "He died happy."

He liked her like this, carefree and lax. After two months of dating, he'd learned that it wasn't her normal. She carried the weight of too many people for a single woman without kids.

"Why were you so stressed?"

She sighed. "I don't know. Everything just built up inside. Ya know?"

Reed rolled to his side and pulled the sheet over the top of them before resting his hand on her flat stomach. "Same buildup or new buildup?"

"Both. I had this new client come in. What a shit storm this is going to be."

"Oh?"

"Yeah, she's thirty-six, stunning . . . under all the makeup and bruises."

A muscle in his arm twitched. "Her husband is hitting her."

Lori glanced at him, blew out another long breath. "Hitting? No, beating the crap out of her. Who does that?"

"Not a real man."

She rolled on her side, tucked the sheet higher over her breasts. "It's hard. I wanted to grab her hand and run her to the nearest police station."

"She doesn't want to press charges?"

"He's a very powerful man. I've learned that powerful men have a way of getting away with everything. She's right in being careful about who she tells what."

"But she came to you."

A tiny, satisfied smile crossed her lips. "I do know people. People that can protect her while she severs herself from his life."

He couldn't imagine.

"She doesn't even want his money. She just wants to get out." Lori shook her head. "How can someone be an eight-year punching bag for someone else and not want them to pay?"

"If she were my sister, I'd kill him."

Kindness swam in Lori's eyes. "You're a good man."

"Not always," he confessed.

She took his words as nothing more than humility and patted his hand over her waist. "How did she not see it before they were married? If she'd come to us before saying *I do,* we would have flushed this out before the wedding."

"What do you mean?"

She ignored his question as she finished her broken thoughts. "What am I saying? There is no guarantee. Look at Trina. None of us had a clue about Fedor's instability."

He knew all those thoughts linked inside her head, but he was lost. "Back up, babe. What are you saying? It's your job to determine if someone is suicidal?"

"With Alliance, it is."

"Am I supposed to know what Alliance is?"

"Alliance is Sam's service. She matches eligible clients with a wife, or a husband, but those aren't as common."

"Like a dating service?"

Lori looked directly at him. "This stays between you and me."

For a second he considered telling her to keep her secrets, but then he'd have to confess his. That halo she'd placed over his head was slipping way below the waist. "Of course."

"There are men out there who need a wife . . . temporarily."

The pictures in his home and all the lines he'd drawn between Lori's friends and her . . . and Samantha Harrison. "Like Trina's husband?"

"Right. Fedor wanted to reassure his mother. He knew she was dying and didn't see the harm in marrying just to make the woman's last days happy."

Like snow falling in exactly the right place, everything started to come into focus. "And what did Trina get out of this?"

"A paycheck for a year of her life. The relationship is on paper. That's understood. Nothing physical."

"And that works?"

"Most of the time. There is the occasion where the marriage works."

He rolled on his back. "Shannon . . ."

Lori huffed. "You didn't hear that from me."

"Jesus . . . Avery?"

"Everyone got out of their marriages everything they wanted."

"Except Trina."

Lori pushed a strand of his hair out of his eyes.

"Fedor wasn't supposed to take himself out. And Alice certainly wasn't expected to leave everything to her daughter-in-law. So, yeah . . . I've been a little more stressed than normal."

His heart started to pound. "If Ruslan Petrov found out about this, he could really screw up everything."

"Yeah, which is why Sam wants all this security. But I don't think for a minute he's on to anything. He's a bully."

What an utter cluster fuck this was.

Noise from beyond her bedroom caught their attention. "Well, hello . . . did someone lose their pants out here?"

Lori cracked a smile and buried her head in his shoulder. "Danny."

Chapter Twenty-Six

Reed placed both hands on the wall in his office and cringed. Lori made a decent living working the legal end of Alliance alone. Million-dollar mergers from which she made a percentage. No need to go to court. No need to file extra papers. Write up a prenuptial . . . execute a prenuptial.

What a scam.

Only none of it was illegal that he could see. There might be a question of morality, and certainly in the case of Trina Petrov, someone, somewhere was going to question the legality of a fake marriage resulting in her ending up with half a billion dollars. And yes, Paul Wentworth and his fake wife, Shannon, wouldn't be very credible if the facts leaked to the public.

He had the information his client needed. Not the proof, but enough to deliver, collect a check, and walk away.

Reed knew, without a second look, he wasn't going to deliver this information to Senator Knight. She'd find out the public facts. Lori Cumberland worked with the rich and famous, and she was the lawyer to write up and execute the prenuptial. Was it legal for a lawyer to represent both parties? He jotted down a note for himself to research. He was relatively sure it was, but wondered if there were any loopholes.

A low hum on his desk told him the devices he'd planted in Lori's home were picking up voices.

He moved to turn it off. He already had the information he needed.

"I'm not leaving," he heard Danny say.

Reed hesitated over the button.

"You're sticking around because you want to protect me. Noble, and I appreciate it. But it isn't needed."

"Don't go, Dan. C'mon," Reed prodded the air as if his chant would somehow go through space and hit Lori's brother in the cerebellum.

"You just fired Cooper."

"I didn't fire him!" Lori's voice rose.

"I don't see him following you around anymore."

"Danny . . . stop. I'm fine. You're cramping my style."

"Ha. Is this about making a crack about Reed's pants on the living room floor?"

"Oh, Lord, do you have to mention that again?"

Danny laughed. "Seriously, sis. I think it's great you have a guy in the mix. If you have company, maybe a tie on the door. We can work this out."

Reed found himself smiling. *Are we in college?*

"I stopped putting ties on doors when I was in law school."

"Yeah, but it worked," Reed muttered to himself.

"It's a great system," Danny said.

"You've been here a month. I love you, but I don't want anything to come between us."

There was some noise. Danny's voice sounded farther away.

Reed turned up the mic.

"And I love you too much to leave now. I'll risk pissing you off until I know you're safe."

"Danny!"

"Lori! This isn't negotiable, oh Mighty Lawyer. I wouldn't be able to live with myself if something happened and I wasn't here."

Reed tapped a nervous finger on his desk. "I always knew I liked you, kid."

Lori's voice traveled. "You're annoying."

"You love me anyway," Danny called after her.

Once a month, usually at Sam's Malibu estate, she and Lori met and discussed current and prospective clients of Alliance.

At that exact moment, they had ten marriages in various stages. Two of which were walking the edge of voiding their contracts because the relationships had become physical. And so long as a child wasn't a result, Alliance and the contracts signed were in effect if either party wanted out on the agreed upon date. They'd built in nearly every clause, including death. Although Trina's situation wasn't covered. Something Sam and Lori discussed over a bottle of really good Sangiovese on her back porch overlooking the Pacific Ocean.

"You know I'm not happy about you telling Cooper to piss off."

Lori rolled her eyes. "I'm American, I don't tell anyone to piss off."

Occasionally, an English saying would leak through Sam's words.

"You know what I mean."

"Petrov is smoke and mirrors. He's spinning around in Munich and Prague, trying to drum up money. He isn't watching me."

"He's dangerous."

"I know this. We've gone over this. Trina is the one who needs security, not me. I have cameras and intercoms all over my house. My office is secure. I'm good." Lori quickly changed the subject. "Trina deposited money in the account."

"What?"

"The amount that Fedor was due to pay when they divorced."

"She didn't have to do that," Sam said.

Lori shrugged. "Technically, we did our job."

"That's not how I feel."

"Me either. It feels like blood money."

"Neither one of us pulled any triggers."

"I still think we should have known Fedor

wasn't stable." How many times had Lori kicked herself about that fact?

Sam topped off their glasses of wine. "Let's just hold on to it for now, pay for her security . . . whatever she needs. If we get through the year without any more from her father-in-law, we'll donate the rest to suicide awareness or something like that."

"I like that idea."

"How is it working out with Avery in your building?"

"I never see her. She's been in Texas more than in LA. She and Trina really hit it off."

"I'm thankful for that. I missed the drama at Wentworth's fundraiser. Gabi said it wasn't comfortable."

"We need to do an intervention with Shannon . . . or find her a date." Lori spent the next thirty minutes and the rest of the bottle of wine discussing the possibility of creating an actual elite dating service.

"You're suggesting we screen potential suitors as closely as we screen temporary spouses?"

"Anything less and we're nothing more than an online dating app. And when marriages end, like with Shannon, we offer unlimited dating service. Make sure they have a man on their arm for events like she had last month."

"Fake dating?"

"Or the real thing. We'd have more clients.

We'd need more staff . . . none of which would know the truth about Alliance."

"I like this idea, Lori."

"I do, too. Maybe it's because I'm getting my sexy on with Reed, but I hate to think of anyone without someone to play with."

Sam sat back, her unruly red hair blowing in her face with the wind off the ocean. "How are things with Reed?"

"They're really good. Almost too good."

"Why do you say that?"

"When was the last time *too good* lasted for me?"

"When was the last time *anything* lasted for you? I was starting to think of you as the one-night stand lawyer."

"It's expected when you're a divorce attorney."

"Says you. I'm glad it's working out."

"Me too."

Sam's housekeeper came outside. "Is Ms. Cumberland staying for dinner?"

Lori shook her head. "No. I've gotta get going."

"You sure?" Sam asked.

"Hot date."

Lori stood and gathered the papers off the table.

"I'm going to have a small dinner party next week. Can I count on you bringing Reed?"

Lori calculated how many people in her personal life had met Reed and decided the risk was worth it. Besides, he'd already met Sam.

"Let me know the date and time, and I'll ask him."

She swung her purse over her shoulder. "Oh, hey . . . did you or Gabi get ahold of Susan Wilson?"

Sam hesitated.

"The woman who approached me at Wentworth's fundraiser."

"Ah, yeah . . . Gabi is working on that."

"Perfect." She kissed Sam's cheek. "We'll talk later."

Lori needed a night out of the city. She'd hinted that she wanted to see where Reed lived. That wasn't going to happen.

Not yet.

If ever.

The pit he was sinking in just kept getting deeper. There wasn't a way to walk away.

Not that he wanted to.

Every time he looked in the mirror, he cringed. His mother wouldn't be proud, his sisters would probably disown him.

The hardest part was going to be the fall. The moment Lori realized why he was in her life, and the look she'd have on her face . . .

So here he was, putting off the inevitable. Every day was a search to find out how to dig himself out of the hole he'd fallen in.

Hell, he'd kick his own ass if he could.

It was times like this he wished he was Catholic so he could walk into a confessional and scrub all the sin away.

He ran a hand through his hair, grabbed his duffel bag, and stormed out the door. The drive to her condo normally focused him.

Not today.

He texted her from the turnaround. I'm here.

Running a little late. Five minutes.

He took a minute for himself before putting the Jeep into park. He waved at the doorman. "Just picking Lori up."

The guy waved him on.

A wave to the desk, a smile to the security guard, and he was in the elevator.

He knocked twice before Danny answered. "Hey, Reed. She's getting ready."

The keys in his hand dangled on his thumb. "Thanks." He smiled, looked around the room.

"We won't be back tonight," Reed informed him.

"Yeah, Lori told me."

Reed nodded. What was taking her so long?

"Want something to drink?"

"I'm good." He wasn't good, he was anxious, edgy.

"Danny?" Lori walked into the room wearing jeans and a snug T-shirt.

Hot . . . she was so fucking hot. Had he ever seen her in denim? He didn't think so.

"Hey." She snuck up on him while his brain was processing her ass in jeans and kissed him quickly. "I could have met you downstairs."

"That wasn't how I was raised."

She walked back toward her room. "Just need to grab my bag."

Did those hips swing as she walked away?

Damn, he was in trouble.

Danny slapped his arm. "Hey, that's my sister."

Reed turned toward him, arms at his side. "You might as well deck me now."

Lori's brother burst out laughing.

"No, really."

The laughter grew until Lori walked back into the room. "Did I miss something?"

Danny grabbed his sister's suitcase, shoved it in Reed's hand. "Go, kids. Have a good time . . . and remember"—he waved a hand in the air between the two of them—"use those condoms. Safe sex is the only sex to have."

Lori walked out the door first.

Before Danny shut the door, Reed turned. "Seriously, dude. One free punch, anytime."

Instead of a fist, Danny slammed the door in his face; laughter followed them down the hall.

The hotel was on the coast in Santa Barbara, just a couple of hours north. The longer they drove, the more the muscles in her back started to relax. "I love the city," she said out of nowhere. "But I need to escape it a couple times a month or I go crazy."

"Have you ever considered moving?"

Had she? Not really. "It fits my lifestyle right now."

"Santa Monica is a little of both. Just city enough, with an ocean to calm your nerves when you need to just look at nothing."

"So why Santa Barbara? Why not just take me to your place?"

"I'm a slob."

"You are not."

"I am. Never make my bed, don't have a maid."

Okay, she did have a maid service. But in her defense, she was almost never home, and when she was, the last thing she wanted to do was push a vacuum.

"My bathroom is never a mess after you leave, and you don't leave the seat up."

"My mother and sisters drilled that in."

"Good for them. Danny is awful."

Reed glanced at her, returned his eyes to the road up the coast. "I'm glad he stuck around."

"He's annoying."

"You love it."

"I'm tolerating it. He needs to move on soon or we're going to be at each other's throats. I don't like being in the position of judging his lifestyle."

"Then don't."

"If he wasn't living with me, I wouldn't. But when you're faced with a dreamer, day in and day out, when you've somehow been delivered the practical gene, it's not possible."

"Your brother is a good guy."

"I couldn't agree more. He wouldn't hurt a flea if he knew it was in pain. He opens doors for women, says thank you to the waiter . . . and tells old women how beautiful they are."

"Sounds perfect." Reed's voice held a slight edge.

"He isn't employed, Reed, a nonstarter. His idea of the future is whether he can afford the tacos at the local shack or the one-buck menu at McDonald's. It was cute in college, which, by the way, he has been to and graduated with a freakin' degree in engineering. But no, that was a way to get through school. I swear he grew up in the wrong era. Should have been a hippie in the sixties."

"Does he do drugs?"

"A little pot, I think. Not that often. At least not since he's been in LA."

Reed bobbed his head as he changed lanes to get around a slow-moving car. "I get it. You're good for him."

"How so?"

"Look at you. Successful, driven, you have your life together . . . friends to anchor you. Keep showing him that happiness and he might want it for himself."

She hadn't thought about it that way. "He does seem a little different this time."

"This time?"

"He shows up every couple of years for a few weeks . . . flitters in the guest room, on the couch . . . then leaves with a note saying he'll see me for turkey. Not this time."

"Because he hasn't left?"

"Because I don't think he's sticking around waiting for the next great whatever to pull him away." And it wasn't like he was asking her for money or anything. He just stuck around. Yeah, he ate her food, but it wasn't like a teenage kid that left the cupboard with nothing but crumbs.

"He's sticking around because he cares, Lori."

She wanted to blow him off.

"Is that so hard to believe?"

"That he cares? He's my brother, he's prewired to care."

"Yeah, but this is beyond a family obligation. This is when it counts."

Her vision tunneled when she turned her eyes on him.

"Are you going to jump on the *you need a bodyguard* bandwagon again?"

"You do."

"Let's change the subject . . . oh, I have one. Have you ever used a dating app?"

"No." His answer was too quick.

"Yes, you have."

Reed didn't meet her gaze.

"There is nothing to be embarrassed about. Lots of people use them."

"A friend of mine asked me to sign up to see if his girlfriend was cheating on him."

"Was she?"

"Yes."

She paused. "What did he do?"

"He dumped her."

"While you were on the app, did you go out with anyone on it?"

"Lori?"

"Yeah?"

"You need a bodyguard."

She groaned and pointed out the window. "Oh, look . . . a unicorn."

Early fall in Santa Barbara had some of the best weather in the country. Not only was it still warm during the days, but the nights didn't get the memo that fall was descending upon them.

The resort hotel Reed arranged had every amenity a couple seeking an evening away from home could want. An open-air lobby greeted them with massive circular tables with floral arrangements that towered five feet. The warm breeze off the Pacific and fresh scent of the ocean calmed Lori's nerves after the drive.

They walked through manicured gardens and meandering pathways flanked by palm trees and lush green shrubs and the ever-prevalent bougainvillea until they arrived at their oceanfront suite. They walked through Spanish-influenced arched stucco columns and heavy wooden doors into luxury.

"This is stunning," Lori exclaimed as she dropped her purse on the bed and crossed to the French doors that opened onto a balcony. Once outside, she rested her hands on the railing, closed her eyes, and let the sun drench her face.

Behind her, Reed dealt with the bellman who helped them with their bags.

Reed moved behind her, circled his arms around her waist, and rested his head on her shoulder. "I don't think I'll ever look at the water again and not think of you," he confessed.

Her insides did one of those girlie things that happened when someone you cared about took your relationship to another level with just a few words.

"Me either."

His chest rose and fell on her back. "Sometimes I wish we could just stop everything going on around us for a moment in time."

"Like now?" she asked.

"Yeah, like this exact moment."

Only he didn't pause, and the clock kept

ticking. "Pool, beach, spa? What is your pleasure, Counselor?"

"How about some pool time overlooking the ocean?"

"Perfect, all the love of the ocean without the sand." He kissed the side of her head and moved back into the room.

She watched him walk away. Something was bothering him that he wasn't talking about. By the end of their stay, she would flat-out ask him if he didn't fess up.

They swam, soaked up the sun, had a couple of umbrella filled froufrou drinks, and even managed to talk politics without so much as a cross word. They took their time showering together, concentrating on all the good parts.

By the time they sat down to dinner at the five-star restaurant the resort offered, Lori felt as if she'd been there for a couple of days instead of a handful of hours. "I really needed this," she said for the hundredth time since they arrived.

"Every weekend should be spent on vacation," he told her.

"But when would you go to the store and finish all those necessary chores you put off all week long?"

They sat drinking wine as the sun sizzled over the ocean. And just when she thought there might be a cooler breeze than expected, one of the waiters arrived to turn on the patio heater to ensure they were comfortable. “Okay, how about every other weekend on vacation?”

“I like it. There should be a bill on the congressional floor mandating it. Imagine how productive the workplace would be if weekends were really days that you spent *off?*”

Their storybook night, complete with making love with the moonlight shining in the open French doors, ended too soon. As she drifted to sleep in Reed’s arms, she decided that whatever was bothering him would wait until breakfast. Maybe a restful night would take away his edge.

Chapter Twenty-Seven

All night he'd wanted to confess. The trip was his way of taking her miles from home, where she couldn't run off, where she had to listen to his story and how he'd managed to get where he was. And somewhere, in all his fucked-upness, he would convince her he wasn't a bad guy.

Only now, she was sound asleep in his arms, and he was staring out the open window, letting the sound of the ocean keep him company.

He'd tell her in the morning.

Slowly, his body sank into the mattress and his mind numbed enough to sleep.

A buzzing woke him hours later when the sun started to brighten the morning sky. Half-awake, he recognized his cell phone was the source of his alarm. Because the ring had been silenced, the only sound was the buzz and vibration on the bedside table. He rolled over, planning on ignoring it and enjoying the warm body snuggled next to his, when the thing went off again. He flung his arm out, grasped the thing, and took a quick look at the flash on his screen.

Eyes blurry with sleep, he had to squint at the picture text that came through. When it came into focus, his resting heart rate shot high.

A picture of his office wall, the one hidden behind a double-framed map, was open wide and staring at him. He touched the power switch to blank the screen of his phone and looked down at Lori, who was still fast asleep.

Careful not to wake her, he slipped from the bed, put on his boxers, and walked outside. He opened the picture again and took a better look. It was his office, his notes. He checked the number on the phone. It was local, but no one he knew.

Who is this? He sent the unknown intruder a text.

> Have you heard of honor among thieves, Reed?

He waited, not completely sure who played this game. It does appear that this is much bigger than one widow.

> Sasha.
> I'm flattered. I'll be in touch.

He didn't bother to see if she'd text him again.

The cold space beside her when she expected something different woke her. Lori reached out, didn't find Reed, and opened her eyes to see him sitting beyond the doors as the sun rose.

He tapped his cell phone against his thigh in silence.

She tucked her hand under her head and watched him without words.

The weight of her stare turned his head.

"You're up early," she told him.

"Did I wake you?" His words were polite. His tone was off.

"I think it was the silence."

He picked himself up off the chair and moved into the room. "I can order coffee." He crossed to the phone on the small desk.

"I'm okay right now."

His hand hesitated over the phone.

"What's wrong, Reed?" she finally asked.

He hung his head between his shoulders. "I don't want to do this," he muttered.

Lori repositioned her head. "Do what?"

"This," he looked at her. "Have this conversation."

"Whatever it is, we can talk about it."

He shook his head, looked out the door as he sat on the edge of the bed. "I can't stand the thought of you hating me."

Air caught in her lungs, and she sat up in the bed, pulled the sheets up over her chest. "Why would I hate you?" Her mind scrambled for a reason. "Is there someone else? We never talked about being exclusive, if there is . . ."

"No. No." He still didn't look at her.

"Then what?"

He pulled in a long slow breath. "I was a cop. Joined the academy as soon as I turned twenty-one."

"Okay. Why . . ." Her mind scrambled, trying to think why this was an issue. "Did you commit a crime and get thrown off the force?" And even if he had, he didn't appear to be that man now.

"Nothing like that. I left." He rubbed his cheek. The scar she'd noticed when they first met came into view. She didn't even see it anymore. Never had she asked about it.

"What does this have to do with today?" She pulled her knees into her chest and wrapped her arms around them.

He closed his eyes. "I didn't meet you by accident."

Her pulse started a rapid tap, and the smile she'd been keeping on her face slowly faded.

"I was on that ship in Barcelona to follow you and the women you were with."

Lori dropped her eyes from his back and looked everywhere but at him. "Why?"

"I was hired by a private party to conduct an investigation."

"You're a PI?"

He nodded.

She pushed her back up against the headboard. "Hired to follow me?"

"Yes, kinda."

"Kinda? Who hired you?"

He turned his head and winced. "That isn't important."

"The hell it isn't. Did Petrov—"

"No! It wasn't him."

Who? For what reason? Lori looked down at herself. Naked under the covers after one of the most romantic nights she'd ever had in her life. "You seduced me to gain information?"

He reached for her, but she pulled away without him touching her.

"I didn't plan this."

Her jaw dropped. "You didn't *plan* this. That makes it okay?"

The hair on her head stood up, and her breath came in short pants as the dream she'd been living in crushed around her.

"This isn't anywhere close to okay."

Her nose flared. "Did you get the information you needed?"

He didn't answer her question with words, but his eyes betrayed him.

"Oh, God . . ." Hysteria sat so close to the surface she felt it snapping her sanity. "What was so valuable that you had to screw me to get it?"

"It was never like that." He reached for her again.

Taking the sheet with her, she scrambled out

of bed, forcing him to move so she could wrap it around her.

God, she was so stupid. There were no such things as coincidences. Wasn't that her motto in court, in her life?

"Why are you telling me this now? Why not just break it off and move on?"

"Because I care about you."

She shook her head and forced her tears back. "Don't say that. You have no right," she yelled. "Who hired you, Reed?"

"It's safer if I don't tell you."

She took one step toward him, hand in the air. "You no longer have the right to care about my safety." She spun around, held the sheet up as she grabbed her clothes off the floor.

"Listen to me," he said as he moved around her.

She backed away.

"There is someone else following you."

"What?"

"And I think she's working for Petrov. You need a bodyguard, Lori."

Her chest rose and fell so fast she was seeing stars. "How long have you known this?"

Guilt hit his face and stuck.

"How long, Reed?" She asked in short, staccato words.

"France."

She nearly dropped the sheet as she reached for her head. "France?" Tears started to fall.

"I'm sorry, Lori. Just listen to me, I can explain—"

She turned on him, marched into his space, and pulled her shoulders back. "Don't." Her finger poked him hard in the chest, and then she fisted her hand and pulled it to her mouth to keep from screaming.

"You were a job, but you've turned into—"

She pushed him away. "Fool me once . . ." She glared at him. "Once."

The sheet fell to the floor and she pulled on her clothes.

Reed called her name as she scrambled around the room, collecting her things. "Lori."

Raw tears ran down her cheeks.

"I'll take you home."

She didn't honor his suggestion with a response as she all but ran out the door.

At the desk of the hotel, the smile on the woman's face fell when Lori ran toward her. "I need the hotel car."

"Right away, Miss."

"To drive me to LA."

The woman looked around. "It's for local—"

Lori swung her purse on the counter. "It's an emergency." She opened her wallet, pulled five one-hundred-dollar bills from a hidden compartment, and put them on the desk. She looked behind her to see Reed running toward her with his bag.

“Please.”

Without words, the woman walked her outside and to the back of the town car.

Once the car pulled away, she heard Reed yelling her name.

Chapter Twenty-Eight

Reed's first thought was to call Danny, but then he switched gears.

He picked up speed on the freeway in an effort to catch up to the black sedan taking Lori home. The desk and valet at the hotel delayed him long enough to give Lori a fifteen-minute head start.

The phone through the system in his Jeep rang several times before Cooper picked up.

"Cooper."

"It's Reed. I need you to be at Lori's when she gets there."

"Is she okay?" The tone in Cooper's voice said he was waking up.

"No. I fucked up. She's not thinking straight."

"What the—"

"I'm sure you'll hear the details, but what you need to know is she is still being watched. Petrov has a woman following her. Five seven, looks like a Russian movie star, complete with an accent, although she spoke at least two languages. Who knows how many more. So she might be able to disguise herself."

"How do you know all this?"

"Not important. Just be there, Cooper. Lori should be back home within the hour. If she won't let you in her place, park yourself in the hall."

Reed disconnected the call and weaved through the light early Sunday traffic.

Twenty minutes into his drive, he spotted the sedan and slowed down.

He kept pace several cars behind, not that he cared if Lori knew he followed her home. Once they hit the city, he pulled in closer, running red lights to keep up.

The driver pulled into the turnaround at Lori's building and opened the door.

She'd put on sunglasses, even though the sky was littered with low clouds and fog.

He'd crushed her.

Lori lifted her head and stared directly at his car, parked on the opposite side of the street. She paused, lifted her chin, and walked away.

Reed's grip on the steering wheel turned his knuckles white.

He had no one to blame but himself, but the need to punch out his frustration overwhelmed him. It was times like this he wished he'd taken up boxing. He could throw himself into a ring and let someone beat the crap out of him, just because he deserved it.

Tears overwhelmed her until she hit Ventura. That's when she noticed Reed lagging behind. She had considered asking the driver to speed up, but to what end? Reed knew where she lived. He knew where she worked, and he knew her secrets.

Once inside the safety of her home, she slammed the door, closed her eyes, and leaned against it. She slid down the door until she was sitting on the floor, her knees to her chest, and cried.

How stupid. How could she be so stupid? They met at a bar on a cruise ship. She remembered their first look, the first flirt. He said he'd looked at the bill to capture her name and follow her around. Even joked that he was stalking her.

She fisted her hair in her hands as she held her head. Everything felt so normal, completely by chance.

But it was all fabricated.

Everything.

"Lori?"

She lifted swollen eyes toward Danny. Cooper stood at his side.

"What are you doing here?" she managed to ask.

"Reed called me."

She forced her jaw to stay closed and squeezed her eyes shut, as if that alone would erase him from her mind. She scrambled to her feet, leaving her purse, which had spilled all over the floor, and her suitcase where she'd dropped them, and stormed to her bedroom.

Inside, she wiped her tears away with the back

of her hand and smelled him. The scent of Reed was still on her skin.

"Damn it."

The blouse she wore was silk, one of her favorites. She yanked it from her back and marched into her bathroom. There, she filled her wastebasket with the clothes she wore. She stood under the hot stream of water until it turned cold, all the while thinking of everything that had happened since she met Reed. They'd made love in her shower, on the counter in the kitchen, against the damn front door. Never again. She vowed to herself that she'd never again allow a man to enter her personal space. Burning the clothes she'd been wearing when he used her for the last time was easy, cheap, but moving wasn't an option.

She tossed on an old shirt and panties and crawled under her sheets. Thankfully, her cleaning service had been there since Reed visited last. The thought had crossed her mind that she needed to make some calls, make sure Sam was aware that Alliance was compromised. She needed to order their private investigator to find out who Reed Barlow really was. If that was even his name. Had she ever seen anything with his identification on it? There were photo IDs on the ship, but she couldn't say for sure she ever glanced at his. They charged things to their rooms, didn't need credit cards. When they went out, he paid in cash. No ID needed. And no need for a waiter to thank a Mr. Barlow.

A soft knock on the door stopped her stream of thoughts.

"Go away."

"It's Avery."

A tiny click and the door opened. Without asking, Avery walked in and crawled up on the bed beside her.

Those damn tears returned. "He lied to me."

Without asking questions, Avery opened her arms and Lori crawled in. "Just cry," Avery encouraged her. "We'll figure out how to kick his ass later."

Lori hiccupped and sobbed.

In a biometric safe under the back seat in Reed's Jeep was his gun. He removed it and tucked it into his waistband before entering his apartment.

He considered the lock on the door, one he had reinforced when he'd moved in but knew it wouldn't take him a full minute to break into. A twist of the handle and sure enough, it was unlocked. No reason for Sasha to cover her tracks when she'd already admitted by photograph that she'd been inside.

Still, he crept into his own place with his 9 mm poised. It was time to stop being a PI and start being a cop. He pushed the door open, waited, and swung in. No one pointed a gun back. Still, he moved slowly, room by room, closet by closet, under the bed.

Nothing.

He returned to the living room, closed the door with his foot, and set his weapon on his kitchen table. The room looked relatively normal with one exception.

A bottle of champagne sat on the counter, open, with a wineglass carrying some of the contents of the bottle.

Red lipstick stained the rim of the glass.

Beside that was a burner cell phone.

Sasha.

Not only had the woman broken into his home, but she drank the champagne he'd forgotten to take with him up to Santa Barbara. And she'd sent him the message from his kitchen.

He left the glass and phone alone with the intention of having them dusted for prints. He still had friends in the department who owed him a favor or two.

In his office, the out of place element was his hidden wall. She'd left his camouflage wide open.

He'd modeled his evidence wall after the one in the police station from when he was on the force. They'd post pictures, notes, evidence, and where it was collected like a road map. Every time he looked at it, another piece fell into place.

It had worked for him then, and it worked now.

Except now he was solo and only a Home Depot door lock and a grumpy next-door neighbor protected his place when Reed wasn't there.

He grabbed the metal trash can by his desk, turned it upside down on the floor, and started ripping apart his evidence.

Lesson learned.

One at a time, he fed the contents of the board into his shredder until it was nothing but a memory and a snapshot on his phone. He didn't need anyone else happening upon what he'd learned.

When finished, he looked around the room. She'd planted bugs. He would have.

He moved to his bedroom, emptied his duffel bag, and proceeded to fill it with clothing to last a few days.

Back in his office, he fished out cash, a new passport, new ID, and a new credit card from a hidden compartment in his filing cabinet. Outside of the slight felony of having identification that wasn't truly his, he wasn't a criminal, just pushing the legal envelope. Or so he justified to himself. He did understand the streets and what he needed to blend, however.

And right now Reed Barlow needed to disappear to do everything he could to keep Lori safe.

He placed a holster on his shoulder, shoved extra clips in his bag. He'd call Jenkins to come over and retrieve the wineglass and Sasha's cell.

He made it to the end of the hall when two men who looked like they lived at the gym stopped him.

"Good morning, Reed." The man who greeted him chewed gum and smiled.

"Do I know you?" He calculated how fast he could draw his weapon and what the likelihood was that the men in front of him weren't carrying.

Slim to no way in hell.

"You called my employee this morning." The second man was all business.

Cooper.

His pulse slowed slightly. Lori's people, not Petrov's.

"Going somewhere?" Mr. Smiles asked.

"My place is compromised," he said.

Mr. Serious nodded toward the stairs.

Without a choice, Reed followed. He wouldn't be able to take them both, so he wasn't going to try. If Cooper was any indication of the kind of men these two were, he wasn't at risk of ending up in cement shoes in the bottom of the ocean.

Inside the parking garage, Mr. Smiles relieved Reed's shoulder of his bag and shoved it into the back of a blacked out sedan. The second man lifted his hand, palm up.

Reed hated being stripped.

He slowly removed the gun at his side and handed it over.

Mr. Serious dropped the clip and removed the round from the chamber before handing it to Mr. Smiles.

Once again, he held out his hand.

"Fuck." Frustrated that he was being disarmed piece by piece, Reed shifted from one leg to another.

Mr. Serious wiggled his fingers.

Reed removed a smaller weapon from his left leg, one California didn't like people to own.

The process was repeated for all three of Reed's guns and one pocketknife.

Mr. Smiles winked before settling in the driver's seat while Mr. Serious slid along the back seat beside Reed.

"Where are we going?" Reed asked once they pulled onto the street.

"Someplace *less* compromised."

Chapter Twenty-Nine

Once Lori stopped crying, Avery made her get dressed so she could drag her away from her condo. Cooper shadowed them while a new set of men moved around her space, searching for more bugs.

This time placed by Reed.

Sam met them with bags of food from a local restaurant and several bottles of wine.

Avery Ubered in ice cream and chocolate.

With all the breakup food covered, the three of them sat around Avery's living room with music playing in the background.

Sam was the hardest to look at. Lori trusted the wrong man, and now everything the woman had worked for was at risk.

"I'm so sorry, Sam."

Fit for the occasion in yoga pants and a big sweatshirt, Sam crossed her legs under her. "Okay . . . you've said that, now let that go. Whatever Reed did, or is doing, isn't on you."

"I trusted him."

"We all trusted him," Avery said from her kitchen, where she gathered dishes for their lunch/dinner/whatever meal it was when you only ate once in a day and planned to be pissing drunk by rush hour.

"No more sorry, no more self-blame, got it?" Sam used her mom voice.

"Got it." She'd just have to say all that to herself.

Avery placed the plates on the coffee table and started to open boxes of spicy Thai food.

"What happened?" Sam finally asked.

"He took me to Santa Barbara to break it off."

"Douche," Avery muttered.

"He's not a data processing anything. Unless you call a spy someone who process data."

"Reed's a spy?" Avery stopped dishing up the noodles.

"He said he used to be a cop, and now he's a PI." Lori watched Sam for her reaction.

"Cooper hinted that he didn't think Reed was in any field that required hours at a desk," Sam said.

"We should have listened. He was sent to Barcelona to gain information about me. About us."

"About Alliance."

Lori nodded.

Avery started dishing stuff up again. "No wonder he was all serious when Trina was drugged."

"All an act," Lori said.

"I don't know, he was concerned."

"He told me that someone was following me

ever since our stop in France. Probably the entire time we were on the ship."

"Miguel? Cuz that guy—"

"He said it was a woman," Lori told her.

"Did he give you a name?" Sam asked.

"No, and he wouldn't tell me who hired him either, or why."

"So what did he tell you?" Sam asked.

"Just that he was hired to find information about all of us. And that he thought the woman following us was one of Petrov's hired hands. That I was still in danger."

Lori looked across the room to where Cooper attempted to blend with the wall. She knew he was listening. Which was fine. All the information Lori had would get back to the Alliance security team anyway.

"He knows about Alliance, Sam."

"You told him?" Sam asked.

God, if she could take back the pillow talk after all the sex that night. "I was discussing a new client whose husband is beating her up for sport, and how if we'd done a character profile and background check, we would have caught how screwed up this man is. Next thing I know we're talking about Trina."

"It wasn't like we didn't all talk a little about our lives when we were in Europe," Avery reminded her.

"I know. The night he and I were talking about

Trina, he had this look on his face . . . like someone watching a movie and finally figuring out all the holes in the story. I should have realized then what he was up to."

"What did you say about Trina's marriage?" Sam asked.

"Just that we'd done all the background checks and Fedor slipped through. He figured out the rest. I didn't confirm or deny any of his conclusions about Shannon or you," Lori told Avery.

"Hey, I don't care. Bernie would probably be fine with the world finding out."

"Paul won't," Sam said.

Lori squeezed her eyes shut. "I screwed up."

"Enough, Lori. He's the private investigator. He knew enough of the pieces to draw the information from you." Sam reached over and grabbed an unopened bottle of wine. "Now, let's start at the beginning, everything you can think of, both of you, about what Reed overheard, and what he knows. I need to know which clients are at risk."

Instead of some dark corner in a warehouse, Mr. Smiles and Mr. Serious pulled into the driveway of a simple suburban house in Tarzana. They entered the house after driving into the garage. Mr. Smiles disengaged a house alarm and went around the kitchen, turning on lights.

Reed knew heavy surveillance when he saw it. Cameras were in the ceiling, his guess was microphones captured the conversation. It was a kinder version of an interrogation room. He wondered if there was a double mirror somewhere with someone behind it.

Mr. Serious's phone rang, and he moved into a living room to answer it.

"Sit," Smiles told him.

Part of the other man's conversation drifted into the room.

Smiles turned to the refrigerator and removed a soda. "I'd offer you something, but this really isn't a social call."

Reed huffed. "I took you as the good cop."

"Ah, c'mon. We're both good. It isn't like we forced you to come with us."

Mr. Serious returned, leaned against a counter, and crossed his arms over his chest. "Reed Barlow doesn't exist," he said.

"Sure he does, he just has a different name."

Smiles turned a chair around and straddled it. "What's your name?"

Reed hesitated.

"I'll make it easy." Smiles lifted his hand across the table. "I'm Rick, and this charmer is Neil."

Reed extended his hand, and for a good fifteen seconds he and Rick shook hands in a way that would have broken bones for a mere mortal. The desire to shake out his hand to return the circulation was huge, but he squelched it. He opened his mouth and Neil spoke.

"You have one chance to get the name right."

Or what?

"Lori deserves to know who screwed her over."

Rick knew how to punch below the belt.

"Michael *Reed* Barnum."

Neil glanced at what Reed assumed was a camera and then back to him.

"Who do you work for?" Rick asked.

"Does Alliance use private investigators?" he asked, knowing full well they did.

"Alliance?" Rick played dumb.

"Fine, but how would you feel if your PIs went around blabbing about you?"

"What were you hired to find out?"

"Everything, anything."

"About Lori?"

"It started as an investigation on Shannon in an effort to find dirt on her ex."

"How did Shannon turn into an investigation on Lori?"

Reed didn't answer . . . wasn't even sure he could.

Rick looked at Neil. "This isn't going to get very far."

"I don't know either of you. For all I know you work for Petrov."

Rick lost his smile. "I should hit him just for saying that," he said to Neil.

Neil shrugged like it wouldn't matter if Rick made good on that threat or not.

• • •

"I fell hard." Lori heard the slur in her own voice. "I mean, I wasn't looking at wedding dresses, but I started to draft a prenup."

"That sounds like love for a lawyer," Sam said. She was sipping her wine, while Avery had no problem trying to keep up with Lori.

"How could I be so stupid? So many coincidences. So many things that just didn't measure up."

"Love is blind," came from Sam's logical and sober side of the room.

"Screw love. I'll just switch teams."

Avery pulled back. "Don't look at me, I like guys."

Lori felt the first real smile of the day. "He screwed me just to get information."

Avery lifted her glass in the air. "Hey, I got screwed for fifty grand."

Lori blinked. "Bastards."

Neil didn't blink. Reed was convinced the man was half robot.

The only reaction was when his phone went off.

"Yeah," came one side of the conversation. "Keep looking."

He hung up, stared at Reed. "Michael Reed Barnum, former decorated police officer. Left his badge when he and his partner, Luke Mallory, were ambushed."

"We were set up by our own guys. I couldn't trust anyone anymore, so I left."

Rick and Neil exchanged glances.

"It isn't fun when one of your own turns on you," Rick said.

"All I ever wanted to be was a cop. Private investigation seemed the next logical step."

"Which you're licensed to do," Neil said.

"I'm a pillar of honesty."

Neil pointedly looked at him.

"With a few chinks in my armor."

"Okay, someone needs to start trusting someone here or we're never going to be able to protect Lori," Rick said to Neil.

"Is she all right?" Reed asked.

Rick held up his hand, reached for his phone. "Hey. You're with them?"

He paused. "No, he's here. We're chatting." Rick laughed. "Maybe he'd like to hear that, hold on."

Rick handed over his phone.

Reed held it to his ear. Cooper spoke in a low voice. "Remind me to punch you when I see you."

"Get in line." Reed was certain one was forming.

"Yeah, there is one. Lori is pissed. And you know what they say about a woman scorned."

Reed heard voices in the background. Female voices.

"Is she okay?"

"You tell me."

The voices in the room became louder, as if he'd been put on speaker.

Lori was drunk. *"I fell hard, I mean, I wasn't looking at wedding dresses, but I started to draft a prenup."*

"That sounds like love for a lawyer." Reed didn't recognize the voice.

"How could I be so stupid? So many coincidences. So many things that just didn't measure up."

Every time Lori spoke, he cringed.

"Love is blind."

"Screw love. I'll just switch teams."

He closed his eyes and kept listening, even though he knew she deserved her privacy.

"Don't look at me, I like guys," he heard Avery say.

"He screwed me just to get information."

"No, I didn't."

Rick took the phone from him.

It took several minutes for Reed to move his lips. "I won't tell you who hired me. They're not the ones you should worry about, anyway."

"We're listening," Rick said.

For the next hour, Reed revealed everything he could without using the senator's name. He told them about Sasha and how she was on the flight to Texas, how she was the one to watch.

"That's not her name, I'm sure. I've attempted to get into the passenger list on the cruise, but I doubt it would be of much help."

"What did Rogelio and Miguel have to do with any of this?"

Reed shrugged. "Coincidental . . . thieves. I spent an extra day in Barcelona searching for them. Their names weren't on any list, good or bad."

"Aliases."

"Right. Crime rings frequent ships like the one we were on, preying upon those first-class passengers who didn't bother bringing fake jewelry on board. The scam works well because of how few crimes on the open sea can be prosecuted. My guess is Miguel and Rogelio knew the names of the single, rich women when they boarded and targeted them."

"Just like you did," Rick said.

"My target was Shannon, and not to rip her off. I told you that."

"Which means Paul was the target."

"None of the women said a thing about the governor. I concluded that he hired a bride," Reed announced. "Lori didn't tell me that, Shannon didn't either."

"Did you tell your client?"

"No."

"Why?"

"Because it would incriminate Lori."

Rick and Neil did that silent look thing they'd been doing all afternoon.

"How so?" Rick asked.

"She represents both parties in these marriages. And although that isn't illegal, there is a question of ethics. I didn't look into individual cases, mainly because the only ones I can say are part of this deal were those of Avery and her husband, Trina and the dead guy, and Shannon and Paul. I don't have to tell you both how tight your security is. I'm not ashamed to say I tried a few hacks to get into her files, but it wasn't possible. And before you damn me for that, I didn't care about the information I'd find, I wasn't going to use it anyway. I wanted to know how safe Lori was being."

"She's safe."

"I found that out. But what I would have looked for was loopholes. Reasons for the bar to go after her."

They did that silent look thing again.

"And you found . . . ?"

"I'm not a paralegal, but one thing that stuck out was timing. If these contracts are signed back-to-back, where either party hasn't had time to look it over, or seek other counsel, they could be voided. In cases like Avery, chances are neither party would consider turning back on their contract, but in cases like Trina . . . who knows what Petrov would do with the information."

He paused.

"And since all of the marriages and divorces are public record, as well as their settlement agreements, Lori's case files would blow up."

"And those cases would be brought into question," Rick said to Neil.

"I'm guessing anyone willing to part with several million dollars for a facade doesn't want that information public."

"I need to call Blake," was the only thing Neil said all afternoon.

"And I need to find Sasha," Reed said. "If she's working with Petrov and she's managed to put any of this together, she's going to try and gather evidence."

Rick stood, turned the chair back around, and pushed it under the table. "I'll go with you."

"I work alone."

Rick pointed to his chest. "Oh, I'm not your partner. I'm flattered, but thank you."

"I'm serious."

Rick lost his smile for all of two seconds. "Me too. You see, you haven't earned our trust yet. And until you do, you and I just became besties."

"I told you everything I know."

Neil had already left the kitchen with the phone to his ear.

Rick crossed to a kitchen drawer, opened it, and removed a pistol and a magazine. He checked the chamber, seemed happy with what he saw, and holstered it at his side.

"Wait, you're not armed?"

Rick winked. "Why would I be armed?"

Reed peeked around the corner toward Neil's back. "Neither of you were armed."

Rick tossed Reed one of his guns, he caught it.

"That would be felony kidnapping."

Holy crap.

Rick returned Reed's ammo and his other weapons. "How did you know where I lived?"

Neil stepped around the corner. "Where did you place the bugs in Lori's home?"

He wanted to lie.

She was going to find out, and that hate she'd been spitting with fire in her eyes when she'd walked away was going to burn holes in him from miles away.

He gritted his teeth as he spoke. "There's a wire basket on her kitchen counter full of wine corks."

"And?"

"A tracking device in the trunk of her car. Looks like a pen."

Neil turned to talk into the phone.

"Dude, she is going to hate you."

Reed started toward the garage. "Are we going, or are you going to just stand there and remind me what a douche I am?"

Chapter Thirty

"What are we watching?"

Reed had his unwelcome partner park up the street from a mail center. "I managed to acquire a credit card number from Sasha. It was sent here."

Rick peered out the window. "What makes you think she's ever coming back?"

"She might not, but until she uses the card, it's all I have to go on."

"How often have you been sitting here?"

"Whenever I wasn't with Lori. And when I was, I had a colleague helping out."

"I thought you said you didn't like partners."

"Colleague, not a partner."

"How sure are you that she works for Petrov?"

The question made his head itch. "She knew of Petrov . . . and she knew of the person who hired me."

"So she's good at what she does."

"Yes."

"How soon will we hear from your contacts with the fingerprints?" Reed told them about the wineglass and cell phone.

"Takes a day to run through the database. The fact she had the card sent here points in the direction that she might be local."

"That was my guess, too."

Rick looked at the military-style watch on his arm, the kind that screamed waterproof, had a compass, and due to the size of the thing could probably be eaten as an MRE.

"I take it you're not the patient sort."

"I don't like sitting when I could be doing." He reached for the handle on the door.

"What are you doing?"

Rick popped the trunk, put something in his pocket, and winked as he walked past the car and into the storefront mail spot.

Twenty minutes later, he waltzed out of the building, tucked behind the steering wheel, and turned the engine over.

"Where are we going?"

"Food. I'm hungry."

"What did you do?"

Rick did a U-turn in the middle of the street and drove back the way they'd come. He removed his cell phone from his pocket and opened a screen.

Reed couldn't help but laugh. "You managed to put in a camera in only twenty minutes?"

"No, I did it in ten, but I needed to open a mailbox, and that took a few more."

"You guys are good."

"We like our toys," Rick told him.

"Who else can see this?"

"Headquarters."

"You sound like you're in the CIA."

Rick cringed. “No, thank you. I can’t stand paperwork. Private security offers us the opportunity to work without red tape.”

“How many people do you provide private security for?”

Rick snickered. “Why? Looking for a new job?”

Reed stared out the window as the world sped by and didn’t answer the question.

Late, hungover, and really happy she wasn’t due in court, Lori inched into her office with dark sunglasses covering her bloodshot eyes.

She sat in her pool of self-pity and bathed in alcohol and carbohydrates for twenty-four straight hours. Now she was determined to push the man who had all but taken over her life for months over the edge and let him go.

“Coffee,” she told Liana as she walked by the reception desk. “Nothing but emergency calls today. Reschedule my meetings. Tell them I’m ill.”

“Wow, you look like crap.”

“It’s a good thing I like you,” she said as she walked away.

It took over an hour and two cups of coffee before Lori could read one e-mail and make sense of it. She and Avery had taken the man-bashing train long and hard, while Sam had gotten off by seven in the evening to get to work on the problem. Lori would have felt guilty for pushing the problem off for an entire day if not for Sam's continued support of her plight. *We've all been there. Take a day or two, then put on those big girl panties and let's get to work.*

"Lori?" her secretary quietly called her from the door. "Sam is on the line. Should I have her call back?"

The blinking button on the phone caught her eye. "I got it."

"Good morning," Lori answered.

"How is that headache?"

"Befitting the occasion, I'm afraid."

"Lots of water."

It hurt to smile. "You didn't call to give me hangover tips."

"Right. I hope you freed up your day."

"I have."

"Good. Let's start pulling files. I need you to tell me what the time frame was between acquisitions of our payees to when they saw and signed the contracts."

Lori wrote a note. "Why?"

"It's been brought to my attention that if we had our brides and grooms signing contracts within a week or less of seeing the contracts, the agreements may come into question, since you represented both parties."

"I didn't always represent both parties."

"Then those cases don't apply. Just pull the

ones where you were the only legal counsel."

Lori saw the connection and possible problem through the fog in her brain. "Since when did you become a paralegal?"

"Someone brought this to my attention."

Lori didn't even ask. "Let me know if that someone needs a job. I'll get on this. Have you spoken with Shannon?"

"Carter has called Paul and is arranging a meeting." Carter was the preceding governor of California before Paul took office. His marriage to Eliza, Sam's right hand in Alliance before she became first lady of the state, was how Paul learned of Alliance in the first place.

"Fine, you speak with Paul, I'm calling Shannon."

"Talk soon."

Lori left a message on Shannon's cell and let her secretary know to patch the call through when she returned it.

For the next three hours, Lori pulled files and placed them in three boxes. At risk, a week or more, and second representation.

Reed was prepared to disappear for a while to find Sasha. With the intervention of Neil and Rick, that didn't pan out. Researching anything online or making calls while in his apartment, however, was out of the question. There was no way in hell Rick and his people didn't help themselves to placing bugs in his space. And until the threat against Lori was over, he was fine with it. He deserved the invasion of his privacy. He was equally sure his Jeep was on the radar. But that didn't stop him from finding the bugs and learning their capabilities.

When his phone rang at six in the morning, four hours after he'd gone to bed, he was surprised they'd given him that much time to sleep.

Only it wasn't the Rick and Neil team that called.

"You're an asshole." It was Avery.

He rubbed his eyes and sat up in bed. "I know."

"You should be castrated and strung up naked in the town square where mounds of fire ants can feed off you for months."

"Oh, wow, you've given this some thought." And now the image was stuck in his head like an earworm.

"You broke her heart."

That image hurt more.

"I know."

Avery paused.

"We're plotting your demise."

He needed coffee. "A slow and painful one, from the sound of it."

"A deserving one."

She said nothing for a moment.

"You know what really bites, Reed?"

No, but I'm sure you're going to tell me. "What?"

"We liked you. We all really liked you."

He needed Jack Daniel's in his coffee. He heard his mother's voice in his head. *If you're sorry, say it, mean it, own it, and do something about it!*

"I am sorry."

"Really?" She didn't sound convinced.

"More than you know."

"Then prove it!"

She hung up without hearing his reply.

"I will."

"How close are you?" Ruslan made each word sound like a command with the thickness of his accent.

"I've engaged. I will have what you need by the end of the week."

"Irrevocable evidence, my dear. Not gossip or speculation."

"I'm working on it. All my bait is sitting in wait until someone bites. And they will bite."

Ruslan looked out over the cold, gray skies of London. "These are not people you have the opportunity to frame twice."

"I understand that."

"Until the end of the week."

He disconnected the call as the clouds opened up and gave in to the rain. "Patience," he told himself. He'd come this far, he wasn't about to pounce without the guarantee his plan was moving forward.

“What do we have?” Sam sat across from Lori with stacks of files.

“Let’s start with the core players.”

Sam turned one of the files around. “What am I looking at?”

“Avery and Bernie. Our first contact with Avery was six months before Bernie showed up. We wrote up the prenuptial, presented it to Avery, made a couple of adjustments. No second attorney was brought in. Avery signed it two weeks after the final draft.”

“And they took two months to plan the wedding.”

“Right. So there isn’t any loophole for their agreement to be voided. Now, here is Shannon and Paul.” Lori pulled another file out, this one thicker. “No second attorney, and the agreement was signed within five days of presenting it to Shannon.”

“That’s because Shannon’s family ran in the same circles as Paul. It wasn’t a stretch that they could have known each other and fallen in love.”

“Doesn’t matter. This could be a sticky one,” Lori said. “If Shannon wanted to dispute the agreement, say she didn’t have time to properly go over it before signing it . . .”

“Shannon wouldn’t do that.”

"No, I don't think so either," Lori said. "But if she did, we would have a problem. Especially now that there is no safety net for litigation if a case like this was thrown into court."

Sam took that in and looked down at the third file. "Trina and Fedor."

"Yes. Not only were we the only representation, the agreement was signed within three days, and their marriage took place within two weeks."

"Sticky."

"Considering the payer is dead and can't deny or confirm anything if someone brought this to court. This could end up in court for years if Ruslan or Alice's surviving relatives attempt to void Alice's will based on a fraudulent marriage between Trina and Fedor." Lori's blood chilled.

Sam's lips pushed together. "What are all these?"

Lori attempted a grin. "Starting with your marriage to Blake . . . here are all the files of players we don't need to worry about. Although you and Blake were married three days after the contract was signed, you had separate attorneys."

Sam offered half a smile. "So these are good."

"Yep. And in this pile are the cases with only me on file as representation, where the contracts were signed eight days or longer from when they were presented."

"All good?"

"Yep."

Sam laid her hand over a dozen other folders. "And these?"

"At risk. Easily rectified if we were to have them re-sign or make a small change to their current contract. So, after going through the files, I have some good news and the bad news."

"I'm listening."

"The good news is, Alliance doesn't have to take the fall."

"I don't see how that's possible," Sam said.

Lori pointed to her chest. "I do. I'm the one that will be brought before the bar. An investigation will shut down my practice—"

"Absolutely not."

"We don't want Alliance blown open."

"We will lock it down tight."

Lori waved a hand at the files. "Every one of those cases are public record."

Sam picked her file out of the pile. "The only thing public about this one was my wedding." She grabbed several others. "All of these are happy marriages. As for the rest, we tackle the current cases first. Have them re-sign."

"And the others?" Lori asked.

"Nothing. Don't act guilty of anything . . . we're not. Nothing here was illegal."

"Lawyers are brought up on ethics. We seldom break the law." And that was where Lori was screwed.

"We know Petrov is after Trina . . . that is the

case we need to focus on and do our best to make sure no one ever finds out the truth behind Fedor and Trina's marriage. Carter is having lunch with Paul today."

"And Shannon made it clear she had no intention of making any further claim to Paul." Lori started to pace.

"It's only right I take the fall if it comes to—"

"Sit down, Lori. No one is going to fall."

Lori was leading with emotion, while Sam was deducing from the facts. In the back of her head, all she could think of was how none of this would have been brought up had she not gotten so close to Reed and said too much.

Chapter Thirty-One

Reed's ass had melded to his desk chair as he searched the Internet for pictures from the cruise to get an image of Sasha. Trying to find out the names of the people on the airplane he had shared with Lori en route to Texas was a waste of time. TSA had shut those things down like the locks at Fort Knox.

Pounding on Reed's front door shook him from his caffeine coma.

He reached for his gun, loaded the chamber, and slowly walked to his door.

"Put it away, Reed."

Sad that Reed had already learned the sound of Rick's voice.

He relaxed the grip on his weapon and opened the door. "What now?"

Rick ducked his head into Reed's apartment. "Dude, you need to clean up around here. Women hate slobs."

"Everyone's a critic." He opened the door wider.

Rick didn't bother walking in. "C'mon."

"Where are we going?"

"Sasha used the credit card."

Reed shook the dark away. " 'Bout time." He

ran through his apartment, turned off his computer, grabbed his cell, his keys, and put on a jacket to hide his gun.

"Where are we going?"

"Beverly Wilshire."

"She checked into a hotel? We can't be that lucky."

"She bought a drink in the hotel bar."

"Anything else?" Reed asked.

"Just the one drink, the charge batched through at midnight," Rick told him.

"So she could have been there anytime yesterday."

"She could be there right now. And since you're the only one who knows what she looks like, guess what you're going to be doing?"

"Barfly?"

"No, that's my job." Rick reached over to the glove compartment, opened it, removed an earpiece. "You're across the street."

"What if she leaves through the garage?"

Rick looked at him as if he was crazy. "Really? Name one woman who can resist shopping on Rodeo Drive?"

"Someone who doesn't have money?"

"Like that stops them."

"Fine."

So as Rick walked into the finery of the Wilshire to pretend to be some kind of businessman, complete with a copy of the *Wall Street Journal* and a laptop, Reed loitered on one of the most prestigious corners in America. The only thing he was missing was a piece of cardboard asking for change.

"Can you hear me?" Rick asked through the tiny earpiece.

"Unfortunately."

"This is a nice place. Might need to take the Mrs. here."

"You're married?"

"Best woman ever. Okay, log into the Internet."

Reed removed his phone, kept an eye on those coming and going from the hotel as he multi-tasked.

"Type this in." He rattled off a series of letters and numbers that made little sense. But once he pressed enter, Reed found himself on a secure site.

"It's asking for a password."

Rick started laughing. "The number four and the words *fire ants,* capitalize the last letters."

The earworm Avery had placed started to sing again. "Very funny."

"We thought so."

The password brought on a video from inside the hotel bar.

An elderly couple walked out of the hotel, and he immediately dismissed them.

"I'm moving you around. Let me know if anyone looks familiar."

The camera swiveled around the room. Not one patron had a feature worth remembering. "Nothing."

"Okay . . . keep the webpage open but save your battery. I'll clue you in when someone new walks in."

It was Reed's turn to laugh. "So I stand on the corner and you act like the crazy man talking to himself in a fancy hotel."

"I'm bigger than you. People ignore crazy when you're bigger than them."

Reed couldn't argue that.

"Does this street ever close down?" Reed asked his unwanted partner through the mic.

"If you sold shoes at a grand a pair, would you close the door?"

"That's just crazy."

Reed glanced back down Rodeo Drive, his eyes landing on the storefront of Jimmy Choo.

A woman walked out carrying bags in both hands. Apparently buying one pair at a time wasn't acceptable in some circles.

He was about to look away when his eyes fell on a woman with olive skin, dark hair, big sunglasses . . . she carried herself with poise, her head just a little higher than everyone around her.

"I think I see her."

"Where?"

"She's headed into a shoe store." Reed looked

at the opposing traffic. No way to jaywalk with so many cars buzzing by.

"Keep your distance," Rick instructed him.

"Do you think I'm new?" Reed crossed the street and blended into the crowd.

It didn't take long before she walked out. The woman looked left and right before putting her sunglasses back on.

Reed released a sigh. "Not her."

"We draft up everything. Consider every possible scenario before you file."

Lori watched as a nervous Ana Maghakian paced her office. "He won't know I'm here?"

"Not until we tell him. By then we need to have you out of the house." Preferably with some kind of restraining order, but that wasn't likely, since the wife wasn't willing to press charges.

"If I move my stuff out, he's going to notice. He's controlling."

"Most abusers are."

"I'll have to move when he's out of town."

"Do you have a house staff?"

"Yes."

"Do they have regular days off?"

"Of course."

"So which days of the week are the most quiet?"

"Tuesday is my housekeeper's day off, and the groundskeepers are there every day but Monday."

"Cook, driver?" Lori rattled off a few more occupations.

Mrs. Maghakian mapped out her household routine while Lori took notes.

It felt as if she were in the thick of a crime in progress. Then again, her life had turned into some sort of a soap opera of late.

"Do you have someplace secure you can go?" Lori asked.

"I have money. I've managed to put enough away for this day."

Lori leaned forward on her elbows. "I'm not talking about a hotel. I'm talking about someplace he can't get to you."

"What's more secure than a hotel with witnesses and cameras everywhere?"

Lori placed her pen on her notes. "What do you anticipate your husband doing when he learns that you've left him and filed for divorce?"

Sheer fear filled the other woman's face.

"We need you safe. I know people that can help you."

"I can't go to some shelter."

"Do I look like I work with a shelter?" Lori didn't mind pulling strings for women like Ana.

An hour later, with more billable hours than any psychologist, Lori managed to plant the seed that Ana would survive her current situation, she just needed the right resources, resources that Lori could recommend.

It was empowering to have something to focus on other than her life, even when she knew it wasn't the healthiest of practices to put all her energy and emotion into one client. Truth was, Lori had placed all of her focus in the whole of her practice. Yet at the end of the day, when she was alone in her bed and her brother's snores drifted to a low roar . . . Lori sensed him. Reed was embedded in the walls of the room, the scent of him in her bed, her pillows. A doctor would tell her she was imagining him there, but she'd deny the doctor's logic. Reed had left an imprint on her life that lasted beyond any relationship she'd had before him.

The knock on Reed's door at six in the morning didn't even shock him.

There was only the groggy walk to the door resulting from the dreams that had haunted him most of the night. He opened it with a push and turned his back on the man beyond.

"Coffee?" Rick asked.

"Please."

"Great idea. Get dressed."

Twenty minutes later they were parked outside of the signature green and white storefront.

Rick had put the car in park and stared at the coffee shop across the street for ten minutes before Reed asked, "What are we doing here?"

"Yesterday, while we were playing cloak-and-dagger on Rodeo Drive, your friend used her credit card here."

Reed glared at the entrance to Starbucks with a groan. "This doesn't make sense. She's too smart for this."

"How so?"

"She picked the lock on my apartment without leaving as much as a speck of evidence. The wineglass was clean, the cell phone was about as traceable as a hooker's case of VD. She's not this stupid."

"You think it's a setup?" Rick asked.

"She's leading us here. The question is why? Is she trying to distract us?"

Instead of answering, Rick made a call.

"It's me. Everything good there?"

Reed heard the male voice on the other end of the phone but couldn't make out the words.

"Alert level up one. Notify Neil." He hung up.

"Who was that?"

"Cooper."

"At Lori's."

Rick took his time answering. "Yes."

Reed focused his attention out the window. "How is she?"

He was slow to respond . . . like a metronome on a piano.

"She's spending a lot of time in her office."

"Work is good." And if she was working, she wasn't in tears over him.

As the morning drummed on, the coffee shop across the street started to take on a life of its own. It didn't help that Reed hadn't managed even one cup before being dragged out of bed.

"This is a waste," Rick said.

"She's leading us around," he agreed. "Tell you what, one pass through and we backtrack."

Rick brought his cell phone to his ear while Reed pushed out of the car to satiate his need for caffeine.

Morning coffee rush hour was in full swing.

The tables in the coffee shop had yet to fill, but the line was six customers deep. Instead of standing in line, he walked to the bathroom. Sure enough, when he left the restroom, only two patrons were waiting to make their orders.

Then he heard it . . . a voice, very deep and distinctive.

He turned.

Red hair, petite . . . a voice that should be on the radio or doing voice-overs.

Sam . . . Lori's partner.

What the hell?

He turned back toward the hall to the bathroom and dialed Rick.

It rang several times before he picked up. When he did, he answered with a demand. "Regular coffee, black."

"Sam is in here."

"What?"

“Samantha.”

“I know who Sam is . . . what is she doing in there?”

“I don’t know, but I have a feeling we should.”

Out of the corner of his eye, he noticed Sam sitting at a tucked away table. A woman sat in the opposite chair, her back to him. Not Sasha, he could see that from where he stood. This woman was a little larger, her hair a little lighter. Her profile suggested a similar gene pool to Sasha’s, but that was about it. He had a feeling he’d seen her before but couldn’t place her.

Rick walked in the front door like a bull in a china shop.

“Lordy, Lord, Lord, I could use some caffeine.” Rick said the words loud enough to get everyone’s attention in the place.

Including Sam’s.

Rick smiled at the woman in front of him and nodded with a wink.

There was a brief moment of eye contact, and Rick placed a hand to his head. “Just don’t think straight without a little coffee.”

He was next in line.

“What can I get you?”

“An ultralarge grande, verde . . . whatever it is you call your biggest cup of coffee. Just coffee. Cut off any of that froufrou stuff. I’ll let the women in my life sweet talk me, I take my coffee bitter and black.”

Reed saw the moment in Sam's body language when she switched gears. The fact that she hadn't jumped up from the chair to say hello to someone she knew said she didn't want the woman with her to know.

"Our coffee isn't bitter," the barista said.

"Well, if I leave it in my car as long as I usually do, it will be cold and bitter by the time I suck it down."

Reed stayed hidden while Sam ended the conversation with the woman.

There was a quick back-and-forth before Sam shook the woman's hand and the unknown woman turned and walked out.

Like a switch, Rick's character jolted back to baseline, and he abandoned the coffee he'd just made a show of buying in the barista's hands. "Who was that?" he asked Sam.

Reed walked around the corner, and Sam saw him for the first time, her expression going from concerned to panicked.

"A new client."

Reed stepped forward. "For Alliance?"

Sam looked between the both of them, then to Rick. "Yes."

Ah, damn . . .

Rick bolted for the door and called behind his back, "No new clients, Sam. Lock it down."

Reed followed him out the door.

Chapter Thirty-Two

"Sam's on line two, she said it's an emergency."

Lori accidentally pressed the wrong line. "Sam?"

"I'm on hold for—"

She disconnected the man on the line, pressed the next one. "Sam?"

"Lori?"

"What's happening?" Her heart was pounding. Sam didn't cry wolf, and emergencies were never mentioned unless it was.

"I need to know exactly how you met Susan Wilson."

"The new client?"

"Not a client. I scheduled a quick meeting to get a feel for her. Before I had an opportunity to really speak with her, Rick and Reed showed up."

Lori's head spun. "Reed? What was he doing with—"

"I don't have the details. They ran out the door. The woman is obviously not who she says she is. No new clients on either end until further notice. Now tell me again how this woman approached you . . ."

Once the call with Sam was over, Lori pushed away from her desk and stormed into her lobby.

Her resident loiterer glanced up, smiled, then looked back down to his book.

"Cooper!"

He snapped his eyes up.

"My office. Now."

Liana looked around as if a cloud of crazy had descended upon the office.

She stormed past her office door, waited for him to close it before she began. "Where is Reed?"

Cooper blinked a few times but didn't answer.

"I know he's with Rick . . . why?"

"You should probably have this conversation with Neil."

"Nobody *converses* with Neil. The man sits there, listens until you run out of words, and then walks off."

Cooper opened his mouth to argue.

"Cooper! Spill, now."

He bobbed his head a few times, ran a hand through his hair. "He's working with the team to find this Sasha woman."

"Working with . . ."

"Reed is the only one who knows what she looks like."

"We can't trust him," she all but shouted.

"So far . . . that's not completely true." Cooper spoke with slow, careful words.

"Oh my God . . . have you ever heard the phrase, 'fool me once, shame on you'?"

"Yes, but—"

"No buts. He's a lying piece of dirt. He bugged my home. Tracked my car." *Broke my heart.*

"He did all those things. You're right. However." He paused.

Lori spun around, marched to the window as if it offered some sort of sanity.

"Neil and Rick think he can be trusted."

"Idiots."

They lost her.

Reed ran after her while Rick jumped into the car. They didn't make it two blocks before she was swallowed in a sea of people.

Rick drove slowly along the parked cars on the busy street with his window rolled down. "Anything?" he yelled.

"No." Both hands on his head, Reed spun in circles.

"Was that Sasha?"

"No."

Several cars were attempting to get around Rick, and honked and shouted as they weaved around them.

Reed gave up and got into the car.

They drove around the block several times.

"Which means Sasha is leading us to this woman."

"A woman who now knows our faces."

Rick tapped his hands on the steering wheel. "I

don't think that's the point. We know her now."

"And if she was attempting to be one of those Alliance brides to get on the inside . . ."

"Yeah," Rick said. "That's my thought."

"So either Sasha doesn't want the competition or . . ."

"Or she's helping us out."

"And if that's the case, then *this* was the woman we needed to be on the lookout for yesterday."

Rick muttered a curse under his breath, pulled an illegal U-turn, and made his way to the Beverly Wilshire.

They left the car with the valet and split ways when they entered the lobby. "You watch the elevators, I'll check the garage."

Reed took his place against a wall. With each ding of the elevator bell, his pulse hitched up a notch.

Ten minutes later, Rick sent a text. Not in the garage. Sweeping the common rooms.

With each click of the second hand on his watch, he knew they'd missed her.

His phone rang.

Unknown number.

"This is Reed."

"She's already gone."

"Sasha." He spun in a circle and took in the people in the lobby. "Who is she?"

"That's irrelevant. You've made her. She won't be back."

"Why are you helping us?"

"Consider it a professional courtesy."

"One you'd like payment for in the future?" He knew how this worked.

"You're bright. Now please take that Neanderthal out of the hotel. There are more players watching than you've seen, and that poor girl doesn't need to end up dead because she failed."

"What the—"

She hung up.

Reed made a straight shot to the lobby doors, his eyes peeled for Sasha. He dialed Rick. "She's gone."

"Do you see her?"

"No. Meet you at the car."

Later, sitting in the Tarzana home, drinking much-needed coffee, Rick was all smiles.

"Why are you so happy? We lost her, both of them."

"I appreciate efficiency, and this Sasha chick . . . efficient with integrity."

"We don't know that."

"Don't we? You said yourself she was too smart to use a credit card in a bar or coffee shop. She stopped Sam from confirming Alliance, prevented someone on the inside who could potentially blackmail any number of people."

"And ruin Lori," Reed added.

"I don't think your Sasha is working with, or for, Petrov."

"I'm doubting that, too."

"Yet she has all the information she needs to headline the blackmail list."

"And she's not using it. Why?" Reed asked.

"Holding it for future use? Her own needs . . . who knows," Reed said.

"Who gains by infiltrating Alliance?" Rick asked.

"Sam and Lori need to be answering that question. They have the client list."

Rick reacted to the ding on the microwave and pulled out leftover pizza. He dropped it in the middle of the table and reached for napkins for the two of them.

"You ready to tell us who you were working for?"

Instead of giving a name, Reed took a slice and wrapped the cheese that was melting off around his finger. "You're smart. Who won when Paul and Shannon married?"

"Paul. And Shannon, in the long run."

Reed bit into his lunch. "And who lost?"

"Senator Knight." Rick lost his continual smile, chewed his pizza slowly as the information sank in. "I hate politics."

"She'll hire someone else."

Rick ate half his slice in one bite, talked around the food. "By the time she does, the girls will figure out a way to make what she finds irrelevant."

"The girls?"

"The women of Alliance."

"Lori and Sam?"

Rick laughed, swallowed his food. "Sure," he said, not really answering Reed's question.

He knew she didn't want to see him . . . or hear his voice. But that didn't mean he couldn't at least get a glimpse of her.

After he left the Tarzana home, he drove to Lori's complex and parked across the street. He wasn't there five minutes before his phone rang.

"I just need to see her," he said to whoever was calling.

"Take a picture." It was Neil.

He hung up.

Five minutes later, it rang again.

"Go away."

"Listen, creepy dude." This time it was Rick. "You're not going to get her back by spying on her."

"I'll leave once I see her."

"You have it bad."

He tossed his phone in the passenger seat after turning off the ringer.

When her car pulled into the valet, Cooper jumped out of the driver's side and turned directly toward him.

What are you going to do?

Unlike Cooper, Lori didn't seem to expect him

there and didn't notice him staring from half a block away with a pair of binoculars.

She removed her briefcase from the trunk, along with a box of what looked like homework, and the bellman took it from her.

He could smell her if he tried hard enough.

Taste her if he closed his eyes.

And when she turned and walked through the doors of her complex, and all that was left was the heat imprint of her skin, Reed closed his eyes.

Chapter Thirty-Three

"I don't have it."

Petrov slowly rubbed the edges of his fingers against the Colombian cigar. "That isn't the right answer," he said into the speakerphone.

"I need more time."

"You're out of time."

"Wasn't it I who told you about Alliance? Wasn't it I who led you to the lawyer in the first place?"

"The lawyer who is physically surrounded by security and cameras. A lawyer who has managed to tighten up one loophole after the other in less than a week. A paltry woman who is no longer the easy target you claimed she would be." The cigar snapped in his hand.

"Another week."

"Belinda, do you know what I do to people who disappoint me?"

"These things take time."

"Four days."

"Petrov!"

"Four. Days." He ended the call and rang for his help.

"She's a loose end. Take her out in three days, sooner if she makes contact."

A half nod and his guard backed out of the room.

Petrov looked at the broken cigar in his hand before crushing it inside his fist.

All week long her head was buried in work. The evenings ended late, without so much as a skip through the Internet for a few minutes of mindless nothing. But Friday evening was cloaked in a lack of purpose. She had nothing to occupy her mind. At Sam's insistence, Lori, Avery, Shannon, and Cooper boarded the Harrison jet and flew to Texas, where they met Trina at the airport.

Fall snapped the heat index into submission, making the transition from the dry heat of California more bearable.

Lori greeted Trina with a hug. "It would have been easier had we sent for you."

"But not better," she replied.

Shannon stepped in for a hug. "You look great."

"Texas agrees with me, who knew?"

"Ladies?" Cooper flanked them, while Trina's fulltime bodyguard walked in front.

They piled into the back of a Suburban and instantly started catching up.

"How is the oil business?" Shannon asked.

"There is so much to learn. It's like school, only no one is grading me."

"And the cowboys?" Leave it to Avery to ask about the men.

"They grow those here like trees."

Avery did a little chair dance.

Shannon laughed.

"Leave me out of that," Lori demanded.

Cooper finished with the luggage and took the front passenger seat before they left the airport.

"I'm nixing anything with a penis."

Carl cleared his throat from the driver's seat.

"Present company excluded," Shannon said for her.

"We didn't hear anything, ma'am."

"How is all *that?*" Trina summed up the entire Reed fiasco with one overused word. *That!*

"Reed's an asshat," Avery announced.

Trina shook her head. "I don't get it."

"There isn't any denying the facts. Reed purposely infiltrated the compound and gathered top secret information to use against us."

Trina turned to Avery, concern in her eyes.

"Don't look at me, I think she's been binge watching *Mission Impossible* episodes."

"Am I wrong?" Lori asked.

Shannon leaned forward from the very back seat. "But he didn't *use* the information."

"You're defending him? His target was you."

"I'm not defending. I'm pointing out the facts. You're the lawyer and facts are your thing."

"How about the fact that he slept with me to get information?"

The car grew silent.

Trina, who hadn't engaged in any of the previous Reed bashing episodes, said, "He didn't use the information."

"That isn't the point!" she snapped. "Whose side are you on?"

"Yours," Trina quickly said.

"First Wives Club or bust," Avery chimed in.

"Girl power," was Shannon's reply.

They all sat in silence.

Then, from the front seat, Cooper snickered. "I kissed my neighbor's best friend just to get the other girl's number."

"How did that work out?" Carl asked.

"Ended up taking the best friend to prom."

Lori rolled her eyes. "Et tu, Brute?"

"I don't like the quiet."

Reed did a double take to make sure he saw who said those words.

Yep, Neil.

"Says the man of so many words," Rick teased.

"He's plotting something."

"That's two sentences in less than a minute. You feeling okay?" Reed asked, his words dripping with sarcasm.

Neil stopped him with a stare.

"I say we send somebody in."

"Do you have a death wish? Petrov doesn't play by any rules," Reed said.

"He has a point, Neil."

"We sit and do nothing?"

"Lori's spontaneous trip this weekend can be one of many to keep her out of harm's way."

Reed looked up. "Where . . . ah, where did she go?" God, he hated being on the outside of her life.

Neil and Rick exchanged words with their eyes.

"Fine. Is she okay?"

Another pass of body language.

"Any more from Sasha?" Rick asked.

"That woman is mist. You feel her in the air but can't see her." Reed's only saving grace in the entire situation was that with all the contacts and toys these men had, they had yet to find Sasha either. He couldn't help but think the only reason he was still in the mix was because the woman had the propensity to contact him. "You can bet one thing about her. She's the nail in Petrov's armor. If he learns of her, he'll either use her for his own gain or eliminate her."

"You think she has something on Petrov?" Rick asked.

"Not sure about that, but my guess is she has information he wants."

And no matter what Reed thought of the woman, she didn't deserve to die.

"My guess is she knows that."

"Hence the mist," Reed said. "Much as I want to find the woman, I'm afraid that will just lead

Petrov to her. And my karma can't take any more women hating me."

He was pretty sure Neil cracked a smile.

It was brief.

Rick looked at his watch. "Don't you have somewhere to be?" he asked Neil.

His eyes shot to the clock in the hall, he muttered something, and double-timed his step out of the house.

"What fire makes that man move so fast?" Reed asked.

"His daughter has a ballet performance this afternoon." Rick raised his hand about three feet off the ground. "Adorable. Gwen would have his nuts in a vise if he missed it for anything but life or limb."

"Gwen?" Reed asked.

"Gwen's the wife." Rick stood. "Which reminds me of mine. And as great as your company is . . . there is someone much prettier that needs my attention."

Reed was surprised they left him in the Tarzana home alone. Even if all the rooms were wired, and someone, somewhere, watched. Since he'd only really seen the downstairs, he took his time looking around. Upstairs, there was an office and two bedrooms.

The hallway walls were trimmed with black-and-white images. He recognized Sam center stage in one wedding photo, and then again in another with the same groom. "You must be Blake," he said to the image. There was a picture of a German shepherd among the photos of the people. He recognized the former governor and his wife. Neil was hard to miss, but the expression on his face was one Reed never thought he'd see. He was staring down at a runway ready blonde. "Damn, Neil. I'm impressed."

On the other wall were several different couples, a few group shots. Reed found the reason for Rick's hasty departure.

Inside the master bedroom were full color canvas images of children. From the oldest kid in their early teens to babies. This wasn't a family of blood, there were too many differences in the faces. No, this was a collection of friends.

He sat on the edge of the bed and tried to figure out which kid belonged to who. And like the old posters of hidden pictures, Reed's eyes blurred as he imagined what Lori's children would look like.

Then he woke up.

He ran his hands over his tired eyes and worked his way home. Before leaving his car, he dialed someone who wouldn't shovel shit over him, someone he could trust to give him real advice.

"Hello."

"Becca?"

"No way . . . my brother is calling me? You never call." His sister did that fast-talking thing that made his head twitch. "Wait, is everything okay? You're not sick, are you?"

"Lord, woman, you sound like Mom."

"Is it Mom?"

"Can't I just call to say hi?"

Becca paused. "Not unless you've turned over some kind of new leaf."

His sister knew him well. "I need some advice."

"Oh my God, you're sick."

"I'm not sick. Geez, paranoid much? You're the older sister, I need woman advice. Mom would just tell me I'm perfect, and if anyone knows I'm not, it's you."

"Wow . . . hold on." His sister moved the phone away, he heard the small voice of his nephew. "No, honey, it's Uncle Reed. Go help your sister clean up the Play-Doh. Okay . . . sorry."

"How are they?"

"They're great. You'd know that if you visited once in a while."

"I haven't been good company."

"Like that's ever changed," she teased. "Now what is this about a girl?"

The sobering current of his relationship with Lori spilled out, minus any incriminating details. And when he was out of words, he finished with . . . "I want her back."

Becca paused, and then laughed. "Wow. There is screwing up, and then there is what you did."

"Becca."

"Okay, all right. You need to stack the deck . . . you are going to need her friends behind you or you're not getting anywhere."

"What about her brother?"

"Please, if someone did this to Rachel, you'd tie the man up in Times Square and throw rocks at him."

The repeated image of fire ants made an unwelcome appearance.

"Fine, her friends."

"And if this woman grants you five minutes, you need to make damn sure those minutes count. This does not sound like a woman who grants second chances. You're going to have one shot, so make sure you know exactly what you're going to say to make her stick around and listen."

He could do that. "Right. You're right."

"One more thing."

"Yes?" he asked.

"Flowers die, chocolate is fattening, and jewelry is a rich man's gesture."

"I'm not a rich man."

"It might mean something, then. Could go either way."

Reed smiled at the image of his pragmatic sister sitting in a room full of Play-Doh and cookies while she delivered advice.

"Love you, Becca."

"Love you, too, pipsqueak. Good luck."

Chapter Thirty-Four

Reed answered his phone without looking at the number.

"The favors keep adding up, Reed."

He dropped the fork that was halfway to his mouth. "What the—"

"Warehouse." Sasha rattled off an address as he scrambled to find a pen. He wrote the information down on his hand.

"Is it Lori?" he asked.

"Her brother. Who all of you overestimated to be able to fend for himself." Reed's brief relief was followed by renewed panic.

"Why Danny? He doesn't know anything."

"Leverage. Desperate people do desperate things. Might wanna hurry. Petrov's men are coming for the woman holding him, but will think of him as collateral damage and take the shot without asking. Bring backup. I draw the line at killing anyone for a job."

"How many men?"

"She has two, I count three of Petrov's goons. None of these men have tasted a carb in five years."

"Stay out of the way."

"Ahh, you care."

He hung up in reply.

He walked right up to the terribly hidden camera in a vent, stared at it, and read off the address. “I don’t know what you guys are made of, but now is the time to bring it. They have Danny.”

And Reed was out the door.

His phone rang as he peeled out of the parking lot.

“Talk to me.”

“Sasha’s tip. They have Danny.”

“Who?” Neil asked.

“I’m guessing the woman Sam met with and two of her players. Minimum of three coming in to take her out.”

“And Dan?” Neil asked.

“She wants him alive. I doubt the others will care once bullets start flying.”

“We’re en route. You need to hold back.”

“The hell I will.” If something happened to Lori’s brother . . .

“Reed.”

“Bite me.”

“Fine, then at least duck.”

Lori and the girls were a tad cooked after the three-hour flight. The weekend had been exactly what she needed. Good friends, great conversation, and reflection did the job of refocusing her attitude.

They were waist deep in a conversation about the best series on Netflix when Cooper turned off the freeway after a brief conversation on his phone.

She ignored it and listened to Avery sing the praises of some fourth-dimensional world thriller based in the seventies.

"So the kid lives in the walls?" Shannon asked, trying to grasp the concept.

"No, in another dimension that parallels our world. But the thing that rules that world can seep through the walls."

Lori noticed the freeway they were on and questioned their path. "Are we dropping Shannon off first?" Even if they were, they were going the wrong direction.

"Change of plans." Cooper looked through the rearview mirror.

Lori followed his gaze, noticed a sedan close behind them.

"Are we being followed?"

"They're with us."

Both Shannon and Avery turned to see what they were talking about.

"Why?"

"There's been an incident."

Gooseflesh rose on her arms. "What kind of incident?"

"I don't have the details. I'm taking you to the safe house."

"What's going on?" Avery asked.

They pulled directly into the garage of the Tarzana home Lori had frequently visited in the early years of Alliance. More than one employee had lived in the house, and while it wasn't a traditional safe house, it was equipped with every possible monitoring and detection system available.

Cooper walked in before them, silenced the alarm, and waved them through the door.

Blackout curtains prevented anyone from seeing activity inside. The old windows had been replaced with bulletproof glass. The house was a kind of pet project for Neil and his team. They renovated from the inside out, placing sheets of metal between the walls to help stop bullets. While there had never been an actual shooting incident in the house, it had seen its fair amount of high-action drama over the years. Hence all the protection.

Cooper ran upstairs.

"What's going on, Lori?" Avery asked.

"I don't know." She had a bad feeling.

"What is this place?"

"The original headquarters of Alliance. Sam lived here before she married Blake. Eliza . . . Neil's wife, Gwen. Most of the employees have lived here at one point or another."

Cooper double-timed down the stairs, this time holding a very large, very angry looking rifle.

Avery sat down hard on the sofa. Shannon placed a hand on her shoulder.

Somewhere in the back of her head, something rang repeatedly.

"Lori, is that your phone?"

She pulled out of her daze and found her purse.

"Hello?"

"Ms. Cumberland." She didn't recognize the voice.

"Who is this?" Her question drew the attention of everyone in the room.

"I have someone here who wants to talk to you."

Air rushed into her lungs.

"Say hello . . ."

"Screw you."

"Danny?" The sound of her brother's muffled voice stopped her cold.

She heard the sound of someone hitting flesh.

"Danny!"

Cooper moved beside her and forced her to tilt the phone so he could hear the conversation.

"Yes, yes . . . I have your little brother. I'm quite sorry about his nose."

"What do you want?"

"So cooperative, perfect. All I need is a signed copy of the contract Samantha forgot to give me last week."

"A piece of paper."

"Well, that and perhaps a copy of Katrina

Petrov's file. That would be gravy. Yes, I think your brother's face can be spared further damage with the simple click of the mouse."

"I'm not at my office."

"Well then, you might want to get there quickly. You have thirty minutes." The line went dead.

Lori grabbed her purse and started toward the garage.

Cooper cut her off. "Where are you going?"

"My office. I have to go to my office."

He placed both hands on her shoulders. "No, Lori. You're not walking into a trap."

"They have Danny." Her eyes were wide, autopilot was talking, and logic wasn't entering her brain.

"And they will have Danny and not you, until we extract Danny."

"What are you talking about?" She pushed around him.

Avery ran in front of her. "Hey, *Mission Impossible* woman . . . stop and think like a lawyer."

Lights from outside lit up the living room as a car pulled into the driveway.

Shannon walked to the window and pulled back the blinds. "It's Sam."

Lori ran around the others and met Sam at the door.

"They have Danny."

She placed both hands on Lori's face. "It's being handled."

The image of Danny laughing as he joked about Thanksgiving and turkey legs brought tears to her eyes. "What do you mean *handled?*"

She pulled Lori to the couch. "Reed got a call."

"Reed? What does he have to do with—"

"Neil and Rick are on their way to get him out now."

"I don't like this," she cried.

Sam looked up. "Shannon, how about some coffee. Avery, there's food in the fridge."

Both women took the cue and left the room.

Sam ducked her head in. "Neil and Rick are going to get Danny out."

"You're sure?"

"They haven't failed yet."

"And Reed . . . where is he?"

Sam blinked a few times.

"Sam?"

"He's there, too, Lori. On our side."

Lori looked over to where Cooper stood by the window, his AR-15 held loosely in his arms.

Let them live . . . please, God, let them live.

Chapter Thirty-Five

He jumped out of the Jeep, running.

Sandwiched between a cardboard factory and a building warehousing something in the fashion industry sat the botanical warehouse Sasha identified as housing Danny. It was Sunday, and the unions did a great job of making sure work halted for the weekends. Outside of a few cars scattered around, there wasn't any outside activity.

He felt the mist known as Sasha nearby.

He practiced evasive maneuvers in an effort to not give away his position as he moved from building to building. The sporadic windows of the botanical warehouse were close to the eaves of the two-story building. None of which were accessible to him . . . or anyone else.

He swept his eyes over the rooftops and didn't see movement.

The massive door to the warehouse was open by an inch. Instead of considering that route, where he would have placed a guard if he were holding someone hostage, Reed looked for other options. The north side of the building presented itself.

Out of his wallet, he removed two pins—the click of the door being relieved from the lock sounded like a gun. He froze, fearful the sound had given away his position.

Deep breath.

Inside, the low hum of voices brought him forward.

"Say hello . . ."

"Screw you," he heard Danny say.

Reed peered around a pallet of boxes containing glass vases. The woman he'd seen at Starbucks stood in front of Danny, who was tied to a chair. Two men approximately the size of baby elephants flanked him.

"Yes, yes . . . I have your little brother. I'm quite sorry about his nose." The woman's English accent caught his ear, but her words screwed with his heart. She was talking to Lori.

The desire to point, aim, and shoot was one of the hardest things he'd ever denied himself.

He moved to another row of pallets. His eyes moved to the eaves of the building. Sasha said there were three more men.

Where are you?

"So cooperative, perfect. All I need is a signed copy of the contract Samantha forgot to give me last week." The woman's voice turned away.

At this angle Reed saw Danny's face. He had one eye open . . . and damn, that nose was going to hurt in the morning.

"Well, that and perhaps a copy of Katrina Petrov's file. That would be gravy. Yes, I think your brother's face can be spared further damage with the simple click of the mouse."

He could hear the desperation in the woman's voice.

"Well then, you might want to get there quickly. You have thirty minutes."

Movement off the west eaves of the building captured his attention.

Holy shit.

He pushed against the back of a stack of boxes, causing the glass inside to rattle.

The room stilled.

Out of the corner of his eye, he saw the woman nod in his direction.

Reed turned to remove himself from the thugs' path to find a gun pointed at his head.

He froze. The grip on his gun loosened.

"Move, asshole."

Two things calculated in his brain at the same time. The man with the gun in his hand wasn't in this for more than money, or else Reed would already be dead. Second . . . Sasha's information was wrong, and Miss Wannabe Alliance Bride was working with more than two men. In his head, he added a plus one to Miss Bride's list. Now the question was, where were Petrov's men?

The man holding a gun to his head had a repaired cleft lip . . . and the surgeon had an eyesight issue. A foot to his back had him stumbling into the center of activity, surrounded by Danny's bleeding face, two thugs, and a nervous woman with a gun.

"Well, look what we have here."

"Reed?" Danny wasn't focusing, Reed could see that by the way his eyes swam around in his head.

"That's so sweet . . . you're here to save the baby brother."

"So full of yourself." Danny's words no sooner left his mouth than one of the men beside him punched him in it to shut him up.

Mr. Cleft Lip didn't flinch when blood splattered his three-piece suit.

"Let him go," Reed told her.

"Now why would I do that?"

"One hostage is all you need." And if she untied Danny, the guy might stand a chance when the bullets started flying.

"Two is so much better."

She signaled to the other man beside Danny, who, along with Mr. Cleft Lip, moved in and grasped his hands.

Tied down equaled death . . . and Reed wasn't prepared to die.

Academy training erupted from the depths of his memory, he twisted his body, brought both hands around to capture the gun, and crashed into the man holding it. At the same time, shots fired from above and below.

The man beside him took a hit, flung back.

Reed had one linear focus.

Danny was a sitting duck at the county carnival, just waiting for someone to take the prize.

Lori's brother focused just enough to grasp the situation and pushed his chair over with his feet. He hit the floor and Reed swiveled around.

Without a gun directed at his brain, he ducked low, grasped the backup gun from his leg, and moved toward Danny while shots rang out around him.

As he crawled, a bullet split through the leg of the chair, forcing him to look up.

He dodged left, avoided the heel of Cleft Lip's shoe, and a shot rang out before Reed could swivel his weapon in the man's direction. When Reed looked up, he saw the shape of a woman in tight, ninja-style black clothing blowing a kiss from the rafters.

Sasha.

Reed rolled out of range, leveled his gun to Cleft Lip's chest, and froze as a bullet from behind him took the man down.

His pocketknife made quick work of the rope around Danny's wrists before Reed dragged him behind a stack of boxes for shelter. He was out cold but had a strong pulse. The knock on his head when the chair hit the ground looked like the cause.

Away from the chaos, Reed looked up toward the ceiling. Two men, covered in black from head to toe, ducked in and out of sight.

The woman in charge lay in a river of her own blood, eyes wide and lifeless.

Cleft Lip was down and the other two men who had beat the shit out of Danny were shooting toward the front of the building.

"We need to get out of here," Reed said to Danny.

A box above them became victim to a spray of bullets. Reed slapped the side of Danny's face. "Danny, wake up."

His head rolled on his shoulders.

Reed shoved his shoulder under Danny's arm and took his weight. "C'mon, man, we need to move."

It took serious effort, but Danny started moving his feet, even if his head wasn't in the game. Backing out the way he had come in took Reed from an inside shooting range to an outside shooting range. Two men in suits were back-tracking out the front door as they sprayed the inside of the warehouse with their semiautomatic weapons.

Distant sirens filled the air, and the men in suits fled like cockroaches in sunlight.

The screeching of tires and lack of gunfire gave Reed the opportunity to slump beside the building. Pain registered in his left arm. His jacket sported a perfect hole, and warmth ran down the inside. He flexed his bicep and cussed. "Damn it."

From the corner of his eye, Reed caught movement when a figure walked toward him and tensed. Danny had passed out.

"You okay?" the voice was modulated with a device to mask its identity.

While he couldn't say for sure, the build of the man talking appeared to be Neil.

"We're fine."

Sirens grew closer.

"Go, I'll handle the police," Reed said.

The masked man lifted a hand in the air, signaled someone else. "We were never here."

Reed lifted a thumb in the air, and the man was gone.

Lori paced like a caged animal. Every minute felt like an hour.

By the thirty-minute mark she was wringing her hands, and her stomach was ready to explode.

She watched her cell phone, knowing that when it rang, the woman holding her brother would know the papers weren't coming. None of this was worth her brother's life.

None of it.

A cell phone rang, and everyone in the room jumped.

Lori looked at her silent phone.

"Hello?" Sam asked into hers.

She released a sigh that sounded like steam from a power plant. "Okay. Yes . . . I will."

Sam lifted her chin and slowly smiled. "They're safe."

Avery grabbed Lori's shoulder.

Shannon slumped on the couch.

"Reed is with Danny."

"Is Danny okay?"

Sam kept smiling. "I know they're alive."

Which didn't mean unhurt.

Lori grabbed her cell and dialed Reed's number.

She could barely hear him over the sirens.

"Lori?"

"Is Danny okay?" She paused and yelled the question into the phone a second time.

"I can't hear you. Hold on."

She heard voices in the line.

"They're taking him to Memorial. But he's fine, Lori. Don't panic." He hung up.

Lori marched to the door and turned to the others. "C'mon."

Reed slapped the back of the ambulance carrying Danny to the hospital. The kid's bells were ringing hard, but he'd recognized him, which gave Reed enough to know he was going to be all right.

Reed's identification and weapon were on the hood of the commanding officer's car.

Lights swirled around as over two dozen squad cars and twice as many officers combed over the scene.

Officer Chow picked up each piece of evidence, one at a time, and dropped it to make a point. "Retired PD. Concealed carry permit. Private investigator. Thirty-eight revolver."

"My nine is somewhere in the building," Reed reminded the man.

"Right, and you want me to believe that an anonymous call brought you here, where you found your girlfriend's brother tied up and under the gun of the dead woman in there."

"Ex-girlfriend. And the woman had at least three men with her that I saw."

"Right, the dead guy who managed to disarm you and two more that fled."

"That's right."

"And who were the others?"

"I'm telling you what I saw. It was like a fight club, all suits, heavily armed. Shots rang out, she went down, and I didn't stand around asking questions. By the time I pulled Danny out of the building, I heard you coming, and the place emptied like rats running to freedom."

"I'm going to need a formal statement."

"I know the drill, Chow."

"And I'm holding on to this." He picked up Reed's weapon.

"It wasn't fired."

"And your nine?"

"Unless someone in there fired off a shot, it wasn't used either."

Chow's gaze dropped to Reed's arm. "Did you take a hit?"

Considering his left arm was rather numb, he felt safe nodding. He shrugged off his jacket, winced at the pain of his sudden movements.

"Might wanna get that looked at."

The ambulance had already left. "I can drive myself."

Chow looked over Reed's shoulder. "Not unless you have four spare tires."

Reed cringed before he turned. Someone had decided inflated tires and doors without holes weren't a good look.

Chow called another officer over while he gathered Reed's ID and returned it to him. They had a brief conversation before he nodded toward the car. "Get in. I need to ask the other witness some questions, anyway."

"Ms. Cumberland?"

Lori jumped up from her waiting room chair and followed the nurse into the emergency room.

"How is he?"

"Your brother is fine. We just brought him back from a CAT scan."

"Is there anything wrong?"

"We don't have the radiology report yet." The

nurse pushed past a curtain, and Lori stopped in her tracks.

"Oh, Danny."

"I'm okay." His face was packed with bloody gauze, a welt up one side of his head, and his eyes were already purple. "It's better than it looks."

His smile was so pathetic Lori found herself laughing. "I'm sorry . . ."

"I'm good. Great drugs here."

She sat beside him and grasped his hand. "I love you."

"I love you, too."

"I'm sorry."

"Stop. This wasn't your fault."

She dropped her head to his hand. "I thought they were going to kill you."

"Look." He moved his hand. "Not dead."

One of the nurses walked in. "I'm going to clean your cuts and redress your nose."

"Sounds fun," Danny joked.

"Ma'am, why don't you step out for a few minutes."

"Do you want me here, Danny?"

He lifted a swollen eye to her. "So you can feel more guilty? I don't think so."

She stepped into the hall and leaned against the wall. She should probably call her parents, let them know what happened.

A familiar voice brought her attention down the hall.

Reed.

He stood beside a uniformed police officer, and a man who wore a badge on the belt of his suit. One of the ER attendants pointed her way.

Reed caught her eyes.

The suited officer walked her way, smiled when he approached. "Ms. Cumberland?"

"Yes."

He glanced over her shoulder. "Your brother's in there?"

"They're fixing him up."

He nodded.

From the corner of her eye, she saw Reed being led to a wheelchair, she saw blood.

"Do you know what happ—"

"Excuse me." Lori half ran toward him, only stopped when she knelt by his side. "Are you okay?"

His soulful eyes melted as they looked at her. "Flesh wound."

She reached out and pushed away at his shirt covering the hole in his arm.

He winced, turned a little white. "How is Danny?"

"Cracking jokes."

"Good, that's good." Reed looked over her head, leaned forward.

Her first reaction was to retreat, but he held her arm and kept her in place. His lips moved close to her ear. “Answer their questions, just keep Alliance and Neil’s team out of it.”

The scent of him, his nearness, brought tears. “Okay.” She placed a hand on the side of his face. He leaned into it.

“Okay, Mr. Barnum, time to clean you up.”

Lori stood and let the nurse take him away.

The doctors kept Danny overnight and released him into the solid care of Nurse Lori and Nurse Avery. Between the two of them, he didn’t have to lift a finger.

Sam brought over a care package complete with the latest gaming system and a half a dozen popular titles. When Lori saw it, she laughed. “He isn’t twelve.”

“Are you kidding me? This was Rick’s idea.”

Sure enough, when they gave it to Danny, he was as giddy as a five-year-old at Christmas.

Avery worked to set the system up, with Danny giving bedside directions. Lori and Sam left them to it.

“How did you handle the police?” Sam asked once they were sitting.

“They asked what I knew. I told them I received a call demanding files of my deceased client. I knew they had Danny. I panicked, was too afraid to call the police.”

“They bought that.”

“I never once thought to call the police. It

wasn't a lie. I told them I'd received an indirect threat from a client's family member and took the precaution to hire a bodyguard."

"Did he ask who the family member was?"

"Of course."

"And?" Sam asked.

"I pleaded attorney-client privilege. The detective reminded me that people were dead, that Danny could have died . . . Reed." She hung her head.

Sam held her hand.

"Ruslan's thin threats would never hold up for a restraining order. If I could prove Ruslan was behind this, I would tell the police everything."

"I can't imagine that will hold the police back."

"I don't know. He seemed appeased, made a comment about my boyfriend being a PI who managed to extract my brother from a room full of hired mercenaries without more than a bullet to the arm. All without discharging his firearm."

Sam smiled. "We do have a few friends inside that can let us know if this investigation is moving forward or sealed."

"If they link Petrov to this incident, my name will be brought up."

"And if that happens, we do everything we can to nail his ass to the wall." Sam took a deep breath.

"I'm glad it's over."

"Me too. Who knew arranging marriages would have led to all this?"

"We've all learned some valuable lessons." Reed's image flashed in her head. She shook it free.

"And on that note," Sam paused. "Alliance has been a great beta program."

Lori narrowed her eyes. "What?"

"Beta . . . a test to a new venture."

"What new venture?"

"An executive matchmaking firm . . . where one may or may not need a prenuptial agreement."

"Alliance with a twist?"

Sam grinned. "We'll figure out the details later. We suspend new acquisitions indefinitely to ensure this can't happen again."

"Probably the smart thing to do."

Sam stood, her high heels clicking on the hardwood floors. "Rick wanted me to relay something to you."

"What?"

"He wanted you to know that they've been working with Reed for more than a week to find Susan Wilson, or whatever her name really was."

"He felt guilty."

"I'm sure he did. Rick also said that if you were his sister, he'd encourage you to give Reed another chance." Sam kissed her cheek and headed for the door.

"Sam?"

"Yes?"

"Thanks for everything."

She tilted her head. "You took all the hits for this one, you have no reason to thank me."

Danny's and Avery's laughter rang through the house.

Chapter Thirty-Six

Two Weeks Later

"Okay, the first official meeting of the First Wives Club is coming to order." Avery needed a gavel. Lori made a mental note to buy one for her and have it engraved.

"Didn't our first meeting happen in Spain?" Shannon asked.

"Okay, our second official meeting of the First Wives Club," Avery conceded.

They were in Avery's condo, having a wine and cheese meeting. Trina had flown in, happy to spend a weekend in LA.

Shannon poured wine and handed everyone a glass. "What is on our agenda tonight?"

Trina laughed.

"We have two very important items to discuss, and we need to start our bylaws."

Shannon leaned over, pretended to talk quietly, when everyone could hear her. "Man, she's taking this seriously."

"I'm learning from Trina, our resident student of business."

Trina lifted her glass in acknowledgment.

"Okay . . . rules."

"We have rules?" Shannon asked.

Avery rolled her eyes. "Everything we say here is confidential unless otherwise stated."

"I like that," Lori said.

The other two chimed in.

"We meet every quarter."

Trina leaned lifted her glass. "If the wine is always this good, we should meet more often."

"Every two months?" Avery amended and wrote it down.

"We vary the locations, with one meeting each year over a long weekend or a week."

"I apparently have a home in Costa Rica on a beach, and another one in Germany," Trina added.

Avery looked at Lori. "Who says stuff like that?"

"Like what?"

"Apparently I have a home in Costa Rica and Germany!" Avery's snark was full of laughter.

Trina grinned. "I do. I think I'm going to sell the house in New York."

"Not for a year," Lori warned.

The two of them started chatting, and Avery slapped her hand on her knee. "No work. Not during our meeting." She started to write the rule down.

"We aren't voting?" Shannon asked with a laugh.

"I'm the president this year, so I'm pulling executive order."

Lori sat back, tucked her legs under her. "We need to vote in an executive order," she said with a laugh.

"No, we don't." Avery started laughing, sipped her wine.

"Why?"

"Because I said so."

They all laughed.

"Enough rules," Shannon said. "What are our discussion items?"

Avery put her pen down. "Lori brought us all together in Spain so that we could help pull each other along after our marriages. To help find out where we fit next, in life and with men."

"Right." Shannon patted Lori's knee.

"Seems like we need to repay the favor."

All eyes turned to Lori.

She slowly lowered the glass from her lips. "What? I fit, my life is fine."

Oh, no . . . she could sense the glow of an intervention coming on.

"How is your love life?" Avery asked, already knowing the answer.

Her lips pushed together. The image of Reed in a wheelchair flashed before her.

"Quick, who did you just think of?" Avery asked.

Lori wasn't sure she liked this game. "Reed. But we all know how that turned out."

"I've been thinking about that," Shannon said. "I think you need to give that another try."

Lori's jaw dropped.

"I agree," Trina said.

"He really is genuinely sorry for his douche-baggery," Avery added.

"And you would know this how?" Lori asked her.

Avery looked at the faces around the room. "I might have had a couple conversations with the man since he messed up."

"You're talking to him?"

Shannon raised her glass. "I'm guilty, too."

"Oh my God."

Trina lifted a finger but didn't make eye contact.

"Seriously, guys. He made a fool of me, of all of us."

"Do you love him?" Shannon asked.

She started to deny it.

"Do you miss him?" Avery asked.

Lori lifted her chin but didn't answer.

"Would you be happier with him in your life?"

Lori looked at Trina, and her resolve started to crumble. "The point is moot. He hasn't even tried to contact me."

"Would you give him a chance if he asked?"

"A chance would depend on what he said. This hurts too much to go through twice."

"If he messed with you twice, we would run him out of town," Trina teased.

"This isn't Texas." Shannon cut off a chunk of cheese and stood. "But I'll endorse that rule."

Trina took her glass, which was sitting on the table, and stood.

Next, Avery unfolded from her chair and put her pen and paper down.

"Where are you guys going?"

Avery pointed toward her front door. "Out . . . side. I heard a knock, did you hear a knock?" she asked Trina.

The three of them scrambled to the door.

Reed.

His hair was too long, and he'd grown out the hair on his chin and lip just enough to . . . just enough to make her heart skip a little more than it usually did when she saw him. He wore a button-up shirt, slacks, and a splash of humility as he leveled his eyes to hers.

She set her glass down before she dropped it, and wiped her hands on her jeans.

Avery moved past Reed. "Make it count."

He nodded and thanked all three of them before closing the door.

"You orchestrated this?" she asked.

"I had to try something. I can't close my eyes without seeing you. I swear I hear your voice ten times a day. I stare at the pictures of you on my phone while I'm at stoplights."

Lori felt a smile inch onto her lips.

"It's not funny . . . I've gotten two tickets for distracted driving just this week."

Now she laughed.

He dodged a grin and dropped to his knees in front of her. He placed his hands on her legs, the warmth caught her breath. "I screwed up, Lori. What I did was unforgivable. No matter how I pushed the facts around in my head, I never came out on the side of right. And I know I don't deserve you." His voice cracked.

Moisture filled her eyes.

He caught her hands in his. "But I love you. And I can't breathe another day without trying to get you back. I started with Avery. She seemed the most against me. Then I called Trina. My apology to Shannon might have resulted in some kind of blood pact to name my firstborn after her."

Lori smiled through her tears.

"I love you. I'm not giving up until you give me a second chance to prove we belong together. If you tell me to leave, I'm just coming back tomorrow, and the next day. I'll start leaving notes and flowers." He smiled into her eyes. "I'll probably be taken to jail for stalking you, but it will be worth it if you give me a chance. One chance, please." He kissed the backs of her fingers.

She released his hand and brushed aside his hair.

He leaned into her touch, and she leaned in with her lips.

Reed caught his breath and gasped before wrapping both hands around her head and sealing their second chance with a soul-shattering kiss.

Lori leaned back, took a breath. “One.”

He kissed her again.

She pulled back again. “Complete honesty.” She stared into his soul through his eyes.

“Deal.”

“All right.” She smiled.

He lifted her off the couch until her body was molded to his. “You won’t regret this, Lori. We’ll be fighting over turkey legs when we’re seventy.”

She choked on a laugh. “A turkey has two legs.” But good Lord, how she wanted to plan on growing old with this man. Tears ran down her cheeks.

“What is it, baby?”

She tried to hold in her tears. “I w-want to fight over turkey legs.”

Reed pulled her into his arms and let her cry. “Then we’ll throw one away and fight over the one that’s left.”

With her head buried in his shirt, she clawed at the back of him, soaking him in. “I don’t even like turkey.”

Reed’s chest started to quake until his laugh took on its own life. He picked her off the ground and spun in a circle.

Epilogue

Reed played with the tie around his neck, did the around thing, the under thing, and then the give up thing. "Babe?"

"It's not that hard!" Lori said from the kitchen.

"Yes it is," he muttered as he pulled it from his neck, turned the light off, and followed her voice.

He made it two steps into the room and froze. Lori in Christmas red with a crisscross of spaghetti strings where the back of the dress should be rendered him speechless. Tiny white lights glistened off the sparkle in the material and the diamond earrings that dropped from the lobes of her ears.

"No it's not," she said, turning toward him. "What?"

He had to catch his breath. "You're stunning."

Her heels clicked, and the material of the dress clung to her breasts in a wispy caress. Delicate fingertips took the tie from his hands and worked their way up his chest. "How can I deny you with your compliments?"

The scent of perfume stole his thoughts.

"There." She patted his tie after pulling it close to his neck.

"How many single men will be at this party?"

He wrapped both his arms around her waist, played with the back of her dress, teasing her skin.

The Harrison Christmas party would house more brass than the White House. Their wealth and stature didn't concern him at all, what did was the amount of men who would be tripping over themselves to get to her.

"Not too many. Most of Sam and Blake's close friends and family are all married or otherwise engaged."

That made him feel a little better.

"What is it?"

"My inner caveman is raging."

Her eyes drifted down.

"You're insatiable, woman. That isn't what I meant."

She ran her hands up his shoulders and left them there. "What do you mean?"

He hesitated.

"Complete honesty." Those two words had become their mantra for the past three months. The only time he'd pleaded mercy was when she asked if a dress she wore made her look fat. *I'm not answering that question ever. That is a woman's trick question, and if a man ever tells you otherwise, they're high.* She'd started to argue, and he stepped up and did what every man should when a woman asks that question. He slid beside her, pulled the dress off, and let his body show her how the dress made her look. Now, whenever she wanted to be late to work, she asked if something made her look fat.

"Reed?"

"I don't want any of the men at this party believing you're available."

"I'm not available."

"You know what I mean."

She dropped her hand to his cheek. "Reed. I love *you.* I'm not available to anyone but *you.*"

Those words never grew old.

He captured her hand in his, kissed her bare ring finger. "I want anyone who looks to know you're mine."

Her long lashes dropped to her hand and back. "Oh."

And when her smile grew larger, he knew just how unavailable he was going to make her.

An hour later, Reed watched her from across the room as she socialized with Neil and his wife, Gwen. Kids of all ages meandered around the room decked in ties and dresses. He knew somewhere in the house a temporary nursery had been set up with a gaggle of babysitters and nannies at the ready.

Rick blocked his view and extended his hand. "Merry Christmas."

They avoided spilling their cocktails while they shook hands.

"How was training?" Rick asked.

"They kicked my ass." Reed had put aside his private investigator hat to join the security team Neil and Rick ran. Doing so required taking his police force skills to a new level. The boot camp–style training went for a week and ended with a commitment to return every few months for a year.

"Every man needs a good ass kicking once in a while."

"If it helps me protect that woman over there, I'm in."

"Speaking of women, I need to find mine. See you Monday."

Reed zeroed in on Lori and heard his cell phone ring. He nearly ignored the call when a tiny voice told him to pick it up.

"Hello?"

"Merry Christmas."

Sasha.

He stepped out of the noisy room and out under the bright Christmas lights that littered the loggia and backyard overlooking the ocean.

"You left without me saying thank you."

"How sweet."

"Well, I owe you."

"Those IOUs are adding up. I thought you might want to know, word is that Petrov didn't put a hit on your lady."

"Really?"

"No. He did take out his hired hand, however. Can never be too careful on who you work for."

Noise from inside drifted through an open door, he turned to see Lori walking toward him.

"Who hired you?"

Sasha laughed, low and deep. "Alice Petrov."

"You're kidding."

"Before she died. I've been protecting Trina since before her husband died. Alice wanted me to find the truth behind Trina's marriage and keep it from her ex-husband."

"Why are you telling me this now?"

"While finding the truth and being paid from beyond the grave, I found a security team worthy of my talents. If Petrov ever finds me out, I'll need to call in a favor."

Lori moved within hearing range.

Reed lifted a hand to keep her quiet. "You won't have to ask twice."

"Good, now take your girl back inside. She looks cold."

Reed noticed Lori shivering, her arms wrapped around her shoulders.

"I'm considering a little work on my Texas accent, what do you think?" Her last words sounded less Russian and more Texan.

"If you need our help, you know how to find us."

"I'm counting on that."

When Sasha hung up, he shrugged out of his

jacket and placed it over Lori's shoulders. "Who was that?"

"Sasha."

"Really?"

He turned her back toward the house. "It appears Trina's mother-in-law has been hard at work beyond the grave."

Lori paused.

"She hired Sasha to keep your secrets."

Lori's jaw dropped. "Why did Sasha tell you that now?"

"For our protection . . . well, Neil's team's, in any event."

They stopped under one of the patio heaters and warmed up from the crisp December night.

"Should I be jealous of this woman who keeps calling you?"

Reed couldn't help it, he laughed. "There is only room for one woman in my life."

She lifted his left hand and kissed the back of it. "I feel the need to go cavewoman on you."

His eyes lit up, his hand moved under his jacket and dipped his fingers past the back of the dress. "Isn't that out of your comfort zone?"

"I heard once that life begins when you step out of that zone."

How he loved this woman. "Cavewoman . . . I like it. Next year's Halloween costumes."

"Already on to next year?"

"Baby . . . I'm planning the next sixty years."

She lifted her smiling lips to his, kissed him. “I love you.”

Without breaking their lips apart, he said, “Love you more.”

Acknowledgments

So many people to thank, and only one page to do it. First, and probably most important, would be my readers. You crazy kids kept asking me for an eighth day of the week so that I could extend the Weekday Brides. Even my publisher asked if I could pull that out of my hat. But alas, there are only seven days in the week, and as much as I tried, an eighth day didn't manifest. Someone mentioned a Holiday Brides Series, and I thought . . . I might be able to do that. Then I thought, let's make this a divorce bride series. Since yours truly has had the real-life drama of her own divorce in the past couple of years, I realized I could add some depth to the plot line. Thank you, readers, for wanting more, and thank you, Montlake, for seeing my vision.

Now on to the name-dropping.

Thank you, Jane Dystel, for always being there for me, not just as my agent, but as a dear friend. Between a divorce, fire, and floods, you're the one who always checked in.

Everyone at Montlake for their understanding and compassion with all my delays and personal drama. Kelli, my dear, you are a rock.

Denise, aka Divorce Attorney Extraordinaire . . .

thank you for taking care of me, and my friend, during that . . . ah-hum . . . little issue we had to deal with.

To Cecilia, my unexpected travel companion. Your suggestion of that cruise to the Mediterranean is forever in print. Now let's do that shit and have a blast!

And now back to Tracy Brogan.

There are very few stressors we have in this life that top getting a divorce. We cry and laugh . . . and then cry some more. The roller coaster of emotions isn't something you can describe in any clarity and truly make the reader understand. Yet once you've gone through it, even if it's what you wanted, you feel as if you've gone through a battlefield, and those standing beside you when it's all said and done are people you hold tight for life. You, Tracy, are one of those people for me. We have a unique bond by our profession, and again by our personal journey. A divorced romance author almost sounds like an oxymoron. But to me, it sounds like a strong woman who refuses to live an unhappy *happily ever after.*

To the next chapter in our lives. I love you, m'friend. Let's kick some ass and take a few names.

~Catherine

About the Author

New York Times, *Wall Street Journal*, and *USA Today* bestselling author Catherine Bybee has written twenty-seven books that have collectively sold more than three million copies and have been translated into twelve languages. Raised in Washington State, Bybee moved to Southern California in hopes of becoming a movie star. After growing bored with waiting tables, she returned to school and became a registered nurse, spending most of her career in urban emergency rooms. She now writes full-time and has penned the Not Quite series, the Weekday Brides series, the Most Likely To series, and the First Wives series.

Center Point Large Print
600 Brooks Road / PO Box 1
Thorndike, ME 04986-0001 USA

(207) 568-3717

US & Canada:
1 800 929-9108
www.centerpointlargeprint.com